Shedding
NEGATIVE BELIEFS
A LETTER TO HER FUTURE SELF
HOW STRONG IS HER FAITH?

EBONIE T. PRITCHETT

Trilogy Christian Publishers
A Wholly Owned Subsidiary of Trinity Broadcasting Network
2442 Michelle Drive
Tustin, CA 92780

For information, address Trilogy Christian Publishing
Rights Department, 2442 Michelle Drive, Tustin, CA 92780.
Trilogy Christian Publishing/ TBN and colophon are trademarks of Trinity Broadcasting Network.
For information about special discounts for bulk purchases, please contact Trilogy Christian Publishing.

10 9 8 7 6 5 4 3 2 1
Library of Congress Cataloging-in-Publication Data is available.
ISBN 979-8-89041-770-1

ISBN 979-8-89041-771-8 (ebook)

ACKNOWLEDGEMENTS/
DEDICATION

I humbly thank God for His love and mercy during this project. I appreciate the friendly advice, insightful criticism, and mentorship I received during this endeavor. I want to express my heartfelt gratitude to the TBN production team for their outstanding assistance throughout this process.

Although I have invested much personal effort in this project, I am certain that I would not have accomplished my goal without the divine bestowal of knowledge and wisdom. I want to express my sincere appreciation to my younger self, who had the courage to dream, and for shaping the person I have become along this journey. I offer my deepest gratitude to my past experiences that have influenced my development and to the current circumstances that continue to support my growth. I confer my blessing upon all who are reading this discourse, and hope that you will discover the bravery, happiness, and affection encapsulated within these written words. May they impact your mind, heart, and soul, and move you to be and become your greatest self.

Most of all, I am dedicating this initiative to all current and future female followers of Christ. I anticipate that this effort will greatly assist you and will have a significant and lasting, positive influence on our Christian community. I also want to offer profuse thanks to all those who have provided support for my aspirations and accomplishments. May God continue to shower you with all manner of success and reward for your efforts.

PART ONE:

SHEDDING NEGATIVE BELIEFS

A Letter to HER Future Self: How Strong Is HER Faith?

HER Pathway Out

Dear Future Self,

Hey girl, remember that, while employed by the Metropolitan Police Department in Washington, DC, you spent four and a half years worrying about where your career would go? After three years on the job, you solidified your conviction that a career in law enforcement was the path for you, and you made the decision to transition to the federal level. You applied to several government agencies, including two of the largest ones out there. You received a response explaining why your application had been delayed in processing. "It's crucial to note that this agency's hiring choices are the result of a rigorous review of numerous variables." Uh oh. That sounded ominous. You read on, with a sinking feeling. "All applicants for a given post are then evaluated against one another based on how they stack up against these criteria. Since there are few available positions, the competition for them is fierce. In both cases, we appreciate your interest in the Agency and wish you the best of luck in your future pursuits." You felt like they were politely rejecting you.

I remember when I received emails like this, I started having serious doubts and was losing motivation to apply any place else. I was recalibrating my life. Feelings of professional burnout left me crying myself to sleep. I started to feel helpless in my current situation, dreading that I might have to settle for something less than my dream. I developed a loss of interest that led me to repeatedly call in sick to work, go AWOL, and drink more liquor than usual. I was so hurt and convinced that this was where I would spend the next twenty to thirty years of my life—feeling unfulfilled and miserable like everyone else. When this happens, however, I truly believe it is because God wants us to feel very uncomfortable, disturbed, and dissatisfied with the work we are doing—even though, on some level, we would really like to continue doing it. Sometimes we are not just underemployed, but wrongfully employed. Jesus discussed the significance of our discomfort quite often. He referred to those who are weeping, hungry, impoverished in spirit, or facing persecution for His cause as "Blessed" in the Beatitudes. (Matthew 5:1–12) If you're too comfortable, you won't be "hungry for righteousness' sake."

I listened to a sermon by Pastor John Hannah on how 2023 was going to be a "record-breaking year." Here he was, a Christian man, saying we could shoot for our dreams, and be soldiers for God, and that the two were not diametrically opposed. This message stayed with me. As I committed more time to reading the Bible, my faith in God's Word grew. I noticed that it is so easy to accept what flesh, "humankind" (bosses, coworkers, etc.), presents to you (positions, titles, and salaries). It is more challenging to truly pay attention to what God is calling you to do, to listen to your gut, your intuition, to wear your shield of armor, and to march forward in faith—in God and in yourself. Christians understand that they are called into their professions, not through them.

Joshua 1:9 states, "Have I not commanded you? Be strong and courageous. Do not be afraid; do not be discouraged, for the Lord your God will be with you wherever you go."

And we know that God causes all things to work together for good to those who love

9

God, to those who are called according to His purpose" (Romans 8:28).

Self, for years, you've waited expectantly for the coming of adulthood that would finally provide you the dignity, respect, and acceptance you've always craved. And then, you longed for the carefree days of your adolescence when you could play without worrying about what others thought of you. Life is an epic race, and you're here to "win." It clearly states in Galatians that love, joy, peace, patience, kindness, goodness, faithfulness, gentleness, and self-control are all fruits of the Spirit. There is no rule that can stop such behavior (5:22-23, NIV). Self, be genuine. Embrace the chaos. Toss it all behind you. From a young age, you understood that you wanted to take the lead in anything you did. This is your chance.

The lessons you've learned and the

experiences you've had are meant to be yours. As a Christian, you understand that life is more about your experiences than your decisions, despite the desire to believe that we live in a world of options and that our lives are shaped by the decisions we make.

While the future remains an unknown, certain anticipated events will arise. A person may encounter situations when it is not feasible to make prior arrangements or have immediate assistance available for guidance. One must adapt to the prevailing circumstances, assimilate the information, persist in navigating challenges to acquire valuable insights, and, afterwards, confidently persevere. Direct your attention accordingly and stay focused.

When facing an unpredictable future, one thing is certain: unexpected events will occur.

There will be times when it's simply not possible to plan or have immediate guidance at hand. In these moments, we must learn to adapt to our prevailing circumstances, absorb the information presented to us, and persist through the challenges. The goal is to gain valuable insights and then move forward with renewed confidence. It's crucial to focus our attention where it's needed most.

Throughout our lives, we're bound to come across numerous guiding principles or "affirmations," as some prefer to call them. These principles are there to support us, assist us, and show us the way forward. The mere suggestion that we might be vulnerable to harmful, demonic forces when alone doesn't necessarily imply that we must acquire a continual collection of tattoos as reminders of such experiences. By now, your life will be filled with enough of these guiding principles. It's important to remember that, like people, affirmations will tend to come and go. Even with the best intentions, it's just not possible to hold onto all of them. Swiftly acknowledging this reality and doing your best to appreciate your current situation is vital to your ongoing growth.

Even if an event or phenomenon doesn't look like an obvious success, it doesn't diminish its potential influence or significance. Belief in its value is not the least bit foolish. Whether something you've tried has worked or not, it can still have a profound impact and can easily add value to your life story. It's never foolish to believe in the potential of these experiences.

It is vital to maintain an unrelenting firm grip on optimism. Engaging in such activities will inevitably result in some discomfort. It is vital to remain tranquil. Consider the biblical passage found in 1 Corinthians 14:33. The statement posits that God is not the originator of disorder or chaos, but rather the source of tranquility and harmony, as seen in all religious congregations.

The Breaking Point

Self-confidence and strength don't just happen overnight. You must fight crushing self-doubt. Sometimes that self-doubt takes over. Okay, so... you broke down. You hit rock bottom. Take a deep breath. I always advise you to put oil on your head and go on your knees before you start praying. Don't look at the time. Not everyone has the good fortune to hear and appreciate such an experience, so take the time to be like Elijah and wait silently until you hear a quiet whisper, the sound of a still, little voice, which is that of God. Reflect on the prayer of Jabez as he called upon the God of Israel, saying, "Oh that you would bless me and enlarge my territory, and that your hand might be with me, and that you would keep me from harm so that it might not bring me pain!" And God granted what he asked (1 Chronicles 4:10). Just know that God is trying to tell you something. God's visions have imparted a great deal of knowledge to you. Oh yeah, here's that point of no return where you start listening. God intended for you to emerge from your breakdown even more powerful than before. God loves to test His people; this is His precise intention for your ministry Be confident that His plan for you will inspire you to take actions you have never taken before and help you overcome the obstacles you once thought were undefeatable.

When you're feeling down, just remind yourself that you're making progress. Keep in mind that everyone who has achieved greatness has also faced adversity. Don't give in to the stress. You need self-assurance, bravery, resolve, and stamina right now to face your issues head-on.

Isolation is the ingredient needed to achieve your next level of success; and fear not, because, contrary to popular opinion, isolation need not always involve exclusively negative implications or feelings. During periods of solitude, individuals can gain valuable insights into their own identities. The lack of external distractions allows for enhanced concentration, facilitating self-reflection and self-discovery. Additionally, a state of isolation fosters a sense of satisfaction and self-acceptance.

Divine Timing

The glacial pace at which my goals were being achieved left me feeling periodically disappointed. Whenever I felt this way, I found it useful to remind myself that divine timing is always more important than human timing. Jeremiah 29:11-12 is a scriptural passage that has stayed with me. It says, "'For I know the plans I have for you,' declares the Lord, 'plans to prosper you and not to harm you, plans to give you hope and a future. Then you will call on Me and come and pray to Me, and I will listen to you.'"

Since the year 2020, I procrastinated on writing and publishing due to a crippling fear of rejection by potential readers and buyers.

After realizing God had even greater plans for me, I made the choice to resume writing on December 6, 2022. My willingness to acknowledge my impasse gave me faith that God would remove it. Even though the mind was usually the source of the danger, I knew this task would eventually become more crucial. I recall that, in my first conversation with the publisher, I expressed my eagerness to get started. She inquired when I wanted to publish, and I answered that May of 2023 was ideal.

A few days later, she called and asked if I could publish in January 2023, giving me only a few weeks to finish the manuscript. Although I was anxious, I eagerly accepted. A journal filled with thoughts and words prepared me well, and the procedure went off without a hitch. I was aware that I wanted to sow a seed that would end the cycle of tragedy in many families and among young adults, especially those around my age, and that I wanted to be a vehicle for paving the way for the establishment of enduring dynasties, institutions, and legacies. That's why I released my first personal journal titled, Win Win Thinking: A 21-Day Mindset Diary to Maximize Your Personal and Professional Success, which hit #1 bestseller in fifteen categories. After seeing this in print, I realized I was giving individuals a chance to discover their life's work by enjoining them to commit to establishing daily objectives, reciting affirmations, and recording what mattered most to them. I knew that individuals might question themselves, asking, "How will this add value to my dreams and purpose to fulfilling them?" but I trusted that engaging in the suggested process would provide them with their own true and enduring answers.

And hey! Let's not forget, lady, that before Win Win Thinking, you collaborated on an uplifting devotional, "Breakthrough Moments," which was published in late March 2023 and also became a #1 bestseller. A global bestseller, "Uncuffed Voices: Her Story is My Story," features your writing along with nineteen other female law enforcement professionals. And you started your own writing service business entitled InspiredByEbonie, LLC. Thus, there is no need to be so hard on yourself. Hold your head up and listen to your own good advice. Remember that your light comes from God. You need the soul of a hustler for God to achieve the goals you've set for yourself. So just think, how many records have you really broken since the new year began?

Celebrating my True Essence

Self, you have graduated from many areas because you have mastered them! Wisdom is the key to attaining maturity. Wisdom increases when you learn to apply your knowledge to everyday choices and situations.

Do you feel like God has abandoned you at times just because everything seems to be going wrong? Do you think God erred? Or forgot? Maybe you wonder if

He's astonished by your circumstances and pondering how to redeem and repair things, or if that's even possible. No matter what you may be thinking, you must know: The Lord is listening.

Self, we began to understand through this process that the successes in life that you are working toward require the character of a woman, not a girl. When a woman chooses to respond to life situations, she does so with diligence, patience, and wisdom. Excuses are put aside, and she submits herself to the process that God is directing her to follow. I express gratitude to all those who have released me from their lives. It is important to note that if one is unable to cope with current circumstances, they will likely struggle to navigate the challenges that lie ahead. There are those individuals who have identified as acquaintances yet have demonstrated an inability to cope with the challenges and difficulties experienced by others. How did you effectively cope with a significant amount of emotional pain and pervasive feelings of jealousy? Upon revisiting Proverbs 14:30, one encounters the following verse, "A heart at peace gives life to the body, but envy rots the bones." In the book of Genesis, the act of murder committed by Cain against his brother Abel is driven by jealousy. Cain's envy stems from God's preference for Abel's sacrifice over his own. In an early biblical narrative, the text elucidates the deleterious potency and malevolence inherent in the emotion of envy.

Self, you were not designed to stand still and just bide your time. Wait silently but move when the sounds come. Having obedience builds your relationship with God; if He can trust you with that, He can trust you with more.

When you leave a toxic job and the people that come with it, your next steps can seem overwhelming. By taking time to process what happened and move forward thoughtfully, you can transform your experience into sharing your expertise on what it truly looks like to participate in a healthy work environment. This new knowledge can help you start a new career and begin your next position with a fresh perspective. We must look at ways to heal after leaving a toxic work environment and are looking to recover a large measure of professional confidence.

You can learn a lot by analyzing what made your workplace unhealthy. For example, you can more easily determine what you want and need from an employer and where and how you want to set personal boundaries to avoid similar future situations. You'll be practicing coping mechanisms by engaging in this process, so you'll become more resilient as a result. And in future workplaces, you can better understand your role as an employee or manager, which will enable you to maintain an uplifting, enjoyable, and encouraging work environment.

If you weren't appreciated at your last position, you may not know your full professional and personal worth or potential after you leave. Take some time to write down a list of your strengths and accomplishments. Start with the positive character traits that have helped you succeed in work and life all over again. Then move on to listing the strengths, skills, and talents that you brought to your most recent job. Consider making a chronological list of your accomplishments in that position, starting with what you achieved in your first few months on the job. List projects you completed and the biggest obstacles you overcame. Recognize that you are "the movement." Don't lose your identification; trust yourself. If you began to feel like you can't hold the weight, give it to God, and He'll reveal to you when it's time for that shift. He will imbue you with the ability to see positive opportunities through the shift that you didn't see before. You will never forget where you came from; trust me, this is the famous notion that everyone plants inside of their head. How many of us, however, truly stick with it? Be the exception; make your beliefs and dreams a reality by accepting that God is on your side and that "you have this!" You are secure!

I am not the "Norm"

Now girl, you know life has been a study in contrasts: fascinating, chaotic, and entertaining, but also dull and predictable. Normal is defined by Merriam-Webster as "consistent with a type, standard, or regular pattern." Therefore, "abnormal" may be described as "not typical" or "average," not fitting into any one category; it is also considered remarkable. You must have life, dear sister, because even when everything is messed up, you can still find joy in it. Isaiah 54:17 says, "No weapon that is formed against thee shall prosper; and every tongue that shall rise against thee in judgment thou shalt condemn." This is the moment to retreat to your prayer closet of worship and read this passage aloud.

Doubt may continue to rear its ugly head; one may find oneself second-guessing such radical plans for change. Sarah Jakes is quoted as saying, "If the enemy gets to my heart, then he can get to my mouth, if he can get to my mouth, then he can get what I prophesy." There were some who judged me from all walks of life, asking why I would do something so crazy, saying things like, "You're being dumb by leaving a job/career with great benefits," and so on. Keep in mind that even if at the time it seemed like the worst decision of my life, it turned out to be the fulfillment of a long-held wish and the best possible choice at the end of the day.

You're amazing! You made it all the way to Doha, Qatar, adapted to living in a completely different culture, and managed to actually get solid work done at the same time! Who else could you possibly have persuaded to take this walk of faith with you? Bishop TD Jakes said, "It is important to look at this as a very clear understanding of contextualization because when people step into the middle of your story, they misdiagnose who you are, and they make false assumptions on brief statements." They were unaware of your inner supplications, your tears, and your very existence. Don't be afraid to be yourself, girl. All followers of God are likewise entitled to this assurance.

Embracing an Unexpected Detour

If we go graciously, we shouldn't feel bad. However, quitting a career, particularly a good one, might cause remorse.

Though we shouldn't feel awful, our brains are good at making us feel just that. Just know that when a road has shut down, it means that it was a path you previously had access to, but now no longer do. This only means that it is time to take a detour. It's not comfortable, but it's how we become successful in life.

Alexander Graham Bell and Hellen Keller have both been quoted as saying, "When God shuts one door, He opens another." There might be possibilities that act as doors, allowing you to go from one area to another. It is noteworthy that God closed the entrance of the ark during Noah's time until the appropriate moment arrived for it to be opened. This is a clearcut example of an ideological storm that resulted in a flood. It is a profound truth that a flood must run its course; any premature attempt by Noah to open the entrance of the Ark would have been futile, as the opportune moment had not yet arrived. If we demonstrate genuine obedience to the Lord and find ourselves securely inside the boundaries of His divine plan, then we will come to possess the discernment to accept His will when He closes a door, and patiently wait for Him to unveil a new opportunity. Divine providence closes a door with purpose, and, at that most fortuitous of times, it reveals one's next best option. Opening the door to the best version of yourself requires you to face certain uncomfortable or inconvenient challenges; sorrow, pain, agony, false beliefs, and other issues you have cordoned off and shunted to the back row of consciousness must now be confronted and handled. Everyone wants peace, joy, and contentment, but only those who are courageous enough to open the door and stare down their shadow side will be set free.

PART TWO:

DON YOUR PROTECTIVE ARMOR

Protecting HER Peace

Self, you must protect your peace, which means caring for and safeguarding your physical, mental, emotional, and spiritual self – in ways that you define for yourself. Protecting your peace is a personal journey, one where you ultimately make the decisions and set boundaries for yourself that you determine to be in your own best interests. Let's not overlook the most well-known verse that will guide you, sis, Ephesians 6:11-13, which states,

Put on the full armor of God, so that you can take your stand against the devil's schemes. For our struggle is not against flesh and blood, but against the rulers, against the authorities, against the powers of this dark world and against the spiritual forces of evil in the heavenly realms. Therefore, put on the full armor of God, so that when the day of evil comes, you may be able to stand your ground, and after you have done everything, to stand.

"Be sober, be vigilant, because your adversary the devil walketh about as a roaring lion, seeking whom he may devour." (1 Peter 5:8)

Some people don't want to see you win.

Self, how did you deal with so much hurt? How did you deal with so much envy? How did you deal with the stress? The naysayers, the negative people around you every day? My answer would be "I'm anointed for this! I got the oil for this! I have grace to deal with silence and people."

Be observant, reserved, and humble in all places, public and private. If your feet are planted where God told you to be, then even if the environment looks like it can pose a threat, the only way you can acquire everything you need is if you go all in.

Weathering the storms is the key to developing unshakeable, unbreakable faith. When you muster your reserves and remain calm while everyone around you is in crisis, God will comfort you, aid you, and invest you with the ability to carry your mission forward. Others will try to capsize your ship; during those times, be the rock and model yourself after God, the true and enduring Rock.

Although this point is connected to the advice mentioned above, it merits separate emphasis, since other people unquestionably pose the greatest danger to one's inner tranquility. Persist in observing the conduct of others and the emotional impact that they have on your life. Do you often find yourself in the company of those who engage in incessant complaining? Are you involved in a relationship with an individual who consistently belittles you? Do you acquaint yourself with those who tend to engage in gossip and are self-centered? By setting boundaries and reducing the amount of time you spend with those individuals, or by directly addressing them and making your beliefs, limits, and what you will and will not tolerate known, you will soon outgrow their influence on your life. You are doing well, young lady, so maintain a positive attitude!

It is important to remember that establishing limits is a means of cultivating a tranquil existence. Your boundaries serve as a means of respecting your own requirements, objectives, emotions, and principles. Consider the limits you establish as principles to govern your life and know with certainty that these can only be determined by you. As you mature and evolve, what you are and are not willing to accept in and around you will become clearer. Boundaries serve the purpose of ensuring your safety and maintaining a sense of respect during and throughout your growth process.

HER Vision Came Through Prayer

Self, when going through a new transition in life, the hardest thing is to give up your expectation of what it looks like.

I consistently underestimated my achievements, since advocating for myself was never encouraged inside our faith-based community. We were consistently instructed that militating for one's own accomplishments was evidence of excessive pride. For an extended period, I remained silent. Every individual has times of difficulty, intense challenges, and overwhelming situations. Consequently, it is vital that we allow God to transform us until His desired outcome is realized. Attainable visions bestowed by God may be realized; if He challenges us, He also provides us with the necessary resources and methods to achieve a favorable outcome. We possess the means to acquire celestial and transcendent revelations to carry out the divine agenda on Earth. We are entrusted by God with these tools. Prayer and fasting facilitate the process of God shaping us to resemble His own likeness. In his book, My Utmost for His Highest, the evangelist Oswald Chambers asserts that if God really exists and you truly exist, you will inevitably become a perfect representation of the vision set before you. You must be anointed in your present if you truly desire to acquire your most fruitful future. There will be lessons you must go through to prepare you for that later time.

In Acts 10:1-23, Cornelius is in prayer when an angel visits, telling him to go to Peter. And Peter is in prayer when he receives a vision as well. Visions begin with prayer. So, before we begin imagining new missional possibilities, we must start praying.

And the LORD answered me, and said, "Write the vision, and make it plain upon tables, that he may run that readeth it. (Habakkuk 2:2, KJV)

Putting your aspirations down on paper helps you chart the most direct path to success. Knowing whether to say "yes" or "no" based on your own personal principles and vision is a powerful tool for bringing about optimal results, and also helps in anticipating and avoiding problems that may arise. Envisioning is not always through the eyes; sometimes it is through the dreams and mind.

SHEDDING NEGATIVE BELIEFS

PART THREE:

TO MY FUTURE SELF

Self! You and I share an unbreakable bond and connection. We do it by not taking each other for granted, and by holding on to each other at this most critical of times.

Please, dear God, all my life I've searched for this one true, great love, and I know deep in my heart and in the serenity of my soul that I have found it within myself. Thank you for the blessings and for the gift of love.

The degree to which you are attacked yet stand your ground will equal the measure of respect that you command. In the auspicious words of he who suffered greatly, it is stated in Job 1:7, "And the LORD said to Satan, 'From where do you come?' So, Satan answered the LORD and said, 'From going to and fro on the earth, and from walking back and forth on it.' The devil will constantly look for a way to return you to a situation where he can manipulate, second-guess, and employ other such tactics. Remain tenacious and remember that you deserve the love you feel for yourself. Above all, let yourself know and believe that the love God has for you has been, and will continue to endure, throughout your life. TD Jakes stated, "If you have power, you have problems." You were only subjected to your trials and tribulations so that you could learn the level of respect you are expected to give back. Thus, you must keep doing what is best for you and resist the urge to let the concerns and issues of others derail you. Just know that you are now aware of what is best for you. Don't stop thinking; use your mind, but only in a positive way, as you now know how to do. The old doors have closed; they were never meant for you and, besides, new ones will surely open. The angels of God have always been protecting you, and you have leaned on them more than ever. Look to Galatians 6:9: "And let us not weary in well doing: for in due season we shall reap, if we faint not." (KJV)

Continue to put God first. You have been corrected and directed. Denzel Washington, when delivering a commencement speech at Dillard University, is quoted as saying, "Do what you feel passionate about and take professional chances. Don't be afraid to go outside the box; think outside the box, don't be afraid to fail big." As it states in Acts 4:15-22, "Speak on what you know and have heard." (KJV) Live your truth. Start now. Push past your limitations. Know your boundaries. Set your sights, hold God's hand, and move forward into the Light.

Closing Thoughts

Self, speak your reality. You must see your progress. Self, don't crack under pressure; facing challenges requires confidence, courage, determination, and endurance in the moment. Confronting and handling difficulties teaches us how to transform our lives. It provides us with knowledge, wisdom, and the tools needed for growth.

God was able to help me understand who I am, to help me see myself as anointed, and to enable me to be unapologetic when it came to my thoughts, speech, and actions. To get to that point, though, I had to change my prayer life.

I've always known I wanted to assume the role of a leader. I began to understand why my father worked so hard to acquire and maintain the leadership role for which he was so well suited. I always hoped to fill his shoes through my own efforts. However, I see now, more clearly than ever before, that I have my own shoes to fill for the legacy I am building. God has His own plan for my life, and I will continue to heed that still, small voice, walk in His ways, and become the woman I am destined to become. I am inspired, and hope to inspire others, to make a difference and not just a living.

I love you, sis. Many blessings to you and your future endeavors. Keep your happiness and faith so contagious that it spreads to others around you. Yours truly,

The Present You!

Ebonie Pritchett Bio

Ebonie is a doctoral student at Regent University, specializing in Strategic Leadership. She holds a Master of Science degree in Cybersecurity from Saint Leo University and a Bachelor of Arts degree in Sociology from Norfolk State University. Ms. Pritchett received the Order of the Sword Shield National Honors Society from December 2017 until the present and was a member in good standing of the Sociological Honor Society (Alpha Kappa Delta) from August 2011 to May 2015. In 2015, Ebonie relocated to the DMV area, where she discovered her professional passion. From October 2018 until May 2023, she served as a police officer with the Metropolitan Police Department in Washington, DC.

During her many years spent in law enforcement, Ms. Pritchett engaged in a broad spectrum of criminal investigations at both the municipal and state levels. Her firmly established track record has enabled her to assist numerous firms in streamlining their business processes, improving their efficiencies, and completing an assortment of projects, all while strictly adhering to industry-standard safety protocols and measures. As an expert in her field of interest, Ms. Pritchett is regularly required to remain current by participating in substantial law enforcement, protection, and safety-related tasks and procedures.

She is a prolific author who has written and collaborated on a series of inspirational devotions entitled, Breakthrough Moments, Uncuffed Voices: Her story is my story, and Win Win Thinking: 21 Day Mindset Journal to Maximize your Personal and Professional Success.

Jay Horne's

THE

TOME OF AGES

A Novel of Rootworld

PRESENTED BY BOOKFLURRY INC.

The Tome of Ages

The Tome of Ages Copyright ©2024 by Jay Mathis Horne. All rights reserved, including the right to reproduce this work in any form whatsoever, without permission in writing from the author, except for brief passages in connection with a review.

Jay M. Horne, Cover Artist assisted by Dall-e

Cataloguing Publication Data

Horne, Jay M., 1980-

The Tome of Ages / Jay M. Horne

ISBN: 978-0-9963227-9-9

Library of Congress Control Number: 2024902821

Bookflurry Inc. Publishing does not participate in, endorse, or have any authority or responsibility concerning private business affairs between the author and the public.

All mail addressed to the author will be forwarded but the publisher cannot, unless specifically instructed by the author, give out an address or phone number.

Bookflurry Inc.

Bradenton, FL

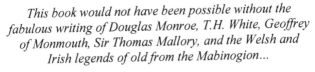

This book would not have been possible without the fabulous writing of Douglas Monroe, T.H. White, Geoffrey of Monmouth, Sir Thomas Mallory, and the Welsh and Irish legends of old from the Mabinogion...

What adventure awaits to any who dare and pull a single thread!

Table of Contents

Author's Note

Often, I am asked where I come up with this stuff. After the completion of The Death of Science: A Novel Introduction to Rootworld, I started to realize what was going on with my novellas.

Those stories, spanning five years, are destined to fall into the clutches of the Rootworld universe. Even my first novel[1], from more than ten years ago, seems to play a part in creating the fantastic universe that we are only beginning to know and love.

With that being said, if you have read any of my earlier novellas, you may know more about Rootworld than you think and possibly more than I knew when I was writing this first official book of the series, as I had no idea that they were parts of a potentially larger whole.

The ideas laid down from the time of legends and during the emergence of Christianity, which my characters have somehow turned on their heads, were always there. I think it was nothing less than the reading I have done since my childhood that helped me associate the possibilities into one megalithic story that will likely span more than ten volumes.

I hope that encourages future writers to read as well because there are still more fascinating and magical things to be discovered than are even dreamt about in my philosophies.

---

[1] Hubudi, Tower Hearts, and Remember were titles the book was published under without the witty and satirical methods I have come so much to enjoy.

Introduction

Time *is* space.

This carries substantial weight for those observing the characters outside these particular tales. Weight, of course, would increase if we approached the speed of light.

It is because space is the fabric of the Universe, and fabric is subject to the calamity known as tearing, that it would go to say that time was also on occasion, in danger of the pitfalls of becoming too heavy for its own trousers.

This is a story of such a time. If Father Time had known that moving so quickly would add extra girth to his middle, he may haven't done so. But it was an amateur mistake, and because he was a substitute nearing the end of his contract, it was bound to happen, even to the best of Incarnations.

His real name was Bobbie, but his parents often call him Karma when he's Globe-side on vacation, and that's because of their child's curious knack of always turning back up when he's least expected.

Being an outside observer[2] all goes in with the business of transforming universes to better outfit the First God's take on things. Because, let's face it, in a nutshell, we are technically his memories. The first God I mean; someone had to experience this stuff!

Embarrassment is something Father Time can put up with, it's only right when he'd grown a bit too comfortable in his station. See? That is how the First God works; he

---

[2] As an observer it is your primary job to just read. Everyone knows about the observer effect and how it can alter the outcome of certain probabilities. In other words, keep your pens off the pages! Terry Pratchett would be proud and would have said something like, "This means that the author doesn't take constructive criticism lightly."

teaches gentle lessons, not harsh ones. So don't be embarrassed for Bobbie. The ensuing humility will spurn him to better enjoy his final years of office and who knows, perhaps a particular female incarnation might have thought the blush on his cheeks was rather fetching, even if his underpants were not.

Understand, that while King Arthur may seem the primary focus in this tale, you must realize that great writers such as Geoffrey and Mallory have well documented a majority of the legend and it is not my endeavor to spar with these historical bards. Though a dual between Mallory and I may finally determine if the pen is indeed mightier than the sword. However, now that the globe is finally catching up, an explanation is long overdue to the people of this multi-faceted universe where science is about to verify the existence of magic.

It was during the time of my King and retinue, that the universe, after biting off more than it could chew, had indeed grown too big for its breeches. So, while not throwing a gauntlet down at the feet of our past greats, I shall stick with their traditions and steer clear of dead metaphors by simply stating that space-time is about to try and bend down and touch its toes[3].

---

[3] Anyone over the age of fifty knows this can be detrimental to the back, much less the trousers.

Chapter One: Who was I?

Imagine a People, congregating. Coming together at desperate times and drawing inspiration from the son of God's crucifixion, resurrection, and departure from the Globe.

Now, imagine no one asking how things went for Hazeus after he went home to Mom and Dad.

I was guilty of it too until, one day, instead of cracking open the Tome of Ages on a dusty old church pew, I spent my summer vacation with the reincarnated druid himself.

Enlightening experience, that, if not exhausting. Evenings were filled with jotting about the day's activities in a blue notebook while the druid listened to 1960s radio and sipped sumac tea. His parting advice was to remember who I was if I should ever know who I am, then I might be welcomed back again.

I pondered that for a season while I scrubbed out the grease traps at a local fast-food joint. There I was staring up at the TV during break time while the ghouls and goblins crowded in for their cheeseburger spooktacular meal deals.

I glanced at the pages of my blue book. Scrawled there was: *Moved seventy-two boulders, caught twenty bottles of wind, identified thirteen plant species. Who was I?* It had been a long summer.

It was Halloween and according to the news lady, a full moon. What a terrible druid apprentice I was for not realizing! I wouldn't normally walk out on a job, but this was a threshold event if there ever was one.

So, I traded in my apron for robes again and set off for the hills to perform a long overdue midnight ritual of past life inspiration.

After a night of spiders in an ancient hilltop graveyard, turns out I'm not only Mathis. This is my third go-round on the pony called Life. My horse has been downgraded from a magical Pegasus with a musical horn, to a Tennessee walker, and now to something called a Ford Taurus, so transportation is a bit different, but at least writing is much easier in this era.

I suspect that you'd agree that magic is finally turning up again. Though, it can be a bit ornery at times. I practically had to threaten the fire to start while summoning the shade of Merddin. Used to be, I could ask politely. Still holds that when you've seen something with your own eyes it's easier to believe.

Things are much clearer now. I may end up back on that old druid's mountain next season after all, since the memories are coming fast as I can jot them down in my blue book. First, I remembered when Merddin declared that magic came from a chaste life. If you asked him[4], he would tell you that when I was Lancelot, it took half a lifetime to convince me of magic. I won't argue being a little hard-headed about chastity back then. Still am now.

If you asked Hazeus, he would tell you that when I was Tom, it took a whole lifetime to convince me of said magic. Albeit he wasn't around as long. Come to think of it, Hazeus also preached about chaste living, but I remember

---

[4] Turns out you can, but you'll have to wait for another full moon on Halloween

that his declaration came right before he decided to return home.

That's not the only thing they agreed on. So, it didn't take long to accept that I may be more than one person in spirit. I can look around and see that what Merddin and Hazeus both told me is still true. Even the one God has many names and faces.

Chapter Two: Hazeus's Return Home

During my present life, a teacher once questioned why it was that the word desert, describing a barren expanse, was spelled with a single 's' while dessert, a yummy after-dinner treat, was blessed with two. When recounting this memory, I suddenly understood.

I was eavesdropping outside of the tent where the great Hazeus of Nazareth was holding an argument with Lazarus. He'd just resurrected the guy whom Mary and Martha were trying to help guide toward reason.

I could hear better if this wind would chill out. The two female silhouettes were projected onto the tent wall. I watched them from outside. *They must be standing on this side of the lantern.* I push the shoulder of my shirt into my eye socket trying to coax out some grit and then try and block the sandstorm with the back of my head as it picks up. You see…

No one ever asks for a second serving of desert.

I can hear Hazeus inside.

"Put that down, Lazarus. There're more pressing matters," he said.

The wind continued to rise and the women's shadows merged and grew as they backed near this side of the tent. The wind finally abated and there came the sharp sound of shattering clay.

"Just a cup or two?" slurred Lazarus. "To celebraaaghh…"

"Christ, Man," said Hazeus as something plopped to the floor inside.

"Please," came Martha's voice. Her silhouette shrank and knelt to pick something up. "Wine is what did this to you in the first place."

Mary's shadow also shrank as she moved within. "Well, dust it off first!" she said.

"Oh. Here," said Martha.

The shadows returned to normal and then there was a slurping sound and a crunch, then Lazarus again, "Argh. Ur, there. Much better."

"Just look at you!" Mary said.

"It's okay," said Lazarus wetly. "There's time for truth tomorrow. Let's celebrate tonight."

I leaned closer and could hear the jar of wine set heavily on the table.

"No," said Hazeus, followed by a pronounced silence. Hazeus's shadow overtook those of the women and another candle was lit this side of him, vanishing all silhouettes. "Look, I've lit the candle at the altar. Do not douse it with compulsions."

Lazarus's voice crumbled at Hazeus's feet, "What's life, withargh—" there was a crunching sound, "Ere. There. This time it'll stay, I promise. What good is life without pleasure?"

Hazeus's voice went down to meet him, "Not a single drink, Lazarus. Promise, me?"

Just then, Martha came out from the tent flaps, and I quickly took two steps away. She was shivering and had a hand on her forehead, so I went over and put an arm around her.

"I feel terrible for the guy!" she said through sobs.

"I know," I said softly. "He's just been raised from the dead and can't even have a decent drink."

"No, I mean he has to keep putting his parts back in place! His jaw, especially." Then she looked at me, her sobs immediately evaporating through suspicion.

"Uh, I mean, Hazeus knows what's best. Trust in his wisdom," I said. Then I saw her eyes drop to my side. I looked down, then slowly hid the wineskin beneath my tunic.

"Ugh!" she said, removing my arm and pulling her veil tighter across her face, then stormed back into the tent. I would like to say I didn't go back to listening in on the conversation, but hey, I had to know if she was gonna rat me out! I didn't want to be the next victim of forced sobriety!

"Lazarus, today we have taught each other," said Hazeus. "Life is more valuable than our compulsions, Friend. If you can value that truth, I can better find reason to continue my own path of righteousness."

I could hear Lazarus sobbing and then the shuffling of feet and robes swishing and what was surely Hazeus patting him on the back. Then again, a jaw being put back in place.

The sand started blowing again.

I was spitting some out when the wind stopped completely and light from inside cast a triangle onto the ground once more.

"Tom?"

It really is amazing how the weather clears when he decides to step out.

"Here," I said, coming around from the side and pretending to be adjusting my robes. "Nature called."

"Let it be written," said Hazeus, "to discipline the body is to feed the spirit."

I quickly unrolled my parchment and set to it with my reed and ink.

"Ah," Hazeus said, stretching out in the silver light of the desert moon, "it's nice when the tears of happiness flow."

My hand stopped briefly while I wondered if he was referring to Lazarus's or his own. I almost teared up myself when Hazeus gleefully poured the wine bottle out onto the sand.

Anyhow, the next two weeks were the roughest, as Hazeus was terribly grumpy. He finally led us on a brief excursion to Ephraim following his storming off after a class and claiming that the questions asked were intentionally redundant and meant to make him look boring.

"I was kinda thinking you were going a little fire and brimstone back there," I said.

"Yeah?" he snapped.

"Uh," I waited until he dropped his gaze back to his sandals, "maybe, not?"

"I know," he said. "You're right. I shouldn't let things get to me. What's it been, two weeks?"

"Yeah. Here." I tried handing him some bread.

"No, it has sugar in it," he said.

"Hazeus, for your mother's sake, you can't stop drinking cold turkey and refuse to eat!"

"I'm not refusing to eat, just refusing to eat the stuff that tastes good. There's unleavened if I'm hungry. This getaway will be good for me. I just need some rest."

"If you say so," I said, sneaking a bite and stuffing it back in the donkey's pack.

He slept away most of his time off until one day receiving word from Mary in Bethany. *Lazarus was drinking again.*

I found myself on the road to Jericho trying to keep Hazeus's spirits up. "People aren't perfect!" I was saying. It wasn't a very good argument for Lazarus. In fact, it was the opposite of an argument, but appealing to Hazeus's compassion was often a winning tactic.

"I think you mean grateful," he muttered. "People aren't grateful."

"Oh c'mon. Lazarus cried tears of joy in your arms, remember? He's just hit a weak spot, that's all."

He ignored me and went on muttering, pretending to be rehearsing. I did my best to steer him in a more positive direction, "Look, have some sweet bread."

He glowered at me.

"Come on, he without sin, remember?"

He watched me while I imitated the adulterous woman shivering and hugging herself helplessly. Tough crowd. I got nothing. "You want to be the only one entitled to throw stones?"

He stopped and the pack mule lumbered on fastidiously. He looked at me, his face lightening. Then he took a bit of bread and ate it while we walked on. But that was the last time I saw him eat.

It was in Jericho that he really got on about chaste living being the seat of power and it only got worse back in Bethany. He didn't exactly condemn anyone for imbibing, nor did he confront Lazarus directly, but by the time we were gathered for the last supper, he was becoming pretty quick to point out the disciples who were indulging in too much food! That, and he was in one of his moods.

"I've always said that I should have been born a few thousand years earlier!" Hazeus said at the supper table among his disciples.

"Well, I've always said I shoulda been born in the Orient," I responded in my usual banter. He'd seen my skill with the nunchucks.

"Come now, Son," said Mary, squeezing his shoulder and pulling his head into hers, "lighten up."

"I just don't fit in," he said sourly.

"C'mon man, everyone is here because of you," I said. All present were surely aware that being with someone who could transmogrify things had its perks.

"Perhaps you should have a drink?" Mary said, letting him have his own space again at the center of the table.

"I don't want one," he said, "someone's got to keep their wits about them."

"Hey," I said, proud I'd learned to pace myself- at least until the sun started setting. It's tough documenting the son of God's miracles when you're too drunk.

"I suppose things didn't have to make much sense to anyone before I came along. Before I showed up, things just, well, things probably just happened!" he said.

"Yes, but they happened to prepare for your coming, Son," said his adoptive mother. "Truly, you should have a drink. Try and relax."

"You know what?" Now he was heatedly directing his voice to the heavens, "It must be wonderful being parents in the spiritual realm." He waved his hand absently turning another cup of water into wine. Then, probably because I'd be the only one to remember a thing come morning, he asked me, "I mean, there wasn't anything material for Mother Earth and Father Time to worry about, now was there?"

I shrugged.

Then he continued aloud to himself. "And yes, they happened for me, okay? And still, they happen for me." He turned to another disciple who was approaching with a cup and some bread.

"Are you going on about your father again, Hazeus?"

"The both of them," Mary said while Hazeus waved. Immediately, the gent smiled and moved back to the end of the table with a hiccup.

"Things do happen for me, and I've told everyone here, that they would happen for you too if you would only quit giving into compulsions!"

This brought a small uproar which worried me, but I stood up to quell it by raising a cup and saying, "To compulsions!" That ended the raucous and turned it into a cheer and then the thunk of wooden mugs loosely in agreement!

"Oh, confound it!" said Hazeus. Then he stood up from his seat, gently pushing away the offerings of bread and wine crowding in on him. "If you insist on whittling away at your intelligences, then go on imbibing, but I refuse to explain again to a bunch of drunks!"

There came a brief silence which Hazeus took immediate advantage of.

"This will be my last supper," he declared, then disappeared in a wisp of smoke.

At least that's what he remembers. What the rest of us experienced was a bit more, er, real, you might say.

Chapter Three: Father Time and Mother Earth

"Hey!" said Mother Earth turning from the dishes. "Don't use your father's name in vain!"

Father Time and Mother Earth knew everything was going to turn out okay. They had seen it. In fact, they knew it with every fiber of their being because, well, reality *was* every fiber of their being. But even Gods can't keep the wool pulled over their kid's eyes forever.

So, when the people were going to crucify Hazeus for refusing to drink wine with them, it was no surprise when he came marching in and demanded to know just what in God's name was going on!

Hazeus stopped at the dining room table and Father Time lowered his newspaper to peek over at his son. "She's right, Son. If you're going to curse someone, curse yourself. One day, you'll learn that everything is your own damn fault."

"Okay…" Hazeus said, but the word came out like a train carrying the world and stopping on a dime. He took a deep breath and reconsidered. His father had a knack for always being right, so he said agreeably, "Well then have it your way. What in my name is going on?"

Yep, now that they had a growing boy, they were going to have some explaining to do. Just as most marriages go, the majority of that explaining was done by the father directly to the wife. But Father Time, as always, was prepared. Some answers were not quite appropriate for a young God, so those stories had been recorded on magic video discs for use at a later, more appropriate date. Up to now, they had tried keeping Hazeus from experiencing ugly things; they hid the adult mvds[5] in the closet behind the false panel with the Christmas gifts.

"Well?" said Hazeus.

Father Time raised an eyebrow in Mother Earth's direction and then cocked his head toward the bedroom. Hazeus watched Mother Earth pull the damp dishrag from her shoulder and drape it over the faucet. Was that an eyeroll? She untied her apron and hung it on the peg by the refrigerator as she walked by. He couldn't help but notice that her eyes were shooting arrows at Father Time the entire way.

When she returned, she had a stack of albums in her arms. Hazeus looked from her to Dad and saw a giant smile spread across his face. Dad folded the newspaper, slapped it on the table, and slid his chair back. Hazeus suddenly felt uneasy.

"Well," said Father Time, coming over and grasping his son by the shoulders, "I think it's time you knew the truth."

The truth? How eager Lazarus had been to give the people the truth. Hazeus had always felt a little truth was best left to speculation.

Dad shook him, tousled his hair, and then took the stack of Mvds from Mom. Then he turned and presented

---

[5] Magic video discs

them to Hazeus. "You're old enough to handle these I should think."

Hazeus glanced at the top one before looking up at his father questionably. He may have read the title had the bright red adult rating sticker not upstaged everything else. His father winked and then reached an arm around Mother Earth's shoulder leading her back toward the bedroom. "Yes," said Father Time, "it's a proud day for a father."

What?
Being a forgiving, honest, and intelligent God isn't just built right in ya know, it takes a good upbringing and Hazeus was in for a few final lessons. It was also then that the son of God would be reeducated about the birds and the bees. According to the sounds that were coming from his parent's bedroom, it was also on that very night that his sister was most likely conceived.

But where did this magical place go, you may ask?

Well, that's the question that needs answering now doesn't it?

The good news is, there is an answer. It's all still right here, in Rootworld. Everything the first Gods created for their children and all the magic that goes right along with it.

Chapter Four: Rootworld

The clouds inside of the crystal sphere turned all staticy after Hazeus placed the album on the turnstile and pressed the play button. The needle bounced along the vinyl surface making little pops and scratches, and something told him that there was more going on than he was imagining.

He would find out that he was correct when his mother's voice emanated from a couple of speakers disguised as golden dragon statuettes built into the cradle of the magiscope.

"One may consider your father rather harsh if you think about the multitude of incarnations that might have been swept under the rug to come up with a working model of our known universe, or even a single ant for that matter," her voice said while the interior static of the device fought to gain purchase on a practical interpretation of what was being said. It finally seemed to decide when a cartoon version of a Lego set was shattered by a hammer, and a broom walked over to begin sweeping up the mess.

"But," his mother's voice continued, "if one were to ponder for a moment from your Father's point of view, they may in turn develop a deep sense of self-love. This of course would follow a deep sense of intelligence from understanding the truth."

The image had gone through a cycle of ants marching into and out of their hill and some complex diagram that might have been an ant's brain, and now was becoming a magic carpet that looked terribly surprised.

"And the truth is," the dragon statuettes purveyed, "there was no rug."

The magic carpet's tassels drooped in a strange display of disappointment before it was unraveled among the magiscope's imagery.

"To understand how your father may have created everything perfectly on the first go-round, one would have to have a mind like Tess Nikola's. A great scientist and inventor of Rootworld."

Now the magiscope cleared clouds away to show a young grey-haired girl in overalls sitting at a school desk with her tongue sticking out from the side of her mouth as she worked in a textbook.

"She was friend of Ian Stein's and eventually married with a few of his ideas[6] to come up with her theory on the MagnoElectric Spectrum."

The text inside of the book that the young girl was working in transformed into a musical ladder that became waves of color and dissolved into a shifting mist of clouds again that began forming a larger image of another person. A young, muscular boy, scribbling equations into a notebook.

"She had the extremely rare talent of being able to picture an invention in her mind down to the minutest detail and even run it through all its successes and failures before

---

[6] And possibly other things

ever building the physical model. In short, if she built something, it worked exactly as she had intended[7]."

Swimming through the spherical lens of the magiscope were various contraptions that Hazeus had no idea about, but he did share a curious taste for the ones that were sizzling with electric lightning.

"Your father did a similar trick."

The images shifted again into a gray miasma.

"You see," continued Mother Earth, "things don't get real until someone runs the gambit."

The magiscope now contained a living image of his father lost in thought. As his mother's voice narrated, the eyes began flicking out reflections of his father's fondest memories, starting with their meeting.

"What he did was," she began, "envision a perfect run of the universe. Forget the perfect run of the Universe. And then—" Hazeus thought he saw a smile crawl across his father's visage as images of his own birth flashed briefly in the placid mirrors, "live a lifetime... to remember it."

The magiscope went grey again and Hazeus thought it might be the end of the record, but then the speakers said pertly.
"And there you have it[8]."

"Everything," the golden dragons continued, breathing to life again, starting with a picture of the globe and flying

---

[7] Ian would say that this talent had nothing to do with skill but rather with sex. As he had engaged in many arguments with Tess and always ended up agreeing with her in the end.
[8] The ultimate truth

down in a bird's eye view within close enough distance to skirt the outside of the great pyramid of babel, "I suppose you could say we are living in his wake so to speak." Then as the scene dropped down to cut eddies across the surface of a great body of water, his mother's face appeared on that surface and said rather sarcastically, "A thing you get used to as a wife. Which is why I always steal his thunder whenever possible."

Then her picture was lost in the ripples, speeding away as the bird's eye pitched and flew over a marketplace of milling people.

"The people down there have already started touting the idea that before our universe was independent there was some endless expanse of waves that our infant universe was bouncing along on in our inflaton submarine[9]."

That made Hazeus look back at the jumping needle along the vinyl track.

"But all of that is speculation on the Globe, where the inhabitants have been drunk for so long they've nearly forgotten describing their God as hovering over the surface of the deep, in a book more than two thousand years old. I mean, c'mon! It's right in the beginning, people!"

Hazeus leaned back on his elbows and wondered at the marvel of it all. How hadn't he realized it before? He was looking into the future! He got real close to the crystal orb and looked down into it.

"We have to remember to give the world a little slack because, Space-time, or the continuum of Time-space,

---

[9] Likely until it was swallowed up by a whirlpool where also likely there lived a kraken.

depending on where you were raised, can be confusing." A book cover materialized with a shadowy image branded into the leather that reminded him of, well, it reminded him of himself!

It was him alright! Right there in line art, burned into the cover and written in gold was the title TOME OF AGES.

"When you've read in the Tome of Ages that God hardened the Pharoah's heart, while in Egypt, to help further sink in a lesson[10], you kind of start to think that God may be an out-with-the-old and in-with-the-new kinda guy, not leaving much room for mercy on innocent bystanders. But one would have to understand that this manuscript was produced in and for a universe other than the original and for far different purposes."

Suddenly there was a horrid screeching and the orb filled with that familiar snow left over from the early background radiation of the universe. The needle had jumped track and was nodding to and fro right off of the edge of the player.

Hazeus reached down to replace it in the cradle but stopped when he thought he felt his stomach rumble.

This brings us to another outstanding truth; that no matter what universe you may find yourself in, or find yourself observing, there are always bound to be gods and they will always need to eat.

---

[10] The Tome of Ages reports that the Pharoah was ready to give up but God said, let the plague continue. And locusts, they're were even more locusts.

While Hazeus is away, I would like to interject for you readers who are wondering how it is that storytellers like me can know all these things. That was a trick that once baffled me as well whenever I was in the presence of Merddin as a young chap at Arthur's side. And once again it confounded me while growing up on books by my favorite authors. You could find me more than once declaring, "This bloke must have been there! It's the only way!"

Well, that's about right. Turns out I was there, and soon you too may remember a little something about your pasts. Time is strange like that. Well, at least the next one in office, anyway[11]. That means gods are strange, too.

In fact, in many texts, man himself has often been referred to as a small god. But if we're talking about the earliest ones like Hazeus and his parents, then we must think inside the box[12].

Not to worry, the Son of Father Time will soon be happily munching on thickly buttered popcorn and returning to the enjoyment of his first Video disc on the magiscope, this time with headphones in, no doubt, since the kitchen is in earshot of his parent's bedroom.

To him, existence is a totally ethereal experience. From any omnipotent being's frame of reference, there would be no physical world except that which they might imagine. And that they do quite extensively. So, nothing is ever destroyed. Things are ever only recycled.

---

[11] And by next, I mean previous

[12] A box of R-rated Mvds passed down from a certain Father Time

Taking out the trash is a foreign idea to the omnipotent. They *are* the bin. Everything in the box, self-contained. Batteries included, if you will[13].

And if that is hard to consider, then think of how we only know reality from a totally physical frame of reference. You might ask yourself what spiritual or invisible world might even exist besides what you can imagine. You can't blame Atheists in that regard. Yet, I know better because I remember.

The only disappointment I've really dwelt on throughout my lives is that it has taken this long for beings on both sides of the equation[14] to respect one another's tangibility.

It can make a person, or God, put a finger to their chin and ponder, like young Hazeus for example, when he saw the impact his life would have on a world appearing in front of his own eyes.

Who knows what he must have been thinking as he ran his finger along the title of a magiscope video disc and read the name Arthur. And who knows whether or not those ponderings held any weight or created any gravity or if they were just intangible musings. Either way, it was at this precise time that in Hazeus's world of science and magic, a savior would be born.

---

[13] And it can get musty in there. But there are creative ways to handle the funk. Just look at the advances and ingenuity in space exploration. Because really... that's what Godding is all about (surviving on your own resources in a vacuum).

[14] And it is in fact an equation. It took Laura Mersini and a couple of friends weeks to make the proper calculations, but it was eventually finished. The exact equation is $Im(1/\lambda) > 0$.

Chapter Five: Arthur Disk One

Hazeus had been admiring the artwork on the album cover and was now reading the back of the cardboard sleeve while the static in the magiscope worked itself out.

Young Arthur knew that he wanted to be rich. He wasn't sure that he wanted to be famous. Regardless, he was brought up to believe that being rich didn't necessarily mean you had a lot of gold or silver but instead were wealthy in other ways. That particular belief would be a thorn in our savior's side until he grew much older and the thorn became a sword.

Would his father simply just have said, "Yes we are rich, Son," when he'd been asked, rather than saying, "We're rich in things, Son, not in gold," then perhaps things would have turned out differently.

Now that our savior is of age, it is plain to see that what his father really meant was, we would be rich, Son, if I hadn't spent the gold on so much blasted nonsense. But what could you expect from King Uther Pendragon, the conqueror?

Oh, just wait... it gets richer. The tale that is, and it begins after Uther decides to cart both Arthur and his sister Morgan off to boarding schools. The boy to accustom himself to wearing dresses and the girl to get accustomed to addressing witches, it would seem.

Don't ask Merle, son of Tal, what hand he had to play in that particular event, because that would only make him cranky.

All Great Stories Begin with Dragons

Inside the magiscope, Sylvia took a long deep breath.

She had been dreaming of food. It wasn't often that a knight came prospecting for gold and Taliesin showed up all on the same morning. This century must be special.

By looking at her, the knight wouldn't expect she was a vegetarian. In fact, all of the chrome that he was wearing made it hard for him to be looking at her at all.

He straightened his helmet to see better.

"Not thisssssss again," Sylvia said. A bit surprised at the hissyness in her voice. Her tongue had grown lazy. No wonder her rumored relation to serpents persisted. She lifted one of her clawed fingers and surveyed the nails. Then casually she glanced down at the insect by her tail. He was wobbling. Perhaps the inseam of his metal trousers was a bit too tall?

She tried not thinking of the visitor, he'd ruin her appetite. Instead, she shut her eyes and re-imagined the plump bush of blue roses from her dream.

While she daydreamed, the knight was about to make the classic mistake that all knights eventually do. If he would only take a moment and think of his position from the dragon's point of view, he may reconsider. But a horsefly rarely considers his position to a man, so, what can really be expected in this instance[15]?

Sylvia didn't care for meat. You don't hibernate for one hundred years on the sustained energy from stick figures in metal underwear. Besides, the chewing burned more calories than the man. Creatures her size needed something

---

[15] One may briefly dismiss the buzz of a circling horsefly, yet when the horsefly bites, it is instinct to swat the nuisance straight away, rather the fly knows any better or not.

a bit more, Rootworldly. Though a decent long sword could be handy as a toothpick.

Taliesin was coming through the veil by way of the waterfall that was hiding her cave. She opened her eyes and looked to the shimmering cascade as the water parted like a curtain over his outstretched wand.

At the same time, our shining hero, having straightened his suit of armor nervously, was mistaking the dragon's disinterest as a threat. He had just built up the courage, or siphoned off enough intelligence, to climb atop Sylvia's tail and raise the sword in preparation of his horsefly's mighty bite. He tightened his grip, inhaled sharply, and ... passed out.

On approach, Taliesin watched absently as the recently animated suit of armor fell backward onto the cave floor with a clatter.

"Playing with your food, Sylvia?" Taliesin asked nasally.

Sylvia's scaly hide shimmered as she shifted. If there had been any plants in the cave, they had immediately wilted.

It's a well-known fact that dragons love treasure. You see, precious stones and golden nuggets take no offense to a dragon's sedentary lifestyle. They are, a dragon's best friend. If you can imagine airing out dirty laundry after a hundred years, you can get a picture, a scent rather, of what it may be like when a dragon, fresh from a century of hibernation, spreads her scales for the first time. The knight had neglected his most important piece of equipment. Taliesin, however, had not. *His* clothespin was firmly clipped on his nose.

"Ah, Taliesin."

He didn't have to ask her to know that on top of being vegetarian, she was also a lithotroph. They were longtime friends.

"You look so different," Sylvia said. Her tail unwinding from the stalactite and disappearing into the dark recess. "Have you been imprisoned again?"

"I like to think it is voluntary," he said. Then, "At least, *I* smell the same."

Taliesin drew the shards of the red ruby from his robes and her lips drew back in expectation. He tossed them up to her and she snapped the tiny morsels from the air.

"Courtesy of my student," said Tal. "He's been up to no good."

When the sound of scales upon coins finally came to rest, they heard the brief snort of the armored man's troubled dreams. "Hub-bub-bub-ub-ub... dragons... and wizards... and such," the knight mumbled before rolling over and sticking his thumb back in his mouth.

Sylvia reached with the tip of her tail and tucked the snoozing champion's cape around him.

"He'll be fine," she said. "I'd sooner eat rocks."

"Indeed," said Tal.

"And Red Ruby from the North Dragon Peaks, this side of the veil no less?" she said, licking her lips.

"I know how you like mineral with spirit."

The large yellow eyes followed the sharp chin down to the wizard's level.

"Oh right," said Taliesin, "you must be famished."

He lifted his wand and opened his mouth, "Um, yes. Now what were those words?"

The dragon was taken aback. She sighed and reared up to stretch her wings while he figured it out. The single flap sent the old man's beard into a twisting tangle.

"Oh yes." He loosened the straps on his leather pouch and pulled a flat stone washer from it. "This will help."

When the wind subsided, he placed the disc on the cave floor and again readied his wand.

Sylvia watched with intrigue.

"Garreg y rosen glass," he intoned proudly and then pulled a fully matured bush of blue roses right through the center of the stone with his wand.

'Just how does he do that?' She wondered.

The large gust had cleared most of the dead air, yet still, the instant fragrance was a welcome guest.

"Oh, that is very nice, indeed," muttered the snoozing knight. Tal nodded in agreement and was just reaching to remove his nose plug when Sylvia bit the entire bush off at the stem. He quickly reconsidered.

Taliesin whipped her up another morsel in hopes that she was waking up on the right side of the cave. In fact, it took him six more bushes, drafted from the other side of the veil, before her stomach lost precedence over her curiosity.

"I guess it has come that time again," she said.

"The world is indeed changing hands," Taliesin said. "But this time, something is different."

"The sword?" Sylvia drew her tail across the treasures piled near the back of the cave. They shifted like sand dunes in the desert wind.

"Arthur has claimed it."

"Your student? The one who's been up to no good, I take it," she scoffed. "Men will never change."

"Just harmless mischief, Sylvia. He was only a boy."

"And ready to be a king?"

"No choice. The son of God had passed through the veil, and it grows thicker by the year."

Sylvia let out a warm breath of exasperation and dropped her head back down on her wrists. "And things were going so well when I went to bed," she said.

There was a clatter of chainmail and iron as the dreaming knight repositioned himself.

"It gets worse," said Tal. "Now an army is amassing in his name just across the British sea."

"In Hazeus's name?" Sylvia asked. "Only these metal clad morons could dream up such blasphemy?"

"Our friend here is but one drop in the huge ocean of Romans bearing iron and steel. I fear our greater threat is religious intolerance. If *that* wave crashes on our shores, we will have no choice but to defend ourselves and the truth."

Smoke escaped from Sylvia's nostrils; liquid-fuel drizzling from the darkness of those living caves. She grumbled impatiently, "There is always a choice. As for truth, it will always prevail. In time, it always does. You expect to thwart the will of God after his own son has turned his back to the veil?"

Taliesin puffed out his chest, "Y Gwyr Yn Ebyn Byd. It's the truth against the world!"

Taliesin circled his wand overhead and from the ether a vision rippled to life. Robbed figures ran, alight with fire, along a beach. Flaming arrows pocked the sky as vessels wedged the shoreline...

"Vivian has foreseen it." He said, "Another battle, Sylvia. Yet, this one comes to draw real blood. This time it will take different tactics if we are to endure."

"What makes you so sure that man will make these terrible decisions without considering the consequences?" She said, trying to look as disinterested as possible.

"Well, I am relatively certain that alcohol is involved," he said. Even wizards have a hard time motivating dragons. "Besides, God has given them leave to do as they please."

Sylvia thought of the dragon's breath[16]. She also thought of the youngling she had lost after it had burned a barn down in Bath[17]. She had thought Tal would have brought it up, but he had not. It seemed some men still had hearts.

"Rootworld is maturing, Sylvia, but the veil is going to shut on the Globe and its children. It is our duty to leave these people with hope."

"Urg." She rolled her eyes.

"Even dragons sometimes act without thinking," he said in defiance to her cold stare.

Just then, from across the cave, came a valiant war cry. "Sir Ector prevails!"

The armored knight had retaken his feet and plunged his sword sharply between two scales in Sylvia's tail[18].

Swiftly, the dragon raised her mighty gauntlet and brought it down on the unfortunate nuisance.

"Eh, hem," coughed the wizzard.

Sylvia glanced back at Taliesin. His wand was raised.

She lifted her hand slowly and peeked beneath with one squinting eye. The man was gone; magicked away back to the armies of Romulus.

Sylvia took to her feet with a long, damp, heated sigh. "I suppose you're right," she said.

---

[16] Despite its name, Dragon's breath refers to the fogs or mists that occur when two worlds are merging or separating. This came about because the world to Dragons, was known as the body of a dragon.

[17] This was in fact, the first dragon ever slain (all for just doing what kids do on occasion)

[18] No more than a mosquito bite, really.

If Sylvia *had* been related to serpents her cheeks might not have been blushing such a violent red, but as it happened, she was related to chameleons instead[19].

"Now, how about another rose bush?" she asked, thwarting all embarrassment.

Tal wiped the fog from his spectacles.

"Okay. But you'll have to save room for the main course, eh, of course," said he.

If Sylvia had an eyebrow, it would have raised.

---

[19] Men found it impossible to replicate the color changing ability of dragon scales when they made shields and other things from them, as they were impervious to heat. The color changing actually is achieved not by sending more blood to heat an area but rather by rearranging a layer of nanocrystals called iridophores. By that technique they can even achieve the color blue like a butterfly. So why would a dragon choose to blush? The simple answer is, well, they're honest, if not soft spoken.

Chapter Six: Arthur

Although I didn't come into Arthur's story until a much later time, I was involved in it, like many of the important characters of his life, from the start. That's to say, in secret.

I sometimes wonder how Arthur held it all together like he did. Oftentimes, he would tell me that he felt there was some unseen force driving his actions from behind a veil. I couldn't tell him how spot-on his observation was. I could only assure him that God's will was being done through him, even if he were fighting against the belief that this new God was turning out to be what everyone hoped.

The truth was, the new God wasn't going to turn out like everyone hoped at all. That would have required humankind to turn out as God had hoped after coming to them in the flesh. Not that gods weren't going to exist in the new world, which was materializing under Taliesin and I's own feet. They were simply going to be different gods[20].

But, in the meantime and during the transition, Hazeus was holding on to the edge of his seat until Arthur's final breath. Only after that breath would Arthur ever find peace in knowing that the first God still held onto his heart and had never gone anywhere.

So, as I tell his story, I do so in reverence, and I urge you to picture a person who exercised more faith than any man who has ever lived. A man who had faith in a friend who he knew loved his wife. A man who had faith in a god

---

[20] Gods with a gag reflex tuned better to deal with real bloodshed. These are gods who can find enjoyment in watching rated-R films while not letting them go to their heads.

he watched shed actual blood. A man who had faith in the blood bond of Family even after it had been shorn away.

This indomitable respect for faith was perhaps why he held it as the true measure of purity and balanced his kingdom on that one decree. Faith in God (however hard that was for such a man) was not enough. It was also faith in his fellow man, even if they be his enemy, that won the field of his life. This story will reveal the reason that the legend of King Arthur and his retinue have survived through history and across veils.

Besides, who in their heart of hearts doesn't miss magic, really?

Arthur's story begins under the watchful eye of a loving god who has no quarrel with curiosity or general boyishness. No quarrel with idleness either; you should see the size of his television.

It was a peculiar existence for young Arthur, being brought up in a Christian monastery where half of the members were Culdees[21].

For people like Mott[22], who we'll soon meet, the news of the coming of our lord had been passed down from less than six generations[23] ago. The druids still had a major presence in Wales and the British Isles while the Son of God had disappeared into the mists. Though they were living in an age of growing papal rule[24], they were still firmly planted in a time of magic.

---

[21] Arch Druids parading around as Arch Bishops
[22] The custodian at Bircham's, though if you were to ask the Abbott who ran the place in Mott's presence, he would remain eerily silent
[23] The Culdees primary objective was in keeping the memories of the old religion through these tales
[24] Pope Gregory (590-604 A.D.)

This was all an easy thing for the Druids and Dryads[25] to understand, as they had begun their stent of sobriety once the lord rose from the dead as predicted[26]. The Agnostics, on the other hand, began celebrating this incredible miracle by following along with a little thing called holy communion. Which was a misinterpretation of Hazeus's final act during the Last Supper.

When Hazeus did not partake of the libations before his magical moment of execution, it was supposed to be an example to all men that even as a last request, you should make a sacrifice of pleasure.

Instead, to all those who weren't personally present, eh hem, that's me on the left[27], and after a long game of telephone, the official scripture came out as drink wine and eat food in the lord's name[28]!

In short, once wine began being served at the altar as a celebration of liberation from sin[29]... Well, does anything more need be said?

On top of that, the Devil brews a mean glass of firewater.

Alas, among all of this confusion there happened to be a boy whose teenage heart remained pure. He was born on Beltane and recently had been receiving a very unique and thorough education.

---

[25] Female druid is technically a misnomer but we are eluding to the peoples that communed with nature and those who did not (not that everyone didn't have that ability, it was just that not everyone chose to)

[26] They'd been celebrating his coming for more than a century and were quick to sober up when Dad finally arrived on the scene

[27] No! The other left!

[28] We won't say that the scribe was the one who drank Jesus' portion on that occasion, but, there you go, we've gone and said it.

[29] I mean who drinks in front of their own father?!

A Boy Amid Worlds

Inside of the magiscope, Arthur was squatting low behind some young yew trees.

When the veil was at its thinnest, he sometimes made out the apparition of his teacher right before everything turned *real* again but not this time. Of course, if his friend Gwain happened along just then and saw him crouching there, he would naturally assume that Arthur was doing any crude number of things that people do while squatting in the bushes, but the real reason he was being cautious was simple. He didn't want to get caught.

Last time he and Gwain got caught mucking about in Rootworld without permission, Merddin had set them against each other in a battle of Litnis[30]. A little friendly competition never killed anyone, unless of course it was a battle to the death. Merddin *knew* that Gwain was his superior in combat. Yet, to be fair, Merddin considered Arthur the more well-endowed in common sense. A trait that's absolutely useless in a game of endurance. Also, a trait not on display when friends are caught in Rootworld, suspiciously near the ladies' Isle of Avalon. *Those dryads hardly wore clothing*, Gwain had said. Being ladies of the lake and all, naturally they were always prepared to get a little wet.

Dying in Rootworld, while not permanent, does however make for quite a start when waking in bed the next morning. Especially when you've not experienced dying there before. You might imagine the surprise of getting blasted by one-hundred-thousand volts of white light and expecting to meet your maker. In Arthur's case, he wasn't

---

[30] A deadly game in which to wizzards bat a ball of energy back and forth until the other loses from sheer exhaustion or lack of skill

entirely sure of who his maker was, with all the Gods he had been learning about over the past seven years. Well, there was Pendragon, his father, but technically he was just his creator, wasn't he?

Sometimes... times like these, he wished that everyone could just forget about the whole business of pulling swords from stones and such. Regardless, having some general direction in which to fly, after getting jolted from his body, may have made his first time a little easier. But there was no sense in complaining; that didn't offer any answers now. And that was the way of things, wasn't it? All of his lessons seemed to further prove to him the same thing: How very little he really knew. I mean, just *how* thin could the veil get before dying became permanent anyhow, he wondered.

He could see a sphere ahead where the fog was aglow with orange light. It was the silver candle that he had left burning in the circle of stones. The tiny flame kept the entrance to Rootworld open while he'd went about his mischief. Not so much mischief as a necessary evil, he told himself. He could see the Janus[31] rod standing by the candle as he crept nearer the circle. He had carved the wooden staff in the likeness of the gatekeeper. It had a face on each side, eyes in the back of its head, you could say, that would keep watch in his absence so no creepy or crawly things might pass through to the Globe in his stead[32].

While he had whittled away at it the night before, Borus had told him that with a name like Janus he should give it two butts to match the two heads. It was

---

[31] The god of doorways
[32] Though the world Arthur inhabited on a regular basis seemed more home to the creepy stuff

quite a crack from Borus. With a name like Borus, well, you can imagine that he is not always the one to excite.

Arthur reached down and worked his fingers at the catch of his belt to free his iron sickle. The damp fog and brine had shrunk the leather around the knot. He was stuck tugging at his belt buckle, another action that would not bode well had Gwain happened along to see; he could practically hear his friend snickering and pointing like an idiot. The distracting thought was enough that Arthur didn't notice when the fog did what fog was notoriously known for doing. It had rolled.

The fog rolled into such a thick mass at his feet that he tripped right over it and went sprawling. He'd have knocked himself clean out had the circle of stones been closed. As it stood, his head hit the soft ground right at the vacancy he'd left on his exit. When he turned over on his backside he thought, 'Good thing I didn't use pumpkin sized rocks like Murdack[33] suggested, a simple trip could kill ya. That was, if lugging the heavy things didn't do ya in first.'

The correct size, according to the leaf totem on circles, was about the size of one's own fist. Arthur's stones, then, were well enough inside the recommendations for safety. His fist couldn't knock himself out, much less anyone else.

The twelfth fist-sized stone was exactly where it should be; one foot outside the circle and to the right, as per the instructions. Of course, he could've always been lazy and used pebbles, but rumor had it that last year a squire had gone missing on Samhain while trying to summon up some shade or another. When it comes to magic, you don't shortcut.

---

[33] Not that Murdack should know, he was the order's tilting tutor and didn't get his burly form by going the extra mile in anything. If he ever did make a circle he'd use the same sized stones as everyone else, if not smaller.

Arthur reckoned since it was the Gods that were the ones judging your performance, it could always happen that Llew Law Gwyffs[34] or King Lyrr[35] might just mistake a measly pebble for another speck of dirt and for no other reason than the fact that they are *the* gods, send you spiraling off into another time and place. It made him shudder just thinking of it.

It was also, for that reason, that when fog started acting too much in character, Arthur immediately made for the safety of his circle. He'd freed the sickle from his belt and scratched an arc between the open stones in the dirt, intoning 'E Gweer!' Then, when he placed the properly sized—if he must say so for himself—stone back into place, the fog immediately vacated his small sphere of safety[36].

He looked down at the moon-shaped sickle in his grip and saw the ground below through the void in its blade. He was here because of that void. If Merddin turned up before he fixed his sickle, there would be Bran[37] to pay.

Sitting there in the clear, crisp bubble of air, he could see that there was nothing in the path where he'd fallen. Whatever it had been had moved on, even if it had been his own two feet. There was never any telling, what, with six ounces of mistletoe tea in his system, tripping was just something that could happen. What he *did* see, just outside the circle, was his prize red ruby of mars which he had just lifted on this daring return trip to the Isle of the Dragon.

---

[34] God of Wind

[35] God of Sea (waves might be confusing, but there may be something to that as well)

[36] Every time this occurred it made him wonder why from this side the protective bubble was, well, a bubble, and on the other side it was always a pyramid

[37] A god believed to provide entertainment in Rootworld and protection on the Globe

The journey from Tintagel to the Needles was a day's ride on horseback, but the funny thing about opening portals and wandering through the dragon's breath was that, with luck, you could fool Time into believing you had made just enough effort to simply be deposited there in mere hours.

And his effort had been no farce! Truly he had believed himself hopelessly lost before coming upon the brittle old tree jutting out by the lapping waves of the channel. There, hanging from it, was the old horn that should summon the ferryman.

The Advice of Friends

A week earlier, Gwain had told him that if he threw the shards of his old ruby into the sea, then Lyr would bring him another. Though Gwain's suggestion had lost a bit of merit when Arthur caught him eavesdropping while he threw the pieces to the waves[38]. He couldn't blame him. Ruby fetched a fair price, and Gwain was always in need of steel. No one broke more swords.

Besides, who was Arthur to decide what was picked up by whom when gifts were left for the gods.

Regardless, they had resolved that the only real hope in finding its twin would be to retrace the steps he took with his mentor a year earlier. Not wanting to wait for Gwain to be free of Murdack's morning fencing and tilting lesson, Arthur had set off to put his latest lessons to good use. The events had brought him through the mists and to the old ferry crossing.

Arthur had waited thirty minutes down by the shoreline after blowing into that dusty cornucopia before deciding just to swim out to the needles for his prize. He had reached the third rocky crag before the current got too treacherous to continue. Climbing up onto the slippery slope he had resorted to desperate measures. Sea water dripped from his jerkin as he lifted his arms high above and recited one of the sacred spells of making.

"A nal nathrock uth vase bethewd ..."

He saw Dragon's Isle rise in the far distance or, was it that the sea level dropped? It was too far to risk swimming. However, beneath his feet, the base of the crag he was standing on was now revealed. It was as if gum had been

---

[38] Eavesdropping was coined during this time for just the reason there was a great spot for curios boys to drop a spying eye from the eaves of a cliff above the cove

whisked away from the root of a rotting tooth. Embedded in the ochre was his replacement ruby.

Resolute, he had then used the blade of the sickle to jostle the gem free, and as the sea came back up to meet him, he secured it in his pouch and began his swim back to the main island.

He had hardly gotten a chance to dry. It only took half an hour of hiking before the fog grew as thick as pea soup and he happened upon the young stand of yew trees. An impossibility, as the hike down took more than an hour and a half! But that was how the dragon's breath worked sometimes[39].

Now, his ruby lay outside of the circle, which he'd already sealed in order to bring down the veil, and his treasure was in danger of being left behind on the island.

He didn't think, but reached out swiftly and captured it.

When his fingers breached the bubble of the closed circle, the wind howled in protest. *When it comes to magic, you don't shortcut.*

Fog flooded into his safe haven and the flame of the silver candle flickered as a tempest made its way through the gully. The young yews bowed as he realized his mistake. The ruby was again in his fist, but the fog grew dark like an ocean suddenly choked with kelp. It went in a spiraling gust up around him.

He looked up at the Janus rod and the faces seemed to glower in disapproval as the staff danced a spiral in the whirlwind. Arthur acted as the candle sputtered out.

---

[39] Especially if a certain wizzard were watching

He shoved his treasure under his tunic and pulled himself up by the Janus rod with his right. He stood up tall and freed the oaken staff, lifted it and the sickle above his head.

"Nid Dim on Dew..."

Then drawing both relics down in an arcing motion...

"Nid dew on dim!"

The thick, rancid, humidity suddenly dropped like a banner in the instant stillness. The fog became dew on the grass, and the sun broke free from over the horizon, casting a golden sheen across the valley as it rose in an animated speed to its apex. Pink ribbons crawled out across the sky, and the yews bristled with life.

Arthur ran the sickle into his belt and removed the ruby from his tunic. He held it up in the sun and the heat from the focused light was immediately on his skin. It was a perfect twin other than a dark inclusion at its center, but it would have to do.

As Arthur probed his way through the thicket and began tottering up the incline to Tintagel, a winged silhouette rolled along the uneven terrain beside him. He didn't have to look up to know that it was Cedric.

Merddin's bird was the only fowl on the planet whose down was darker than its own shadow [40]. The normal excitement that Arthur would feel at Cedric's arrival was replaced by uncertainty. The morning's events had him questioning if the beaked tattletale had been around when he dropped the veil.

The first time that Arthur had met Merddin Emrais was when he'd followed the large raven through the forest.

---

[40] Cedric was so darkly colored that some actually thought he was a shadow. You'd have to be able to be looking both at the sky and the ground simultaneously to know otherwise. Which made things confusing to everyone but the chameleons.

Perch to perch, the huge mass of feathers had coaxed him forward to within earshot of Merddin's lute. When asked about the strange pet, the druid had told him that if there *were* any masters present, it had been the bird.

Now, Cedric lit in front of the treacherous east ridge, his left claw clutching a score of snails.

"Oh no you don't," said Arthur waving his Janus walking stick in the bird's direction.

Over the years, the raven had nearly led Arthur right over the edge of the bluffs in the same game of tag. The sandpaper cackle echoing when he poked his head through thin foliage along the crag. It was just play for Cedric, but something made Arthur feel that the animal was void of sympathy for snail and student alike. It may have been the way it dropped the snails down onto the rocky shore below in order to break into their fleshy centers. A pet like that didn't need spoiling, some of his fondest memories were of Merddin arguing with the confounded bird.

As Arthur emerged from the steep footpath and onto the grassy knoll, he startled a kaleidoscope of butterflies. Now *there* was an animal he could do as a pet. Nothing scary nor magical about them. Well, they were just as impossible to catch as Cedric, and he thought he recalled Merddin saying something about if you killed one now then you may change the course of history in few hundred years. Suppose when it came right down to it, even the most beautiful creatures were dangerous. He thought again of the ladies of Avalon.

The bells from St Materiana's Church were tolling for morning mass as Arthur set off through the knee-high grass, attempting to ignore the fluttering insects. Of course, when your goal is to avoid a butterfly rather than catch it, the things all of a sudden became very friendly. He managed to break free of the swarm without killing too many of his great-great-grand-children and pondered why it was that your thought about a thing carried so much gravity.

If he could somehow work out how to think more positively, or just not think much at all, he may end up being a decent king indeed. Yet, as he cut a line through the plain, he was off to a bad start already. Thinking about nothing more than Mother Theresa setting him to a few barrels of potatoes and may apples over his tardiness.

Chapter Seven: Mott's Order

Mother Theresa was the only nun in Cornwall that could keep St Materiana's church in any certain order other than simply, Bircham's. Materiana's was a vestige of Anglo-Saxon belief but Bircham's Order decreed them part of the rising Roman Catholic church. None of the friars hardly realized what it took to keep the place operating. What it took was six feet of smocked religious habit, a backward veil, and a skin tag strategically marked with a hair on the chin. The friars called her Mott, and when Mott spoke, people did more than listen, they averted their eyes.

Mother Theresa knew what she was doing each morning as she readied herself for mass. Her beauty mark was a brand of personal power. It paid to look that good. What, did people think that more than one hair didn't grow from that mole on her chin? It took work, you know, plucking it religiously. No sense in plucking every last hair though. People might take notice.

The friars were good enough men. A little soft-bellied maybe, but it was only a trait passed down through the generations. The young men do all of the work, while the old men do all of the ... well, she wasn't sure exactly what they did, besides scribble away on that confounded parchment during long-winded arguments over vague rumors.

"Did you hear of the battle between Mecca and Medina? Word is Clovis is claiming Gaul. Have you considered the possibility that Friar Charles' gold and white frock is actually black and blue?" And so on and so forth.

Naturally the boys who used to do all of the fetching, and scrubbing, would grow up to become the friars. They had earned their place. Meanwhile, Mott had earned her place by looking threatening with a rolling pin, and sometimes a hammer. She was, after all, the one who kept the church sign tightened, polished, and perched above the mission entrance. If a friar so much as attempted to hold his title over her head, the title that she held over all their heads may just come crashing down on the lot of them. She smiled at the thought.

Mott took another peek through the loose boards behind where Friar Charles stood upon the dais. He was busy delivering his usual fire and brimstone which she had learned to tune out. Beyond Charles's black mantle, she imagined the argument continued among those gathered in the chapel. *She* thought his frock was gold and white. Murdack was sitting in the front row and the way his face was going wooden, she guessed he too was just realizing that they were short one altar boy.

Now, where was that Arthur? The bells had tolled twenty minutes ago, and Murdack would surely scold the boy upon his late arrival. Morning mass was no place for it, but that never stopped him before. Oh well, if Murdack interrupted again she would just have to tie another knot in his breastplate cords. He could use a gentle reminder to take a little less communion anyhow. If that didn't work, then maybe she could tell Merddin and he could turn him into a toad. There wouldn't have to be much magic involved in that. Again, she smiled.

When Merddin had first come asking about young Arthur, she thought the Bard had been mistaken. It was only natural to feel that way when her best worker was being surveyed as the possible recipient of a higher education. That would mean she would have to spend more time explaining things to Gwain and motivating Borus. Borus could haul double what the other boys could from the well, but half of his time was spent preoccupying himself with the smell of his fingers after a good scratching of his backside, or pulling love bugs apart from their mates.

She may have contested had the druid not produced the boy's birthrights from the end of his magic wand in a minor display of indoor fireworks. The trick had made some dormant flush of heat rise under her cape. Thoughts like that weren't becoming for a nun, but she had to admit, the man had spark.

Chapter Eight: A Wizzard

Mott stepped out of the side door and peered along the dusty cobbles which ran the length of Bircham's chapel. Young Arthur was just coming through the archway of the monastery with a loyal following of butterflies; the light shining off his blonde hair. He flew into her arms like a kite with a tail of rainbow ribbons.

"I'm late," Arthur said from the muffled crease of her bosom.

She pressed the boy back to get a good look at his blue eyes. He was swatting lightly at the butterflies.

"Bless it, these creatures won't be away," he said.

She took the crooked staff from Arthur, leaned it against the stone wall, and unfurled his brown robe in a single whipping motion with her right hand.

Mott gave a gentle wave and mashed the thick robe over Arthur's head, pulling it straight.

"Come now, you smell like you've rolled in honeysuckle," she said, depositing a copper candle dish in his grip. "You've been lucky not to attract the hummingbirds as well."

"Is Murdack at mass?" Arthur asked.

"I'm afraid there'll be no avoiding him. He's already got that look in his eye," said Mott.

"How many barrels am I in for?" he asked, watching Cedric light on the steeple cross.

"Oh, hush now. Your tutor sent word that you are in for some proper education this afternoon. You'll be free if you survive your morning duties."

"Merddin?"

"That's right, now be off with ya before Friar Charles finishes cursing the whole congregation," she said.

Arthur ambled off toward the doors.

When Mother Theresa re-entered her room, a familiar old man was lounging comfortably in her knitting chair. His legs were crossed under his light blue robes, his pointed dunce's hat draped over his most elevated thigh. Merddin was getting a spark to his pipe just as she heard the chapel doors fall shut on the other side of the wall. She couldn't help but peek. Merddin's intrusion could wait.

She peeked through the boards into the chapel and watched as Arthur made his way up the aisle toward the dais. As he approached the front row, where his jousting teacher sat, Murdack's grimace grew irrevocably tight. The old boy wasn't going to be able to contain himself. Another communion, chalked up to Murdack's short temper.

She dared a glance to Merddin who was now puffing away jovially and saw that he had one finger to the sky. A gesture for her to be patient. When he pointed to the crack, she peered back through.

Murdack looked like a cat had his tongue. Twice he nodded in Arthur's direction, but it seemed that his mouth just wouldn't obey his passion. Suddenly master Murdack had developed too much tongue, quite a feat, for his oversized mouth.

Arthur took his place by the dais after lighting his wick on the candelabra. Meanwhile, Murdack sat there unusually silent and feeling defeated. He had a strange craving… for flies.

"It was your idea," said the wizard between puffs, responding to her raised eyebrow.

"T'was only a passing thought, old man!" Mott stepped away from the wall, ducking beneath one of the hanging plants. "Practicing magic in the house of God, it's improper."

"Well, I say, I would do no such thing," Merddin twisted his beard around his index finger. "When it comes to magic, I ma 'dam, am no practitioner, but a professional."

With a huff, Mott stepped to her table and finished breaking the last of the bread into bite-sized pieces.

"It's too soon, I tell you," she said, shaking her head.

"Destiny waits for no boy," said Merddin. "You've had more than enough years to whip Borus into shape."

Mott's fingers whitened with her grip on the serving tray.

"Borus's backside was numb to the whip before it were ever fashioned. Maybe the only thing thicker is his head."

She sighed.

Merddin said, "If we don't act soon there will be no sword left to pull. It's damp on the other side of the veil you know. Rust tends to take, eventually."

"You with your Rootworld and dragons, and destinies," she said, clearly tired of the day-to-day. What she needed, was a vacation.

"We will need witnesses, Mott. You have been the only one at Bircham's that I could count on."

"Aye, well, without Arthur, the only thing I'll have left to count on is me own ten fingers," she said sourly.

"Beg your pardon? You'll also have your toes."

She lifted the tray pointedly. "I must really deliver the communion. Blast it all! What's happened to the wine?"

"Sorry madam, it's been a long night." He unwound his beard and lifted his wand. With a grape-scented voice he muttered a few syllables and before she could object the tray took on a bit more weight. A plum-colored slosh peeked at the rim of the pitcher.

She felt a teenage tingle of desire and slowly set the tray back on the table. "I thought your kind had rules about such things!"

Merlyn struck a wooden match, "Moderation, is the key."

"It's going to take some convincing," said Mott.

"Well, word is around the forest that convincing is your specialty," he lifted the flame halfway to his pipe and stopped, "if I am not mistaken."

"What I mean is it is going to take some convincing, me!" Mott said, the tray shuddering.

As Merddin grasped for her meaning, he recalled a past life as a squirrel during mating season. While he reminisced, the match had burnt down to his thumb. "Ouch! Confound it!"

Shaking his hand to a blur and finally getting ahold of himself he said, "Well yes, of course. Naturally." He pushed his glasses up the bridge of his nose, "Name your price."

With a curtsy that reduced her height from six feet to four and increased her girth, considerably, she batted her eyes. "Nothing less than a very long vacation on the isle of Avalon," she said, "all expenses paid."

"Beg your pardon?"

"You heard me," she said.

"But don't you have rules? Blasphemies and things of that sort? Your being a nun and all?"

"Oh, can it Merddin! Do you see any Romans around here?" she asked, before blousing her habit and turning a few pirouettes. "Sometimes a woman just needs a little magic in her life."

She winked.

He supposed he did have quite the relationship with Avalon. Possibly the fairies could convert a set of drapery or a bedspread into a fitting gown for her, on account that parachutes hadn't been invented yet. There were other ways, he didn't want to consider, that she could ask him to introduce a little magic in her life.

"Besides, convincing I my specialty." She directed his eyes to her rolling pin.

She saw his Adam's apple bounce and then noticed the pitcher of wine suddenly lost a cup of volume.

"Alas, I shall speak with the Lady of the Lake on your behalf," he said. And then he belched.

A Frog in the Throat

Arthur stood beside the dais with his candle dish and snuffer. Murdack was unusually quiet. Borus sat beside him. It was obvious that he had been careless in his fencing instruction yesterday, for both of his ears were crimson. Only one other thing, besides a wooden sword, could cause that much redness. And that Borus had experienced on Mother's Day when Theresa snatched him by the ears for his unruly oration before the congregation.

"God bless all the mothers," he'd said. Theresa, being the singular woman in Bircham's order, naturally assumed he was being vulgar. Of course, Arthur and Gwain knew that was really the best he could do.

Mott came through the entrance with an unusually broad smile and hummed her way between the rows. Gwain placed his candle on the floor and took up the tray of bread and wine while Arthur doused each of their oblations. Mott handed Arthur the pitcher and he retook his place a step down from Friar Charles, who'd upon getting a scent of the libations, was hurriedly bringing his sermon to a close.

Mott ladled out small helpings of the wine to each passing member. Of course, Friar Charles had two full servings while they assembled back to front. The lesser were always in further wont of blessings, and of course, free spirits.

"And be thou blessed," said Friar Charles with each passing patron. "Peace go with you," he continued as the next took their bit of bread and dipped their lips to the ladle. "Of the blood and of the body, blessed be thy name." And then the next, "Thy will be done... by Jove, Murdack!" said he, "Pull yourself together."

Murdack gathered his tongue up from the floor.

"Well, at least he's seemed to learn and hold his tongue," The Friar told Mott.

Murdack rolled the sticky thing and shoved it in his mouth. His attempt at rage came out as a ribbit.

From behind the wall, Merddin Chuckled.

Chapter Nine: What are Friends for?

After their itchy burlap robes had been neatly deposited on the hooks outside Mott's quarters, Gwain and Arthur raced down the slope behind Materiana's to their dugout hut near the corner of the property. Their sandals were left at the door and the two boys went feverishly to work. Arthur's hands were busy seating his replacement ruby into the sickle's blade, when he noticed Gwain had a handful of assorted leaves. His tongue had been cocked from the side of his mouth as he worked.

"Those aren't oak leaves, Gwain."

"Do you really think he'll notice?"

"Considering each letter represents a different tree type," said Arthur. "It's Merddin. He's probably already noticed."

Gwain continued stringing the leaves onto twine in an attempt to make a satisfactory booklet for the Wizard.

"You have had three weeks to get it done," Arthur said, before the ruby found its groove, "Ah hah!"

Arthur held the sickle up proudly.

"Says you with a stolen ruby," said Gwain.

"Pfft. I worked hard for this ruby. Besides, it's practically identical."

Arthur slid a wooden box out from under his bed and unhooked the catches. He folded back the lid, revealing his personal symbols of mastery. Wrapped in a blue cloth was a chalice he had fashioned from mother of pearl. In white, rested a rainbow-colored wand. A vine naturally twisted up its length to the top. In a small green pouch hid a smooth bluestone washer. Arthur removed the red cloth and spread it out on his bed. He placed the sickle on the cloth and wrapped it delicately, depositing it in the box. He clasped the box shut again and turned to Gwain.

"I wouldn't have had to go back for another ruby had you not been using my sickle for your pyromancy."

"How was I supposed to know it would break?"

"I still think you were torturing the ants," Arthur said. "Merddin says no one should touch another's personal symbols of mastery."

"Oh, what's the big deal?"

"You'll see if you touch this box again, I'll set fire to your hair while you sleep."

"That's the only way you'd best me; in my sleep, you know."

Arthur smirked.

A black mess of feathers suddenly took up occupancy on the inner windowsill and announced its entrance.

Taking the messenger's cue, Arthur placed the box on his cot and stripped off the dirty tunic, "I won't argue with you about fencing, but academically, I'm afraid you're outmatched."

Arthur straightened his hair in front of the silver wall-plate above his pinewood chest. As he opened the trunk and removed his Ovydd's robe, he heard Gwain mutter to himself when another leaflet tore.

Cedric clucked impatiently.

Dawning the robe and then shouldering the box of symbols, Arthur pointed to Gwain's project, "On those last two leaves you've written oak but they're clearly poison sumac."

Gwain eyeballed the booklet questionably. He could have sworn that Cedric laughed. "You're joking!"

Arthur opened the door and said, "Guess you'll not find out until tomorrow."

Gwain suddenly found himself scratching.

Home Away from Home

Arthur followed Cedric along the ridge toward Merddin's cave, the wooden box strapped on his back. His green robe had grown dark over the last year with wear. Still, it was precious to him. Mostly because of the care Mott took in helping him fashion it. He'd grown impatient sitting by while she spun the flax, so she had sent him off for the dyes; green grasses on the plain, and fern from the forest. He bore it proudly ever since. Now his ankles peered out from the bottom hem.

Sandstone tumbled away beneath his sandal and disappeared into the frothy breakers far below. Cedric squawked as Arthur pressed tighter to the wall of the cliff. Sometimes the wind along the route to the falls opposed every step. One mighty gust was likely to catch a hiker's hood and lift them right up from their feet and away from safety. But Arthur had come a long way with the God of Wind, and now Lew Llaw Gwyffs was more likely to badger Cedric, as they passed along the treacherous route, than he would Arthur. A fact Arthur was taking a slight enjoyment in.

He sidled along, glancing up every now and again to watch the fragile sylphs send gentle updrafts underwing, keeping Cedric from getting any real purchase. He knew the frustration that could cause firsthand. During his second year, under Merddin's tutelage, he'd spent a spell as a sparrow, and the same little sylphs had nearly cost him his tail feathers at the talons of a peregrine. Now, one of that same peregrine's primary feathers was trapped beneath the sap coating of his rainbow wand. It was his first victory over the elemental forces. No easy feat!

In fact, had Cedric not intervened with a quick grab of his beak, Arthur may not have emerged the victor.

Remembering the event, he closed his eyes and whispered *Y Gwyr*. Then smiled warmly as the wind spirits lost interest and Cedric finally found a foothold on the ridge.

Along the crest, sandstone whirled into dust devils that traced his path forward toward the cave, the steady gust now helping to press him safely to the cliff wall. Before long, he could see a rainbow tracing an arc through the fine spray beyond the blind ahead.

The cave.

Maybe today Merddin would take him into its depths that had remained so secret over all of these years...

Chapter Ten: Merddin's Cave

No other place in Cornwall was as luxurious as Merddin's seaside cave. The inside of a cave would quickly grow unbearable from the smoke of burning torches as little light crawled beyond the damp spray of the shimmering cascade that separated the outside from the in. However, the soft glow instead emanated from fixtures of every shape.

Dim orange light spilled over the chairs, footrests, and bookshelves. In one instance it was coming from the eyes of a skull. On the floor beside the postern, which cradled the unfortunate animal's remains, was a paper cylinder, also glowing with a soft shine. Overhead, a fan turned, kept in motion by some mysterious unseen force.

The furniture was mostly leather, that was, the pieces that weren't piled in hordes against the walls. Animal skins were draped over the backs of chairs and tossed over racks of antlers. A shining cherry wood table with two leaves marked the center of the space, a thing unheard of until the 16th century. Atop this marvel was a spread of fine china, whose origin Arthur only knew from Merddin's frequent educational tales. It had been set for three, which he found odd.

The falling water had been bewitched into a proper curtain by Arthur's symbol of mastery until his attention was stolen away. Cedric was the unfortunate recipient of the blunder. Arthur had nearly dropped the precious chalice, which he had been holding aloft, when he saw the most misplaced item by far.

Mott was lounging in the chair that Arthur had naturally grown to think of as his own, and she was smiling.

As Cedric went to work shaking off the beads of moisture from his oily coat, Arthur's jaw suddenly developed an aversion to staying shut.

An Interlude

A wedge of yellow light cast itself across the surface of the magiscope and Hazeus could see the reflection of the refrigerator being opened in the kitchen. He mashed the pause button on the player and turned around to see his dad's head buried inside of it, accompanied by the clinking of glassware. He must've been up for a midnight snack.

"I don't get it!" Hazeus hollered over the partition, hoping his father was in a decent mood.

The clinking stopped and Hazeus saw his dad's brown hair appear above the rim of the lower fridge door, and then his bushy eyebrows, then finally his eyes. The tanned knuckles of his left hand still held the woodgrain laminate handle. "What's that, Son?"

"I mean, when's it get good? I thought there was supposed to be, you know, grown-up stuff on these mvds?" Hazeus thought briefly that he had taken more offense at his parents' indiscretion in the bedroom that evening than he had at anything he'd seen so far in the magiscope.

He heard his father sigh, then one final clink before the refrigerator door closed and the full-bearded face of Father Time found its height. Then he leaned against the partition. He stood propped on his knuckles against the low wall with a bottle of wine and two long-stemmed wine glasses nimbly crossing each other in the fingers of his left hand.

"It's important, as my son, that you ask yourself if that is really what you want," started his father.

Hazeus dropped his gaze for a moment, but his dad didn't let him feel ashamed for too long. "Once, when I was reading your mother one of my stories and had gotten to the part when the young prince was finally going to ask the young princess to marry him, she screamed, 'Stop! It's a trap!'."

Hazeus was now thoroughly confused and kinda wished he'd not said anything in the first place. His father knew this before he himself did. That was kind of his thing. Also, why when his father said something you didn't easily lose interest since the tact was built right in from the start.

"Not, the marrying, Son," continued Father Time, understanding. "Getting married wasn't the trap your mother feared for the prince, it was the growing up. Growing up can be a trap."

Hazeus thought he might be beginning to understand the moral.

"Take Arthur's state of confusion when he saw Mott in his chair at the cave," said his father, "first you'd have to catch up on how things order themselves in Rootworld. Any student of the occult, be it witchery or wizardry, was taught one thing from the start. Like attracts like here in Rootworld."

Hazeus was getting it now. On the spiritual plane that is how things were. If you thought about something, you got it. It was simple as that. A whole load different than over there on the physical plane where Maggie had produced his living counterpart, making him the only tourist able to move from the Globe to Rootworld on a whim.

Over there on the Globe you didn't just think up a pair of fuzzy bunny slippers if your feet were cold. No, over there you thought of a pair of fuzzy bunny slippers and all of a sudden your feet were freezing and you realized that if you wanted a pair of fuzzy bunny slippers you'd first have to catch a bunny, and proceed to go through a whole lot of gruesome steps that directly opposed the whole point of a comfy pair of slippers to make them in the first place.

Father Time had given him the span of time necessary to come up with this little bit of insight before he continued.

"Exactly like here," he began, seeing the pride in his son's eyes, "Fire is fought with fire, water with water... If you went putting opposites together, you transfigured things. For instance, fire and water make steam; meanwhile the original elements lose all of their power and form. The same went for the sexes."

Oh boy. Now Hazeus was really wishing he'd said nothing. Particularly he'd not exactly ever seen his dad hanging around in the kitchen at midnight with a couple of wine glasses, obviously ready to return to the bedroom for a   nightcap. He could see the understanding in his father's face that was always there[41].

"Look," he said, "boys studied one place, girls another. You just didn't go inviting women into your cave; they could drain the energy of the whole place in a single go. Arthur knew that better than anyone," Dad said. Then he winked. He found his footing and prepared to be back off to bed. But before he left, he added, "Only because he'd once witnessed Mott do something similar with a whole gallon of wine."

Hazeus turned back to the magiscope and crossed his legs. He put his finger to his chin and was almost going to let the whole thing go when it just became too much for him, "Dad?!"

His father stopped with the bedroom door propped partway open. Hazeus's mind was in a state of fury. Were they really drinking wine in there? Is that what adults did?

---

[41] It was right in the space between hair. The eyes and bridge of the nose. If you'd seen Father Time in Minesota you might have mistaken him for bigfoot. Then there was that one time in the Alps when someone fainted as he appeared to them. If they would have realized it was god they may not have, but they assumed he was a yeti instead.

He had just found it so appalling that the inhabitants of the Globe were drinking in his own name that he had quite literally departed their company, so why in, forgive the explicit language but, why in God's, then he corrected himself, why in his own name were Mom and Dad drinking?

"That's easy," said Father Time, before he had even asked[42]. "We're just happy you're home."

The wedge of yellow light became a slit across the surface of the magiscope as the bedroom door clicked closed.

Hazeus deflated back into his own lap and tossed another few buttery puffs of corn in his mouth.

"Hmm," he thought aloud, and mashed the pause button.

---

[42] That's also kind of his thing.

Chapter Eleven: Polite Utensils

Merddin was busy arguing with the tea kettle.

Arthur could tell Merddin was trying to say something, but the ear-piercing cry of a whistle was drowning him out.

Merddin smacked it with his wand.

"Now, I do say," began Merddin, satisfied.

Cedric knocked the wizard's pointed cap askew as he took his perch near the stove. He received a scornful look as Merddin quickly straightened it.

Mott covered her mouth with a tissue, trying to hide a sure chuckle.

"Now, I do—" the kettle started up again.

Merddin frowned. WHACK!

"Now, There's that." He looked now at Arthur, who appeared rather disturbed.

Merddin continued, "As you've noticed—"

SQWAUK!

Merddin glowered at Cedric, this time clearly annoyed.

For once, Arthur agreed with the bird.

"Hmph!" Merddin decreed, giving a great huff that sent the tip of his wizard's hat flopping forward, further setting him into a rage.

"Oh, you tell him!" he blurted to Mott, and went back to arguing with the kettle.

Mott's face was returning to normal from a nice bright pink when she put her hands in her lap. They shared a little smile when, from over the stove, both saw the wizzard pull his hand back after trying to handle the hot-headed teapot.

"I know you weren't expecting to see me again today, Bear cub," started Mott. "But Merddin and I have something to tell you."

She motioned for Arthur to have a seat at the table.

He unshouldered his wooden box and placed it on the table; the silverware shuffled aside to clear him room.

You get used to furnishings having a mind of their own when you've been brought up in the house of Taliesin. It's not a well-known fact that Merddin and Taliesin are one in the same, but all the future history books will show it's so. Also let it be said that Taliesin[43], before he was set adrift on a boundless sea, was once teacher to all intelligences.

If you are going to command the material of time and space, it is only proper to start from the ground up[44]. The most basic things were the easiest to teach; atoms and elements and such. Generally, he just had to remind them to, "Hold yourself together lad!"

You'd be surprised what utensils are capable of remembering. It was the more complex things in existence that were stubborn when it came to learning.

Objects are never shy around Merddin. It is their natural tendency to act to their fullest potential. There's always an aim to impress in the company of your teacher. Though, Arthur's good friend Borus would seem to contradict this infallible law.

While Arthur wrapped up and stowed the chalice, Merddin finally managed to bring the tea; that is, the tea allowed him to bring it over. Much to everyone's relief, it had decided not to give a toot, after all.

"That's better," said Merddin.

A chair at the end of the table stepped back to allow Arthur to have a seat.

---

[43] Also, Merle son of Tael, Ambrosius, The Wizened, and very far in the future, Merlin.

[44] On another plane a young woman named Lilith will be experiencing a similar situation very soon

He obliged, feeling quite like Merddin and Mott were about to stage some sort of intervention. All teenagers feel this way when approached by more than one figure of authority. Naturally they assume words are about to be said about changes their bodies are going through, or feelings they may be having toward the opposite sex. Arthur briefly thought of the business with his ruby, and eyed Cedric accusingly.

"You are coming to an age—" began Merddin.

Here it came. But he thought they'd covered this when he and Gwain got caught spying on the girls on Avalon Isle…

"—when things should be told to you plainly." The wizard looked at Mott for approval.

She nodded encouragingly.

This was quite the news coming from Merddin, who'd said not one thing plainly during his entire life.

Arthur would say anything to be free of this awkwardness. He made a minor attempt. "Hold on a minute," he said. "It took me nearly an hour to cross the bluffs. How did you manage to beat me here after mass?"

Thinking about it now, he just couldn't picture Mott toeing it across the slim ledge. He and Merddin had been over the laws of physics, and let's just face the facts here; Mott normally had an entire church-pew to herself, and it wasn't *exactly* because everyone was terrified of her.

Mott crossed her legs and straightened her smock, nuzzling down deeper into the easy chair.

"And who was it that taught you to use a broom?" she asked.

Arthur's face twisted into an expression of distaste. A broom? A broom? Was she implying that she had flown here on a broom like Merddin may have done?

"Oh, never mind the details," said Merddin, quickly snuffing out the image of a much later time, when he'd been taking one of the Queen's portly daughters to a wedding reception via motor scooter. Let's just say it wasn't something you wanted to get caught doing by the paparazzi. Thank Hazeushaphat that social media hadn't been invented yet!

"We'd like you to know what kind of man your father was," Mott said.

Was, she'd said. Arthur was smart enough to know that people didn't go talking about the living in a past tense, unless they were Merddin, of course.

"You said, *was*."

"You heard me right," said Mott.

Arthur looked down in his lap where he had mindlessly been turning the gold ring on his finger.

"Uh hum," said Merddin. "Let's not go acting like Uther was some sort of Saint. That there is the only thing he sent you with when you were born. He was a great warlord for sure. But we're hoping the education we've provided has taught you to be a leader with wits. A king who relies on right, not might."

This was so much worse than the talk he had thought they were going to have.

"Merddin's right. Blood is where it ends. Just because he left you an heirloom so that you would know you were his predecessor doesn't mean he wouldn't have brought his armies here to challenge your claim to the throne if you'd drawn Excaibur before now."

Excalibur

The magiscope came to a halt on the image of a cross enveloped in swirling mists and the word Excalibur froze in Hazeus's mind. As the mists moved about the fixed image in the sphere, Hazeus began to realize that the lines that decorated the cross were very peculiar.

They made little whirls of their own like one might find in the Celtic book of Kells[45]. The top of the cross was a dark halo, circled with a gold spiral that grew out and down a dark leather grip, the gold tendrils twisting along the handle, inviting a young king's fingers to fit them. The gold lines ran down to a pommel at right angles that drew the eyes to their opposing finales, yet the gold etchings turned back on themselves toward the grip where they would dive beneath the leatherwork of the handle and emerge along the silver blade that was only now being revealed from the depths of the clouded magiscope.

It was a cross, that would be a sword.

The damned sword.

Hazeus felt a pang of grief. Then he thought maybe he was just being silly. But then he thought he may really be feeling Arthur's unease.

Hazeus had left the Globe for the simple reason that he could not bear to watch the men there kill themselves indirectly. But this sword represented the prospect of them killing each other firsthand!

Now, he was getting a terrible feeling in the pit of his stomach as he realized that he might have to watch as Arthur used that sword. He thought about what his father

---

[45] A book that was drawn under such magnification as the naked eye could hardly tell it wasn't a solid line. Fractal.

had said and suddenly wasn't so sure he wanted it to get good. Even if it was just a bunch of made-up stories in the magiscope!

He imagined, just for a moment, that he knew what Arthur was thinking when Merddin joined him at the table and took him by the hand.

He imagined Arthur thinking; can't we just forget about fighting? What is the use of a sword besides trimming the fat from a Christmas bull? And most importantly, where had Hazeus run off to anyhow? Shouldn't he be handling this mess instead of me?

But in the magiscope, he watched Arthur look up and a cloudy memory coalesced to life of when the future king had been younger and standing at the mouth of a giant cave.

Chapter Twelve: Bursting with Pride

Arthur was ten years old and staring into the dark. The dark had been the first thing that Arthur *knew* he was afraid of. It was then that Merddin had challenged him to face his fear for the first time and venture into that cave alone. Now, sitting at the table, his hand in Merddin's, he was certain he was about to face another challenge alone.

"The time has come," said Merddin. "No one stands by who can threaten your claim to Cornwall. But we must act now. Uther bested the Angles in the North, but they will return in heavier numbers. Unlike his son, Uther had no respect for the beings of shade and sea. He was rent asunder by his opposing elemental force."

Arthur considered this, he who was also born on Beltane; a child of fire.

Merddin saw the look on Arthur's face.

"That's right. He and his battalion were brought down by water. A rather inconspicuous spoil of war, wouldn't you say?" He gave time for his student to consider this. "Had Uther finished his training under Arch Druid Embroisias, Lyrr may have been more forgiving when they greedily went for the tainted water supply after the long battle. They were poisoned."

Poisoned! What more would Arthur have to deal with as a king? He was sure he was not ready. Who wants to be the plumpest pheasant atop the highest tree? It's always the first one to be shot with an arrow!

He expressed this concern to Merddin when he saw there was no hiding his worry.

"The pheasant atop the tree is an easy target," said the wizzard. "So don't make yourself a target."

"But isn't the king targeted by all of the forces even beyond the borders of Europe?"

"Ah but ask yourself what the head of the Angle battalion must of thought of your father, and what kind of man he was, for them to taint their own water supply in order to bring an end to his rule. Uther was a great warlord but don't think his life was in much mortal danger during battles."

"This is the problem today, and I've spoken to Murdack about it many times. The leaders are focused purely on winning, whether it be for sport or for glory. If Uther defeated the Angles, why do they have a chance to return?" he paused. "I can tell you why."

"Go on."

"Because the Lords hide behind their shields and armor, impenetrable to the footman, atop their horses. Then when enough common folk have been killed, they cry yield and admit defeat before the privileged can even sacrifice their own blood for the cause!"

"And you can be sure those same lords will be present to try their hands at the crown of Cornwall," Mott said.

"In fact," said Merddin, scooping some sugar into his cup, "Mott is to make sure of it."

"But that is why I cannot see the justice in such war. Lords battle, and common lives are lost, and then they are jousting in friendly sport nay a month later. It is the unprivileged who pay the spoils of war."

"Very good, Arthur." A tear came to the corner of the old man's eye. It quivered there for a moment and vanished as fast as it developed. "Justice, is that an honorable man is to claim Cornwall at last."

Arthur looked to Mott and saw that tear drops were disappearing into the corner of her trembling lips.

It's true that Mott's bosom swelled with pride, though it went unnoticed. As far as bosoms go, hers already existed on the outliers of sizeable possibility. The wise old sage was also full of pride. He was in fact proud of himself for remembering exactly how this was supposed to go. The tear that had made a brief appearance had formed in the knowledge of the hardships he saw before the young boy king. That memory was a bit more painful to recall.

All the blubbering made Arthur feel self-conscious over his secret trip back to Dragon's isle, but the mix of emotions in the cave, here, on the precipice of change, was making it hard to hold back his own tears. Once Arthur's lids failed him, then the real waterworks began. They all cried together; Cedric and the teapot joined in.

Once the deluge of handkerchiefs, which Merddin had produced from his hat, had suffered the deluge of tears, Mott and Merddin's plan was carefully divulged.

While the makeshift family spoke into the evening, Cedric pecked at the corn growing from pots by the stove. He had spent more time wrestling with the silk than enjoying the meal, and at one time was reluctantly rescued by Arthur after turning upside down, entangled on his perch.

Mott's departure was marked when the waterfall darkened to a deep blue shade. The magical poker, brush, and bellows were beginning to craft a fire in the wood burning stove when she brought out a parcel, a final gift to her adopted son.

Arthur pulled the hemp cords and unwrapped the paper. His eyes shined even more blue in the reflection of the gift when he raised it up.

"An education never ends, Arthur," said Merddin, standing behind the high-backed chair.

Cedric hopped to the chair and marched up onto the wizzard's shoulder.

"However, what I am permitted to give you is at an end. It will now be your responsibility to bring all you have gathered to the people of Cornwall. In our order, it is the Bard's duty to preserve the culture, and to preach diplomacy. In this, you have graduated from Ovyyd to Beirdd."

Arthur stared at the finely woven robe and again his heart was full of thanks for Mott.

"You have earned the sacred sky blue!" said Merddin proudly as Arthur went to Mott for a hug.

"There there, Bear cub. Now, let's see it on you before I'm off."

When Arthur came up for air, he was met with his mentor's nod of approval.

Arthur breathed in the scent of the fresh linen; sage, chicory, bellflower, and rosemary. The neck of his new robe was damp with fresh tears. He looked like the wizzard. Well, minus the hat and beard. That is to say that they both wore blue robes, and Arthur's was even a shade richer, as it had just been dyed.

Mott helped him to straighten it up. Like she had done a thousand times before mass. She stepped back to take in the sight of him.

"Now that's a refreshing sight," she said, content. "All's I ask is that you're never beyond fetching water from the well for an old nun. Nothing about a shiny new hat and sword makes one better than the rest."

What makes you better than the rest, she thought to herself smiling, is a good upbringing.

Living with men of the garb gave her a special opinion of men in general. The friars were supposed to be the pick of the litter, but they made 'better' seem to mean, sitting on a high enough seat as not to get your robe muddied by the commoners. Better, in the age of anarchy, boiled down to a more sharply inclined nose, and a stiff index finger, good for directing others to fetch the water, or scrub the font.

Mott took the broomstick, which had walked over from the corner on its bristles, and she began hiking her smock up at the knees.

"A good king understands his people," she said. "And you can't understand by sitting atop!"

Most of the broomstick disappeared beneath the drape of her smock. It made a small grunt when she lifted her feet. Merddin didn't seem to notice.

Arthur wondered if Mott understood how the broomstick might feel at this point, with her sitting atop and all…

Merddin swirled his wand overhead and the waterfall opened a curtain for her departure.

"Mind the weather, Ma'am." Merddin said.

"Oh, a little rain's never bothered me," she said. "You just don't forget our arrangement."

"Yes, yes." He flicked his wand, and the broom began rocking toward the exit with obvious difficulty.

"Arthur, you be home for morning duties. You're not off the hook yet."

The falling water closed behind her, and they watched the silhouette ascend and disappear.

The Rainbow Ladder of Fion

"What arrangement, Merddin?"

"Oh, it's nothing," he said, shaking his head and straightening his hat. "Now, where were we?"

"The coronation," said Arthur.

"Yes. The coronation."

"...and you're sure I am going to be able to pull the sword out when it all comes down to it?"

"As sure as my own two hands took you from Uther's," said Merddin.

Arthur pulled up the sleeves of his new robe. "You have seen my arms, haven't you?"

"My boy, it has nothing to do with strength."

"But how does it know?"

"Well, it's in your blood," Merddin nodded, his eyelids squeezing shut behind his glasses. "Besides, it's your destiny."

"But *how*?"

"Oh, I thought we'd been through this, boy! It's magic!"

Merddin pointed at the figurines he and Mott had arranged on the table. The tabletop had a yearly calendar burned into the cedar surface. His wand was pointing to the clay figure of a sun. It occupied the box marked May the First.

"Here," explained Merddin, "is Beltane, your birthday. A bit further along is the summer solstice, roughly around June twentieth. The longest day of the year, you see. We will have to be at Stonehenge for a proper coronation on this date, it is the only way if you expect Herne to offer you any fealty. Tricky God, that Herne."

Arthur frowned. He felt confident that he already held influence over the elements of stone and sea. He had already mastered two of the three spells of making. The first of which he earned in the depths of the giant's cave at the base of the cliffs of Tintagel. He *breathed* the words of that spell.

Merddin sensed his discord and sighed.

"Try not and worry, Arthur. It is true you are graduating a bit early, but you will be ready for the challenges that present themselves to you along the way. Have faith."

"Faith? You're asking me to believe the sword is going to know who I am, but you have not told me *how*!"

Merddin shook his head in frustration and tapped the side of the teacups urging them to step aside. He muttered under his breath more or less to himself. 'You'd think once a boy had seen Mott fly off on a broomstick, he'd believe anything were possible...'

"Belief imparts reality young bard. If you must know, just remember, like attracts like on Rootworld. It's why we must gather when the veil is at its thinnest, right at the light of dawn." Merddin pointed to March twenty-second, "Between here," then to April first. "And here, while the darkness is giving into the light. Why? Why? Well, Incubation, my dear boy! Excalibur will recognize you."

Arthur then surrendered to Merddin's logic. He had been staring at the clay figure of Excalibur when Merddin said, "Come on, now. Bring your box along."

Cedric gimbaled from his perch and glided across the oriental rug, whose figures moved like toy soldiers underfoot. While the wizzard crossed behind him, his wand stretched out into a staff of old oak. Then, Arthur watched as he fitted his pipe into the end of the old wooden stick and the combination set itself aglow.

"It's a cycle," said Merddin as he used the crooked end of his new staff to scoop up a large iron ring from the floor which served as a handle for the trap door.

"If you wouldn't mind?" he said.

When the new bard took the iron ring in both hands and hoisted away the great plank of wood, he was suddenly struck with nervousness. A wooden ladder ran down the dark stone throat, reminding Arthur much of the well he'd gotten stuck in as a boy.

"Not to worry, Arthur. Indeed, you will be tested again in solitude. All men are. But this is not that day. Follow me."

He watched as the sage used his pole as a handle and agilely navigated the entrance to the dark beyond. Before a moment had passed, they were descending the wooden rungs, Merddin's voice floating up along the silvery stone walls.

"The Pendragon is a cycle. Like time, it flows. You, Arthur, are the head in which the fire of creation is kindled. From Ambrosias, to Uther, to you and beyond. Just as only one can occupy the throne of the distributor, only one can occupy the throne of Cornwall. All stations are passed from one to another, in a never-ending cycle. That cycle takes place in the body of the dragon."

Arthur was stepping onto the stone landing when he responded, "Well, we must be nearing the end of the cycle. Everything going on seems to be taking place closer to the beast's backside than the fore." Arthur waited to see if Merddin would take his meaning, then offered, "it seems mostly excrement now."

"Would you prefer to be in its jaws?" responded Merddin. "A smart man will find that it is sometimes wiser to hold his nose than to raise his sword!"

From deep within the cavern that stretched out ahead, Arthur could see a shimmer of blue light. Merddin started off toward it, holding his staff aloft to illuminate their immediate area.

"Once, in a great while man surprises me and uses the faculties that were gifted him from Abred. It is fortunate that Vortigern chose to open his ears whether than raise his sword when it was I up for the sacrifice."

Merddin turned his face to Arthur under the light of his staff and sneered more gaily than the boy had ever seen. "Oh, you should have seen the look on the court magicians' faces at Mount Erith. Trying to build a tower on an aquifer! Keep using your head lad and people will believe anything you tell them. I gave them so much prophecy they'll bore themselves untangling it. Yestrasmartus[46] eat your heart out!"

Arthur's brow furled as they continued along the tunnel, "Who is Yestrasmartus?"

"He will one day predict the end of the world. But there will be others. Like I said. It's a cycle."

The cavern ballooned out to a huge hollow underground. Merddin once again spoke what Arthur was thinking. "Welcome to the belly of the beast, as it were."

In the center of the chamber was a stalagmite. Three feet in diameter and half a man tall. Possibly, it was the petrified stump of a tree, and sitting in the hollow top was a cool, still pool of water. Above it, suspended in a network of cords, hung a blue globe of glass, a flame flickering from its center like magic.

The light of Merddin's staff dimmed as they neared the pool. The click of the wooden tip echoing with every step they took nearer.

"The Sight is a skill normally reserved by the ladies of the lake, down here, among the shades of stone and sea, you have great sway over those forces that now rally against

---

[46] Yestrasmartus is the lead oghamologist on Rootworld and his prophecies are legendary to many, while to others they have just been another way to lose money at the racetrack

you. Forces that will remain unseen to you while you tarry above in the world of man. If you are to overcome those forces, you will need the alliance of Herne."

Arthur's eyes widened when the name came again. The forest God. The protector of the final spell of making which had eluded him all this time.

"Our time together is coming to an early end, yet you still have one task to undertake as a student of the oak. The hunt. That journey you will have to prepare for alone. All I can offer you is a glimpse into the prophetic pool in hopes that you find some knowledge which will assist you in the coming battle."

"This pool is an oracle?"

"Its power is in its purity. No other well exists like this one. It is water which has never seen the sun and is connected to those running wild, alongside the roebuck, during his journey underground."

Merddin reached out with one finger and touched the still surface. The oil of his fingertip spread out on the rippling surface and became every variety of greasy blue tints.

"As you know, the great circle of Abred began in the waters of Annwyn; all potential started there. This pool is but a mirror. Whosoever hovers over the surface of the deep will see themselves reflected back, but often it is not the person they expect." The wizard searched Arthur's expression for understanding. "It is in seeing one's own reflection that sparks the questions leading to creation. Questions asked by a man who was, who is, and who will be again. If you dare to look, the time is now."

As Arthur peered over the edge of the pool, Herne the Hunted peered back. Atop the bearded man's head was a set of antlers; Arthur's own curiosity looked back at him from those eyes. Then, the being became suddenly distracted and darted out of view.

When Arthur saw that the reflection remaining was suddenly his own, and that the velvety antlers had been replaced by a crown of gold, he strained his eyes in an effort to see deeper into the water, beyond the stone throat of the well. Down where the fingers of blue light failed to touch, something stirred.

Two dots, shining with a light of the opposing spectrum came up from the deep as a piercing purple gaze. The skin of the creature that lurked below was neither flesh nor fish, but it wound round like a serpent. The coils of the thing filling up the urn without disturbing the surface of the pool, and when the head appeared again from within its writhing parts, Arthur again sensed a familiarity in its face.

The beings that were revealed to him all gave Arthur the suspicion that if he were born to another time, under other circumstances, he would be gazing into the pool as them and be seeing himself within.

'Would his skin instead be scales if the reptile had dominated Merddin's ladder of evolution, which he had been so taught?'

The shifting images filled him to brimming with a clarity that grew as he mentally climbed a rainbow ladder. He became so light of weight that his body was lost to him completely and the reflection turned into a waking dream.

He'd been a drop of water.

He'd been a tree stump in a shovel.

He'd been a lizard basking in the sun.

He'd flown high as an eagle.

He'd been a raging bull.

He'd been a man in fetters.

He'd been a babe set adrift on the sea by an unwonted mother.

He'd been a circle of stones, taken down and resurrected.

He'd been a ray of sunlight trapped inside of glass.

He'd been a cloudy thunderhead.

He'd been a bolt of lightning, and then a branch of lightning, astray looking for a place to connect back to the main... or was it better to strike somewhere anew?

He'd been a thought in the head.

He'd been a flaming sword.

He'd been the sword in the stone. He'd been *Excalibur*!

Chapter Thirteen: Quest for the Crown

It had been nine days since Arthur's experience in Merddin's cave. Mott had been keeping him busy, gathering enough herbs and firewood to hold the old men of St Bircham's over during her absence. An absence which she always failed to hold any conversation about.

One thing was certain, the days were pleasant. Though only pleasant to Mott. She was in an unusually good mood, which meant that the friars were out of sorts. Charles's smock had failed to be tailored and the paleness of his backside spoke louder than his sermon on holy days as it peeked through an unscrupulous tear.

The wine cellars hadn't been swept in days, and the recent rain had made a mess of it. Murdack was prodding at Borus and Gwain with the muddy end of a broomstick in his gallant effort of doing a duty normally managed by magic. That is, the magic of a one Mother Theresa and her habitual tidiness. Which had largely gone unnoticed. At least until now.

All in all, St. Bircham's was preparing for disaster. It wasn't often that Mott got a vacation. The place would need to grow accustomed. The monastery might also need a new closet constructed to house all the rolling pins and iron skillets that weren't getting broken over her time away.

At least the tournament in London would keep the men from too much trouble while she was away. Any day that you could keep them off the property of Bircham's was one less day she'd have to make up for upon her return.

She had really wanted to see her boy claim his British inheritance, but there would be time for that later. Besides, Merddin had promised her a chance to look into the magic mirror if she'd ever had the desire to reminisce. She was ready for vacation!

Mott had reminded Borus three days about his duties to friar Charles, and after a fourth, Borus had jotted Ogham letters from his constructed notebook onto leaves and stuck them up as reminders all along the cloister. Later, those ancient sticky notes would cause a bit of rash concern.

And so it was, after she had waved the procession off on their long journey to London and contented herself that all affairs had been set straight at Bircham's, she took up only her wineskin, purse, and tweezers and set off for the foggy shores of Albion where her ship was supposed to be in wait. She left her rolling pin because there was to be absolutely no trouble at all.

Sir Kay

There hasn't been much mention of Kay thus far. A point I would like to remedy, as his role presently becomes rather a large part of Arthur's rise to power. It is, despite popular belief, Sir Kay's good nature, both as a brother and a son, that spurred the Britons into the wave of silence which allowed our noble king to perform his miracle under the watchful eye of those gathered there.

Kay had been the victor in every sport battled that day in the fields near St Catherine's Cathedral. All except for one.

"You mean Kay didn't take the gold in archery?" Borus asked.

Arthur, dressed in his new blue robes, had been trying to loosen a knot in Murdack's breastplate cords that had appeared overnight.

"Hazeus, Mother Maggie, and Joseph!" Murdack barked. "I swear I've grown two inches since last spring!"

"Wider, do you mean, Sir?" asked Arthur.

Murdack   Grunted. On a brighter note, his tongue had seemed to lose a little weight since Borus last had seen him.

"Was it you who took the gold, Sir Murdack?" asked Borus. It was a formality that the knaves refer to their betters as Sirs during a tourney. It was more polite to assume that they would be knighted after the event than otherwise. Really, it was the easiest way to motivate them.

"Of course not, Lad! Who could do anything with Robin destroying everyone's arrows and all that? It's not fair I tell you, and this armor is supposed to be made of breathable joints! Breathable joints!" he stopped to take in a few difficult lung fulls of wind when Arthur finally popped the knot.

"Ah. That's much better," he said, "thank you, boy."

Arthur turned to Borus, "Kay doesn't much like archery."

He thought back to the fateful outing when Kay had lost his arrow along with his best kestrel in the woods. Nimble little Arthur had gone to fetch them both in confidence only to have Kay abandon him at sunset to his fate.

However, Arthur had returned at nightfall victorious, with Kay's bird and Merddin in tow. That was when Arthur had been rewarded with his education. Also, on that day, Kay had really become the second son, even though he would always be the one to bear the weight of all the armor.

"You really missed it, Borus," said Arthur, ladling out a cup of ale for Sir Murdack, "Robin of the wood arrived during the end of the bowing competition and split the final three combatants' arrows directly down the center."

Murdack took the cup from Arthur, sloshing most of its contents onto the ground, with a grunt of indifference. Arthur and Borus watched as he divided the rest of it between his mouth and his beard.

"After that," Arthur continued, leading Borus away and back toward Kay's stall, "he split his very own arrows down the center, too. Two bull's eyes! An absolute win over the field!"

What Arthur didn't say was that later, in a rather odd turn of events, Robin had refused the gold medallion, only to turn around and steal it from Sir Ector and deposit it into a beggar's tin on his exit. In fact, this argument, was among the first Arthur would settle after his unexpected and sudden rise to monarchy[47].

"What were you busy doing anyway, Borus? We were looking for you everywhere," Arthur said before noticing he was talking to himself. "Borus? Hey, Borus!"

"Sorry," said Borus, "It was an interesting pile! You don't see horses like these everyday you know?"

"Nevermind," said Arthur, thinking he might now have some idea. "You really missed some amazing swordplay. A mysterious man named Dapp took the silver without wearing a bit of armor, and only kneeled to Kay on a feigned injury. He was obviously the best if you ask me."

---

[47] You'll be pleased to know that Arthur sided with Robin, though he was no where around to appreciate it. Sir Ector was rather upset seeing the beggar with his gold as this was the second time in a year that he had been within sniffing distance of treasure and been denied.

"Kay!"

"There you are, Arthur!" said Kay, "I've been looking all over for you."

"Looking for me? Shouldn't you be getting ready to take your turn at the Quest for the Crown. You've waited years for this!"

Arthur was right, he had waited years for this, but this past year had not been one of those. After his aforementioned victories, Sir Kay was indeed to be granted a chance at Kingsman ship in an effort to free the sword from the stone. It was customary in the tourney on previous occasions to gather behind the church and watch the victor test his metal, so to speak. Yet, Kay had other intentions. He had fought long and hard this day to fulfill his promise to Merddin and Mott.

Lifting Arthur to his rightful place on the throne would only ensure that the title be placed upon him that history has so far proved to hold firm[48]. Also, Merddin perhaps had promised to reward the man.

Over time, Kay had become quite verbal about his jealousy of Arthur's many magical excursions as this animal or that. For his duty, the wizzard would allow Kay a single transmutation. Specifically, into a certain maiden; an educational experience he'd been pouring over for years. Alas, the few hours he was later granted this reward were spent in private, and for them Kay was forever grateful. Though, some would say he became a bit more dim-witted because of the experience.

So, it was when the crowd had gathered in the churchyard for the victor, and the raucous voices became a sea of noises that Kay pulled Arthur aside and swore to him

---

[48] An honest and loyal knight.

his fealty.

"We both know that it isn't I that is supposed to draw the sword this day," he said. Then he smiled and said, "I think it is high time you replace your sickle with a proper weapon, don't you?"

Arthur looked down at his golden sickle hanging at his side. Then he looked past Kay to where the sword's hilt jutted up. He thought back to one of the great druidic truths. That no war blade be born nakedly in the presence of a druid, and now he was supposed to wield one?

Kay saw the stony look on Arthur's face and said, "It is my duty to bear a rather different weight than yours my brother. Yours I fear may be heavier."

Kay kneeling there on the ground at Arthur's feet was a rather strange occurrence that didn't take long for people to notice. A general confusion was spreading out across the yard chased by a wave of hushed whispers.

Why was the victor on his knees?

The Sword in the Stone

Something wasn't right. Arthur had been warned it was coming, but he didn't think it would be like this. Not at someone else's expense. Especially not Kay's! Suddenly, Arthur felt like escaping to anywhere but here.

Tears were gathered there in Arthur's eyes as Kay continued to urge him to approach the ancient sword. When Arthur finally dared to glance again beyond Kay's stall to where Excalibur stood, he felt the air around becoming the dragon's breath.

He remembered his experience at the magic pool. He had been that sword! He knew all too well this stone…

If there were ever a time when a man were aware of his place in history it was then. The path before him was so immutable that even the ancient giants couldn't have tipped the scales of fate. Kay kneeling. The people hushing. The sword, having been. Not a single part of the experience would yield to his desire to turn and flee.

The time had come.

Merddin

"The stuff of legends is born here, between this world and the next," said Merddin proudly. A young girl, who was holding her mother's hand, looked up to the grassy knoll to see a wizzard who was perched atop an ageing yellow horse. She was the only person who seemed to notice[49].

He was speaking out over the crowd in a strong proclamation and looked very regal in her opinion.

History was being made again. Merddin could feel it. It's only natural when you are yourself a historical figure. Major magic was going to have to happen. Not only because his apprentice was about to pull Excalibur from the stone, but also because another unprecedented event was taking place across the lake. Mott was getting her first foot rub and make-over. Much magic would be needed indeed!

Murdack waved a gauntleted hand at the mist that tickled his mustache with futility. "It is the devil's work I tell you, this mist," he whispered to Borus, who was trying to shoo off the bloodhound which was snuffling at his breeches.

Golden rays broke through the shifting leaves of the grove and moist shadows danced across the marble outliers in the churchyard at Catherine's. A procession still gathered from the eastern woods, passing up and around the rear of the cathedral in hopes of ending up at good viewing angle of the iron relic.

Earlier, this same congregation had crossed the Salisbury plains, keeping far enough south to avoid a perilous midsummer meeting at the Henge. Some things

---

[49] Things only ever require one witness. Reference the observer effect in other footnotes.

seen, refuse to be unseen. When things refuse to be unseen, other things tended to refuse to be believed.

It was well enough that the Romans had avoided the salt flats on this day, as that route was falling into disrepair, else they would have had a hard time convincing one another that a rather large dragon with blue lipstick wasn't perched atop the Tor, her outstretched wings encircling the bluestone oval.

Though, their carefully chosen route wouldn't be protecting them from *all* things magical this day.

Merlyn recollected that it had been five years since the annual quest for the crown found its footing, and in that time, he had seen far more unsavory things than this small congregation had been privy to.

He had frequented the field during war games which had become akin to a good foxhunt. For the lords conducting such battles, the danger in war was about half that of a hunt. The most laborious part of which was the three hours it took before battle, to screw on all the metal plating. And even then, it was the squire who was doing the sweating.

The same safety did not however hold true for the Picts and the Gauls who made up the infantry. It was among them that Merddin used to have the power to avert the bloodshed by simply walking between the seething armies with his hands outstretched.

That was before the veil had been rent asunder and violence had settled in this domain. Yes, Merddin could have gone the way of the Root, but his weakness for mistletoe, mushrooms, and other spiritually altering flora kept his feet firmly planted on the Globe with the rest of the inebriated. This was a grey area to him since his kind had sobered up after Hazues's departure. But, as he put it once to Mott, moderation was the key.

Plus, because someone had to teach Arthur if the Globe was ever to find its way back to magic was a nearly impossible job, he had been allotted certain liberties to cope. Proving the existence of magic through science was a long road, but with the help of his magical and delectable flora[50], chemistry might speed things up a bit. He could only hope.

In the meantime, things were going to be entirely too real. Now, the good foot soldiers; the shepherds, the bakers, the blacksmiths, the messengers, that is where the passion was down on the battlefield. Once the horn blew and the fighting began, the scantily dressed and armed footmen went to their fates in the names of their lords who had long forgotten that pouring their own drinks was an original sin[51].

As honorable as was a foot soldier's loyalty and sacrifice, it never saved them from a potential trampling under the hoof of their own lord's war horse either.

Once the battles were well underway, the massive four-legged tanks would drive their way into the throes and their mounts would cleave at the parties underfoot. But when the fire dwindled from the frontlines, the entitled eyes behind the helmets began to lose interest in competing for their fellow man's right to mortality. At best it sometimes came down to a knight being unhorsed and a couple of metal trashcans walloping one another with metal sticks. But the entitled hardly lost a limb or suffered a mortal wound. That was the job of the laymen.

When the lordship's numbers were unable to support a decent line against danger, the horns would blow, and the

---

[50] And a few select fauna, such as a certain toad whose anus did strange things to consciousness.

[51] In fact, it is dishonorable in many places to pour your own drink. Pouring someone else's drink on the other hand is always alright, and furthermore, greatly encouraged!

numbers would be tallied, and the spoils would be divided to the winners. Then things generally would go back to how they were before.

Men were dangerously segregated by class. Which wouldn't make for certain unhappiness, but unfortunately, being a good sport sometimes meant being a dead husband.

Certainly, now if ever, Cornwall was in desperate need of fair leadership.

Kay had, by then, grown into his twenties, and Arthur was just short of sixteen. Now, this relic which five years hence drew hundreds of knights from Britain, was now only surrounded by just short of three dozen ironclad imbeciles. But the time had come and there would be a king.

If the rightful King could not be crowned by birthright; pulling Excalibur from the stone, then he would have to be crowned by brawn. That had been the decree. By a look at the lot of them, it most certainly wouldn't be brains, Merddin thought.

This was in no offense to Kay; it was just that the old wizzard was one of the only ones who could have a confident chuckle at the whole dire situation. He knew how it would end. In fact, there were only a handful that were confidants in Arthur's true birthright. He was looking forward to seeing the surprise swell across the company when it happened.

There were apt to be many dusty knees and embarrassed lords this day.

And that was glorious!

Merddin looked down at the little girl. At least he hadn't been entirely talking to himself, so he gave her a wink. Then of course, the tip of his wizzard's hat fell in front of his face with a sweaty slap.

And a little girl laughed.

The Sword Speaks

Magical steel peeled forth from centuries-old stone.

This is where things begin to get a little fuzzy when it comes to the history books on the Globe. That's because depending on who you ask, the sound that the sword made coming out would be described in an array as rich as the white light was that day[52].

Beings of all sorts heard different tunes.

The squires all heard the spine shriveling scrape of nails on a chalkboard, if that was, chalkboards had been invented. The boys covered their ears and took auditory cover behind their masters' horses. The elder knights and citizens heard the sound of something they had been waiting for nearly ten years, the confirmation of Cornwall's rightful King. To them, the sound was one of victory and relief.

A few fairies, living in the cathedral gardens, heard the long low roll of thunder[53] and when the sword's tip twanged from the top of the immortal sheath, they'd thought it was the sharp crack of lightning.

Arthur's ears were deaf to all. The sheer adrenaline muffled everything but the feel of the cool leather-wrapped bronze in his grip. Also, he may have been preoccupied by how the ruby in his sickle was putting off a bright orange glow.

Beyond the throng, between a few fallen iron pickets and up on a grassy knoll, Merddin heard the steel song of an old friend.

Meanwhile, all the way from the salt flats, Sylvia thought she heard the sound of lunch.

---

[52] The white light was actually being refracted from the dragon's breath and was playing in rainbows across the entire churchyard.

[53] Tiny ears register high pitches as deeper tones.

Mim

Merddin should have foreseen what happened next.

Knowing what is going to happen before it does is an advantage of choosing your life before you live it and picking your own destiny makes for some pretty good party tricks as well. But you couldn't blame an old man for letting a few things get by once in a great while.

The problem with seeing your life before you start out on the journey is, well, you tend to forget some of the story along the way. The really big events come back rather quickly because it is so exhilarating to remember them. But, remembering why they were so exhilarating, to begin with, was often in the smaller details.

In this particular instance, there were multiple smaller details, because there were multiple big events happening at once. All those details would require a great deal of memory, and even a wizzard's memory is subject to the effects of aging; that would only be fair. Not to mention a wizzard's memory also has the ingredients to every magical concoction, spell, past life, and remedy stored up there. So, there was that to contend with.

The further along Merddin got in years, the more he relied on a dirty word that is so often misinterpreted, and he didn't use it often because it made him think of a time when everything was perfectly organized, and in other words, *boring again*. But faith, however dirty a word, made him no more ineffective. When you've already seen the ultimate outcome, it does little good looking to the past for answers.

Naturally, choices would still have to be made. Not making a choice is just as partisan as having a strong preference. It was a wizzard's job to make those hard choices, because to a wizzard, they weren't so very hard to make at all. Everything would, in fact, be okay either way.

He'd seen it, well, as far as he could remember.

Which brings us to the question of how then *does* a wizzard make those rhetorical decisions. Merddin was about to undergo this process once again. So let us tag along.

When Arthur held the magic sword overhead and the red ruby of mars exploded in a grand flash of light, time stopped for the wizzard. Things were only just starting to get moving again when Merddin scratched his beard and said, "Oh yes. Now, I remember."

Merddin chuckled when time, and the sound of sidling hooves, came back to him. Some of the horses had been spooked by the blast and their mounts had gotten busy soothing them with shushes and pats.

An infrared haze was slowly fading while photons continued winding their way toward the outward reaches of the churchyard through the mist. When the deep hue climbed the stone wall of the cathedral and snuck over the pickets surrounding the yard, Rootworld briefly merged with the Globe.

The spiritual goings on out on the Salisbury plains, and those occurring in the churchyard became one. Simultaneously, those at the drawing glimpsed the great dragon perched atop the henge, and Sylvia glimpsed the great men perched atop their mounts.

The visions, vice versa, faded with the crimson blast, but not before Sylvia noticed something falling to the moist soil of the consecrated earth.

From atop the Tor, she took to wing.

In the churchyard, the bloodhounds also saw the tiny weevil break free from its ruby prison and fall to the ground. The insect stunk of death and decay. The dogs, however, smelled bacon.

Gwain was holding Kay's beagle taught by the leash and taking up a quick lesson in how hard it was to break a dog's will at the call for brunch.

At once, leashes broke free from squires' grips everywhere, and hounds bounded for the tasty morsel. Nothing draws the teeth of a good dog more than pure evil incarnate.

The dung beetle was already chewing its way into the bitter earth, excreting a soft serving of poo even quicker than it swallowed. This only managed to excite the dogs into a ground-pawing frenzy at the base of Arthur's perch.

It was quite a sight, Merddin's apprentice standing there atop a stone dais, sword thrust at the sky, a multitude of frenzied hounds below him. Yes, mostly as he remembered it. All except that peculiar weevil, marking Mim's untimely release.

Still, Merddin watched with pride as Arthur wielded Excalibur in unwavering focus, despite the unfortunate loss of the ruby he'd worked doubly hard to attain.

The crowd broke from a hushed surprise into cheers.

"Hip hip," they cried.

Arthur followed, pumping Excalibur skyward.

"Hip hip."

The newly minted king met his teacher's exceptionally calm stare where he'd been sitting atop the stone wall flipping through Borus's ogham booklet. It was all coming back faster now. Merddin thumbed over another leaflet and stroked his beard. What to do about this? He was going to have to make a decision.

The old druid struck a note of surprise and threw his arms up in the air, being rid of Borus's itchy abomination then he saw a gentle laugh take Arthur's lips which the throng interpreted as genuine happiness. He could hardly be angry at the boy for having such daft friends.

Merddin shook his head and glanced suspiciously at his fingertips before continuing the internal debate with his brain and the external one with his beard.

On one hand, if he and Sylvia didn't intervene while Mim was but a tiny weevil, that little bugger would burrow its way beneath the cathedral and deconsecrate the land on which they stood, taking her time to fester in the world of the waking. He knew where *that* would lead. That would mean more work.

On the other, if they did intervene, the coronation would be interrupted before the Saxons and Catholics both swore fealty to Arthur. *That* might mean more bloodshed.

More pressing, Sylvia was already in route.

This was one of those moments when a wizzard's choice becomes imperative because no one else would dare to disappoint a dragon.

It was a bloody shame that bloodhounds weren't quicker to the dig, thought Merddin finally. He really wanted to see Arthur's kingdom begin firmly beneath the veil. Perhaps in another life. But wasn't that what he always told himself around this time?

Reluctantly, he lifted his arms and reminded himself quietly what the few brief years of life were compared to the art of perfecting the soul. Then, with a swift inhale and a few more Welsh axioms, he parted the veil.

In Merddin's mind, he heard Sylvia sigh as she banked a hard U-turn in the sky, "Just once, can't we do things the easy way?"

As Merddin lowered his arms he responded

through the ether, "I thought more work on our part would be the lesser of two weevils."

And that's how they do it, you see. As hard as it is to make a decision, or disappoint a dragon, it's just as easy for a great wizzard to make a dragon chuckle.

What was less humorous was what was going on below the energetic gathering of legend. Because, through the dark below, Mim dug with her little weevil claws as age of King Arthur began.

Chapter Fourteen: The Witching Hour

Hazeus was just thinking about how creepy the little weevil looked boring down through the dirt when the magiscope's player-arm ran out of groove and started ice skating around the smooth center circle of the record. It was right about then that a lightning bolt struck outside the window, and coincidentally the grandfather clock began its long march towards tolling out the twenty-first hour.

That was strange, he didn't remember his father calling for rain[54].

He plucked his dad's neck cushion from off the easy chair and laid out flat on his back, more comfortable than he thought he might be on the thin bearskin rug by the fire and stared up at the clock.

Both ornate little iron hands pointed up. Midnight. He had been watching for hours. He thought how strange it was that time on this side of the veil moved slower. Of course, science on the globe would find that time moves slower at higher altitudes, and their house being in the clouds atop Mound Meritites would account for a lot of that difference, but not all of it, surely!

As Hazeus lay there watching the secondhand tick away the early first seconds of morning and listening to the rains encroach from the waterwise side of the root, his eyes grew heavier, and before long he found himself someplace else entirely.

---

[54] And that was something he would definitely remember as it involved bamboo sticks filed with rice, coconuts, dancing, and sometimes his mother.

Tom

"Is this where I get to say I told you so?" I said, from the dark beside Hazeus.

"That depends," said Hazeus, considering a moment that he may be sitting near his oldest and closest friend from the Globe.

"Depends on what?"

Now Hazues was certain it was me, "Whether or not it's worse or better than I expected it would be?"

There was a silence, I let Hazeus wonder for a moment if maybe I had disappeared. Well, disappeared even more so than being totally invisible to begin with.

"It's worse," I finally admitted.

Hazeus sighed.

"I tried telling them!" I said.

I could tell Hazeus was trying to look around, despite the impossible darkness. I sensed his head turn before he said, "Go on. You can say it."

"No, no. I really don't want to give you the satisfaction."

I put my fingers through my old friend's hair and then my palms on each side of his face. Then on his chin and top of his head like a mime, all before grabbing him up in a great embrace which he returned with gusto.

Both of us had stood up from the rather hard stone we were occupying and were standing at arm's length when the sound of blown clay shattered on the floor just near us.

"Crap," said I.

"What? What was that?"

"Not to worry. It was probably the jar I had the gospel stashed inside of."

Hazeus set free with one hand and felt the stone we'd been sitting on, determining it must be a bench of sorts. "Gospel?"

"Yeah," said I. "I wrote it all down, like you told me. Not that it matters, they'll probably be just as likely to believe the dead me as they did the live me."

"You're still on about that?" asked Hazeus. "That's why I said to write it down! It helps get it out of your system so you can move on!"

"Uh, you're lucky you remember it as disappearing in a whisp," there was an awkward silence, "well, let me help you remember what happened on our end."

I listened as Hazeus recounted in gasps and exclamations the entire instant memory of what occurred after his crucifixion. It took less than thirty seconds, but the emotion in those sounds told me he got it.

"You get it?"

"My teaching in Egypt and India didn't help matters, did it?"

"No," said I. "I mean, you didn't learn your lesson the first go round?"

"I was stubborn," said Hazeus. "You know, old habits."

"Well, they figured you came back from the dead."

"I did," said Hazeus, and then spreading his invisible hands and cocking his head he said, "technically."

Then there was another even longer silence. Then we started laughing.

"It still hurt," said Hazeus.

"Well, death does. Even when it comes naturally," I said.

"Nice chap, though," he said. "Where in the hell are we anyhow?" he asked.

"Well," I said, "not hell, but it's definitely not heaven."

"I'm guessing we're on the Globe somewhere. I can always tell by the smell of it."

"You did always have a nose for falsehood."

"Well, right now my nose is picking up a whole lot of frankincense and myrrh."

Suddenly another sound had joined us in the dark. It sounded like someone using a hammer and chisel.

"Tom?"

"Yes?"

"What's going on?" Hazeus asked.

"Promise you won't get angry?" I said.

"Toooooooom?" There was another larger sound like rock cracking and a sliver of yellow light made a thin vein on the roof of the chamber.

"Uh," started I, "well, we aren't so much on the Globe as inside of it."

Now there was a terrible crash and the rock concealing the tomb we were in crumbled to the floor, letting blinding light flood inside. Both of us shielded our eyes. Voices were coming from inside of the blinding sphere of light that marked the cave entrance.

"Stand back, I say," came the voice of an elderly man, "give it time to air out a little."

Another man said pointedly, "I think you mean, to air in, Merddin."

There was an uncomfortable pause from the lighted bubble and then, "Now is not the time for jokes, Chancellor, please bring Arthur."

Hazeus sighed, seeing the guilty look on my face for the first time in centuries. "You didn't?"

I was busy twiddling my thumbs.

"You did," said Hazeus looking back to the cave entrance where he could now see a wizzard in a blue robe leading a scrawny looking young man into the chamber. Their forms were silhouetted against the outside, making the light a bit more bearable now.

The two figures came more into focus as they neared. The wizzard had a bundle under one arm and walked with a staff. The young man ambled along behind him, stooping to peer beneath the exceptionally tall wizzard's arm.

"They can't see us," I said.

"Huh?" asked Hazeus.

"They can't see us," I said.

"A point," said Merddin loudly just as Hazeus was about to say something, "that I will shortly remedy."

"Who is he talking to?" Hazeus asked me at exactly the same moment that Arthur asked Merddin, "Who are you talking to?"

"He's talking to me," I said at exactly the same time Merddin said, "I'm talking to Tom."

Hazeus and young Arthur both looked terribly perplexed.

"And who is that?" Hazeus asked me at exactly the same time Arthur said to Merddin, "And who is that?"

"It's uh," said both Merddin and I in unison before Merddin stopped abruptly and said sharply, "Now won't you stop that?"

His irritation was only further agitated by the tip of his hat falling down in front of his face.

"Stop what?" said all three Arthur, Hazeus, and I together.

"That!" thundered Merddin striking the floor with the end of his staff. Arthur took a few silent steps backward and decided it better not to say anything further, at least for the time being.

"Well," I said, after a moment, "that's no way to treat the son of God you know."

Merddin looked in the general direction of my voice and flipped his hat back to a state of normality. "I think," said Merddin a bit calmer now, "there is a place for jokes and a place for anger, and now is the time for neither."

Then Hazeus and I watched as Merddin unrolled the bundle on the floor and started making little piles of its contents in front of the bench at our feet. "This should help ease the tension," said Merddin working.

Hazeus elbowed me and said, "Told you, frankincense and myrrh."

Merddin continued and Arthur crept a bit closer now. "It should also help us see you, if you would be so kind as to sit on the bench."

I looked at Hazeus who looked at me and we shrugged then sat down.

Then the wizzard lit the incense and little flames crawled across the peat under the herbs causing smoke to begin drifting up. Once the peat had turned into a deep red bed of coals, the wizzard threw a handful of shredded herbs onto them and Arthur's eyes grew wider.

"I can see them," said the young man.

"There," said Merddin, "that's better." He waved for Arthur to approach and have a seat on the stone ledge alongside the wall.

"So," said Hazeus, finally thinking he was catching on. He had read enough sword and sorcery novels to know exactly what it meant to be summoned by someone. "Can he hear me now?"

Hazeus was looking at Arthur, but his eyes flicked back over his shoulder at me, as he was unsure exactly who he should be addressing at this point.

All at once, I said, "I don't know," Merddin said, "No," and Arthur said, "Yes."

Merddin rolled his eyes, clearly on the verge of boiling again and Hazeus said in general, "So which is it?"

Arthur and I saw the look on Merddin's face and decided we'd better wait our turns.

There was silence.

"Well?" asked Hazeus again after a time.

Merddin smoothed out his beard and settled in beside Arthur on the stone ledge. "No," he began, "he cannot hear you, but he is rather adept at reading lips, so as long as the threshold smoke holds out, he will have no problem communicating."

"I see," said Hazeus, and looked at me impressed. Then we both turned back to the student and his mentor. Which was strange, because Hazeus and I had had a similar relationship.

"So," said Hazeus, "I suppose I am to be asked three questions or something like that?"

"Well," said Merddin, "that's what was written on the lintel."

Hazeus looked back at me. I shrugged and silently mouthed him a personal, "Sorry."

"I got that!" said Arthur.

"Now you speak up?" said Merddin, ridiculing his apprentice. "Well be quick about it, before the smoke is gone."

"Let me save you some trouble," said Hazeus standing up slowly. "Look." He stepped through the smoke, and it swirled and stuck to his image, making him look even more solid than before. Then he reached down and gathered up the broken pieces of my fumbled pottery and turned around, glancing over his shoulder at the wizzard and Arthur. When he turned around, he was holding a clay bowl of water.

Hazeus stepped over and placed the bowl by Arthur's feet and sighed. Looking up at him he said, "You must be Arthur."

Arthur nodded.

"Look man, I messed up." Hazeus took off Arthur's sandals and placed them beside the bowl then he dipped into the clay bowl and wet his hands before starting to massage the young man's feet.

"You're going to see," said Hazeus, and he looked sideways so Arthur couldn't read his lips but that I could, "Dad, said it best." Then he turned back up to him, "You're gonna see, that everything is your own damn fault."

Arthur looked at Hazeus perplexed. Merddin seemed to look proud. But Hazeus couldn't tell if Merddin was proud of him or Arthur. This was the oddest thing he'd experienced in all of his Father's creations.

"What I mean to say is," Hazeus continued, "I didn't know what it was all about." Then he looked over at me then back at Arthur, "Life on the globe I mean."

Arthur seemed to be taking this rather odd turn of events in stride.

"I thought if I just explained things to everyone, then everything would turn out okay." Hazeus put down Arthur's foot. "But it only made things worse."

He began washing the boy's other foot then stopped abruptly and said, "It all comes down to priorities."

"What do you mean priorities," Arthur asked.

"You know," said Hazeus, "by the way, that's one question. Priorities. Like, the most important things should come first. In my case, it was myself and my family."

Hazeus wrung his hands and then picked up Arthur's sandals and clapped them together until they were acceptably clean. Then he placed them on Arthur's feet.

"There," he said. "I owed you that much." From his knees he then lifted the bowl in offer toward the wizzard.

"Oh, no thank you," said Merddin. "It's mostly limestone and gravel on the way back to Avalon and I'm trying to put on layers. Besides, I wouldn't want to cause a rift…"

Hazeus gave Merddin's thickly calloused feet a look of pity.

"I have an appointment for a pedicure with Vivianne, as it happens."

"Well, don't say I didn't offer," said Hazeus placing the bowl down and dusting his hands together as he stood.

"I'll be sure to remind Vivianne of your grace," said Merddin.

"Why did you owe me?" asked Arthur and Merddin gave him a look of reproach.

"Mind your questions, boy!" the old man said, sharply.

Hazeus spread his arms, "That's two," he said. Then he stepped back through the incense, which now wasn't so eagerly productive, and he had a seat again. Placing his hands on his knees, he said to Arthur, "I've seen what you will become, and I hate to deliver the burden to you, but it is not going to be an easy journey."

I leaned away from Hazeus and scoffed, "That's no fair! The sight is supposed to be reserved for women!"

Merddin said, "Women, and then there is that Yestrasmartus of the root."

"Nonsense," said Hazeus, "that was all just coincidence. There will always be someone finding fortune in abstraction, especially among such an abundance of it. You know this well, Merddin."

"Ha!" barked Merddin. "I knew it! I knew it!" he said again while stroking his beard proudly. "Quite the performance though."

I crossed my arms in disgust, hoping they could tell I deserved a bit more lenience when it came to telling the future.

"Relax," said Hazeus, "You're not missing anything. You know my father. It's a coming-of-age thing."

"We all have our specialties," said the wizzard.

"Yeah?" I asked, now intrigued, "Then what's mine?"

"You seem to be able to appear in two places at once," said Merddin.

I must have looked terribly confused as Arthur was sitting with his hands in his lap, looking like he was constipated. Perhaps, he'd decided it was safest to keep his mouth shut as to not foul up the last question.

"How can you possibly know that?" I asked.

"Well," said Merddin lighting his pipe casually, and beginning to puff at it. "I've seen it."

"Am I the only one without the sight around here?" I demanded, throwing my arms up.

Merddin went into a coughing fit after burning his thumb on the match. When it settled, Merddin finally re-crossed his legs and smacked his lips together in a sign of utter placidity then Arthur began pointing and making urgent motions towards his beard with his hands. Merddin was looking into his pipe to see if was still lit as he could still smell something burning.

Hazeus covered his eyes with one hand, and I joined in with Arthur in an effort to bring Merddin's attention to his own burning beard.

"Well, confound it!" Merddin hitched while swatting the rogue match from the wiry nest of smoldering grey hair.

Arthur seemed to manage the whole thing without breaking his vow of silence.

"I do say," said Merddin, stroking his beard again and getting comfortable. "This is why I normally use magic. It's less intrusive." He nodded informatively in Arthur's direction who was sitting stone still as if nothing had happened, obviously used to preserving the old man's dignity. Then Merddin began snapping his fingers over the pipe bowl. A few weak tendrils of smoke began eeking up. "Well, I don't like to show off, you know? Now, go on. Where were we?" he said continuing the performance.

Hazeus finally came out from hiding behind his hand, and I said, "You said you'd seen me some place else."

"Oh, yes," said Merddin. "You're Lancelot."

"I'm who?" I said, clearly confused.

Merddin took his time getting the sweet-smelling flowers in the pipe to a good heat. After a couple of long deep drafts from the stem of the pipe he'd begun producing a regular cloud of nice thick smoke.

"I can see how that might be confusing," he said. "If you take my word for it, then you will be considerably easier to convince than your future incarnation that I just managed to brief on the whole ordeal yesterday."

I looked at Hazeus and he shrugged. "I haven't gotten that far. I'm only on disc three," Hazeus said.

"Tell me you at least know about the dragon," said Merddin wryly.

Merddin could see through our fading forms that neither of us had any idea what he was talking about. "Well, yours is white," Merddin told them frankly. "And you can tell your father that it should be written that all father's should heed well the advice of their son's, as they are more likely to speak the truth of life."

"I'm not sure he'd be very receptive," said Hazeus, not certain that he was being metaphorical.

"Wait," said Arthur.

"I'm starting to think we've probably overreached our quota," said Hazeus looking at me.

I said, "Well, to be fair, some of the questions were directed at me."

Hazeus knew what was coming. I could tell that he felt terrible about it, too. But what else was there to do but for him to tell the truth?

"Look," he told Arthur. "After everyone left me for dead, my family took me and put me in a private tomb to rest. Before that I didn't believe in things like pain and suffering. But I had brought it on myself, hadn't I? I didn't realize that everyone would just go on drinking! I should never had condoned it."

I was staring at him trying to resist the absolute urge to say, I told you so.

Hazeus sighed, "But, those Romans, they love their wine. I only made things worse when I secretly left for Gaul with Maggie, but I couldn't bring myself to abandon her after everything I had put her through. People saw us crossing the sea and when the word of a risen Christ caught up with me years later, Maggie had already grown old and passed. It seemed there was a pope raising cups in my immortal name. I had failed totally and there was really nothing left for me to do but go home."

Arthur and Merddin looked at one another. Then Arthur said, "And by home you mean Heaven?"

"Uh," Hazeus said, "it's a bit more complicated than that. Let's just say I needed to get back to my roots. Regardless, I've seen that you are going to be the next living legend and I don't want you to end up like I did. Prioritize, Arthur. Put yourself first. Turning the other cheek will get you only so far when this world has gone so mad! Refuse to take life, my boy. Follow your heart, do not preach to your people but instead lead by example. Inclusion is key. Be a beacon of truth."

"Okay!" I blurted, "Don't tell him too much! You'll give it all away!"

He was on a roll. I could see Hazeus was exhilarated. He probably thought he was starting to understand where all this was going! That, or getting more excited about seeing the end of his show. Either way, it meant time was up.

Visiting the globe isn't like being in Rootworld. You don't have to sleep in Rootworld, you only sleep in Rootworld, well, when you get tired of being there. His excitement was gonna throw the both of us out of this dream in a hurry!

"The spell Arthur! The third spell! Use it and one day you will again greet me as brother!"

I had a hand on his shoulder trying to keep him seated, as Hazeus was leaning forward into what remained of the threshold smoke.

"Where are they going?" Arthur asked Merddin.

"Back," said Merddin.

"Back to their roots?"

I could hear them speaking but things were getting dark as if someone were covering the cave's entrance with wool.

"To the future, Arthur." I heard the old man say, then I thought I smelled burning rubber. "They're going back… to the future," said Merddin right before it was black as pitch again.

Then I can only hope Hazeus heard me when I said, "I told you so."

Back on the Mound

Hazeus had lost Tom and was waking from a dream of being inside of the tomb he'd been occupying. In it, and by the light of a nice hot pipe, Merddin leaned down by the stone bench and picked up a roll of old parchment that was lying among broken clay. He unfurled it enough to see the title, penned in the hand of an old friend. It read, the gospel of Tom.

"Is that what I think it is?" asked Arthur.

"That depends," said Merddin, "what is it that you think it is?"

"You know," said Arthur, "the truth about what happened to Hazeus."

"Doubtful," said Merddin.

"And is that what I think it is?" asked Arthur pointing to a couple of flaming hoof prints among the ashes of frankincense and myrrh.

It was then Hazeus woke to a lightning bolt striking again outside his window in the deep orange hue of a rainy dawn. At the same time, tires were screeching and the magiscope was full of smokescreen. When Hazeus' eyes finally cleared, he saw a silver carriage doing donuts in a cobblestone lot behind some horses that were running atop a strange, wheeled platform before coming to a stop. One of the carriage's batwing doors flew open.

A sandaled foot stepped out and a wiry-haired man emerged in a toga. "Martin!" he yelled, "get her in the carriage! Lightning is going to strike the clock tower in three minutes, and we have to get these horses to exactly eighty-eight miles per hour."

"I'm doing the best that I can here, Doc!" Martin said, dragging the unconscious blonde woman toward the carriage. 'We'll make it, just relax."

"You don't understand," the scientist said, pulling at the sides of his hair and then reaching into the carriage to retrieve a bundle of oats. "Milton is refusing to eat the superfood, and…" he held up the bundle then looked at the horse's feet where they were mounted in the cycling apparatus "Great Scott! His hoof is coming loose from the stirrup!"

Hazeus felt something beneath his hip.

"Oh," he said, picking up and then pointing the remote at the magiscope. He must've rolled over on it during his nap and changed the input to the Aganon Divine Video subscription. His father had been watching a classic. He switched the input back to mvd then he looked up at the grandfather clock and saw the hands sat at four and twenty in the morning. He thought he smelled something strange emanating from his parents' bedroom.

Hazeus stood up and made his way quietly to the window where he could watch the rain. He moved carefully so as not to wake his parents. They didn't like him up this late, or early he supposed. He outta be in bed, but it was the weekend. The rain was coming down, but the clouds were thinning out just enough that the bright white hole above was starting to peek through a bit. He had often wondered what it would be like if he could turn back time, like in that movie his dad had been watching, and go right on through the white hole to come out on the other side.

There were theories on the globe about black holes as astronomical objects and he thought that he might just pop out of one of those. But that was just his imagination, surely! Hey, the rain seemed to be slacking up a little. Maybe he and Dad could throw the ball around a little later if it cleared up.

Hazeus opened the refrigerator quietly and lifted the cardboard lid of yesteryear's pizza, he read the print on the side facing him '*Just Directa your Feetsa to Daddy Green's Pizza*! It was a pizza with beansprouts. Well, at least it was cold. He squirted some ketchup on a paper plate and sat down with a couple of slices in front of the magiscope again.

Chapter Fifteen: The Counterweight of Gods

While Hazeus loads up disc four and before he starts going through the arduous task of picking bean sprouts out of his teeth, let me catch you up on what was going on with me around this time.

As I once mentioned, men have been called small Gods.

This is a term that Merle and I coined back in the Zoroastrian days when we first figured out what was going on with our relationship. In short, I exist so he has someone to blame his mistakes on. He insists, that if I could only understand what he was trying to say, then we wouldn't have to go through all of this again[55].

He decides where and when we will pop up again and pretty much how everything is going to play out. But there has to be someone who observes all of this go down, so that's where I come in. Problem is, we all know what happens when you look too hard at something, especially with a really strong opinion about it. It can start to resemble something entirely different than what it actually is.

This is also known as perversion[56]. If you make that mistake in perception, well, wrong choices tend to be made. So, it's kind of like, if I have an opinion of say, Arthur's beautiful wife, Merle might alter his course just enough to shoehorn my desire in on accident.

You see our first go round together was like a brotherhood. We were born at the same time. Two dragons, he red and I white. This can, at first glance, be a little

---

[55] And then again. But, that's another story.

[56] But we won't say it is the same thing a certain McFly was doing up a tree.

disorienting because the dragons are actually still both alive and well. Hence the existing in multiple places at once trick. But after that incarnation we started being born a little bit further apart each time, which was a good thing and a bad thing in a way.

If you think of a child drawing their first self-portrait, for instance, and the parent looking at it saying, "Well done!" You can start to see how our relationship started out. I had no clue what it was he was drawing at first. Or, er, writing, I guess would be a better way to explain things. Actually, weaving would be totally accurate but you could only understand that if you knew the concept of how and why dragons dance. So, forget that for now.

Back when we were dragons, things made sense. He was knowledge and I was wisdom. He, being born with all of his memories and me having to remember them as we went along, like a couple of hourglasses filling our glass from opposite ends.

When I was Thomas, Merle tried explaining to me the Universe and how it was all supposed to go in its entirety, but I was born not long after he was, so it was kind of like looking at that first self-portrait, if you get my meaning. I wasn't born as smart as he was, so there just wasn't enough experience to me yet to really get all the big words he was using. That's why I was known as the doubter.

But, the second time I came back, I was born a bit later than he was, so it was further along in his lifeline before I ever remembered him. By the time he convinced me of who I was, I had enough experience to understand more of what it was he was trying to say. Gathering the memory of being a dragon in my past was a bit farfetched, but eventually I got on with it when he jogged my memory in a most inappropriate way.

My earliest memories of my second life were of being raised an orphan in the skeleton of an old Shepard's hut on the more windward side of a hillock out in Benwick. Things are often as such with tales of gods and heroes.

Fortune favored me with good looks, and I did not let them go to my head too soon. I was a very disciplined child, if not a busy one. I spent most of my time around the grown-ups rather than the children. Of course, it had the undesirable effect of landing me with the most chores, but it kept my ears burning and got me an apprenticeship with Uncle Dap at King Ban's castle.

I spent three years sleeping in the armory of the castle. And would have stayed there all my life if I had any sense at all. But I was an egotistical young man, and more than anything else I couldn't handle my own failures. Rather than face them like the honorable knight I would one day become, I would run from my problems.

Dap spent countless hours training me and answering my stupid questions while I was supposed to be maintaining the equipment. Don't get me wrong, I did my job well. It was an easy job, and one I would do today if I had the chance. There is nothing like living in a place with every piece of gymnastics apparatus, weapon, and exercise equipment to keep yourself occupied.

I never tired of learning. In the three years at Ban's armory, I ate like a bird, but still somehow gained forty pounds of muscle. I learned to tumble, to fence, to use a shield and spear, throw an axe and all types of blades. I would get tired and lay in the mats for respite and Dap would tell me not to waste my time and to practice other things if I were sore instead. He taught me to juggle and stand on my head.

After the first year, we became friends and Dap began teaching me how to tilt, finding amusement in my suffering. Perhaps it brought back memories of his treatment back in Spain, where he said he was instructed to perform a flip. And when he refused, he was switched until he did the flip, fail or no.

Not that Dap were ever that way with me, but his demeanor was always such that if you disappointed him he might not tolerate you again for a week and then you would learn no more of his secrets. I mean just how did he stand on one hand and juggle a ball upside down? I never saw him practicing! He would just, one day show me another miracle and say, if you keep it up and only listen! So that is what I did.

For three whole years. The best years in fact that I ever knew in life. I did listen. I wanted what Dap had. I wanted to be the best. I became proficient in every weapon and with the heaviest armors. After two years I was his right-hand man, though only sixteen years old. Anytime a nobleman came through to test a piece of armor or equipment, they tested it on me. Dap would laugh, directing me to go harder or lighter on an opponent, much like a baseball coach from the sidelines in modern times. People were his playthings, and I was the remote control.

I didn't mind at all. In fact, I loved it! I was invincible. But all good things come to an end, and as my third year came and went, and my ego ballooned into something unmanageable, even by Dap, I traded my heavenly abode for a tumble in the sheets. King ban's daughter was three years my junior and though it was consensual, our relationship was not one that was going to abide my staying in Benwick. So, I tucked my tail between my legs and left the city. Teenagers will be teenagers.

Regardless, I continued having quite the time sowing my oats in the city and was in quite a tangle of social and moral triangles involving the opposite sex. I just couldn't help it, you see. I couldn't pass a town without a farmer asking for me to lend my strength, and those farmers always seemed to have daughters, and sometimes lonely wives as well.

Anyhow, I never was one to tell a harmful truth. At least until I finally met Merle, son of Tal. If a woman asked me if I loved her, I would assure her it was true. Yet, if she asked if I loved another, I would offer no such truths though I certainly believed the contrary. And on multiple occasions!

What can I say? My first life was not versed in the rigors of dating. As Hazeus's best friend, I didn't exactly have women flocking to me for sin[57]! Yay, I tell you, things may have been going better if I was smart enough to just tell the ladies that I was dating other women before I ever went on and rolled in the hay with them. But that was a tactic I was ignorant of in that second life.

So, when Merddin found me, I was in dire need of escaping my former ties with nearly seven women. Eight, if you count the twins. It is a running joke that my name, Lancelot, was chosen with Merddin's foresight of the predicament caused by my constant poking at things due to my youthful appetites[58]. I found it rather distasteful that he would compare the art of love making to the lancing of a boil!

---

[57] On the contrary, and you wouldn't believe it, but it was the other way round.
[58] Some things are just too right to even bother fact checking.

I have to give it to my brother for it was he who delivered me from shame when I was left to defend my own honor, with a tree branch.

There I was, up a tree and naked as a jay after a gorgeous young lady had asked me to fetch her goshawk. I was a fantastic climber, but I couldn't do it with my armor on.

This is so embarrassing! Once, while recounting this at Merddin's behest to an Arch Druid, he said that my blushing reminded him of a tomato who'd been caught dressing a salad in public.

Anyway, she talked me into removing my armor and sword to climb the tree. Well, I was playing on with her, and we were in a secluded bit of the wood along a trail that I had not seen another person on all morning. Besides some overgrown villas there was none about and I saw an opportunity to bed down another damsel.

She was playing at me and joking that I should leave my breeches and my undergarments as well, as it would make the climb less difficult.

"It is such a hot day," she said to me with her little heart shaped lips. "Surely you'd climb better without all of that burden."

Yeah, well, little did I know, that she had met Daisy from Wittershins, and that Daisy and Sonya were sisters that had a well-trained carrier pigeon between Wittershins and Benwick! And Sonya had had a baby by a young handsome traveler named Lancelot who she'd seen neither hide nor hair of in more than a year's time.

So, there I was up a tree when I noticed the goshawk's foot had been tethered to the branch by no simple means. That was right when it had been my intent to turn victoriously to my sweet lady Elaine with her goshawk and my manhood erect and ready. But, when I saw the piece of chicken wire on that goshawk's foot, I knew something was afoot, besides a goshawk up a tree, and my manhood deflated considerably.

In seconds, there were half a dozen young men approaching from the fields and I knew I didn't have time enough to get down from that tree and especially not enough time to gather my things before they would be upon me, so I tore free a branch.

At this point I would like to point out that I was rather ashamed, nervous, and entirely thinking of nothing but myself. So much so I didn't care that the goshawk was still attached to the branch.

But wouldn't you know it, when I took the branch in hand and turned to head back down that tree and face what might be certain doom, the tree branch spoke!

"You're not intending to draw the blood of those blokes with this here goshawk I should hope," said the branch.

I was utterly bereft of word.

I sat perched in that tree, staring at the branch in befuddlement while the damsel ran out to meet her cohorts for the victory.

"Excuse me," I said to the branch, "but, did you just talk?"

"Not the branch you, idiot! Me," said the goshawk.

So, then I balanced the branch out before me and looked directly onto the goshawk who had been clinging to it with its every metal. It took it neigh a few more awkward moments to settle and regain a rather regal posture. When it did, I felt both stupid and ashamed. If not a little confused. "Funny," I dared to answer, "I thought you were a merlin."

The goshawk ruffled its chest feathers and lifted its chin.

"You certainly know your birds!" said the goshawk. "Now, I am going to suggest that we do something about your ensuing embarrassment."

My foot was in the crook of a branch that looked only a bit more stable than the one freed into my hand. I was under constant threat of not only embarrassment, but it seemed, imminent injury to my backside and other private parts of the anatomy.

Unsure as to whether I should take my chances with a talking bramble against the oncoming throng or take my time arguing with a goshawk, my muscles seemed to tell me that I had better just stay put for a moment and let the bird have its say.

"You could just simply untie my foot and we could both be free of this embarrassment in a jiffy, you know," said the bird.

Now I was shuddering under the sheer weight of the branch and sweat was rolling down my back and gathering in rather uncomfortable cracks and crevices.

"I'm afraid if I let go my hand, we might both tumble to the ground at this point!" I said mindlessly to the branch and bird both at once, still unsure as to who was speaking for whom.

"Just relax, Boy," said the bird. "I've never seen us quite so nervous. Take a deep breath and sit back on that branch there. It will hold and we are quite safe. I don't see any bow and arrows."

"Well," I said nervously. "There's lots of rocks down there, they can do a lot of damage with rocks you know." Plus, I imagined one or two of them had pitchforks.

What was I saying? Was I really talking to a bird? Maybe I'd lost it all together.

"It's the wine," said the bird. "It has a different effect on you."

"The wine—" I thought briefly, "yes, of course! The wine!" I said to the bird. Then I remembered, she did give me some wine before all of this. I usually never drink the stuff because it seems to make people slow.

"Yes."

"What's that?"

"Yes," said the bird, "it does."

"What?"

"It makes things slow."

"What, the wine?"

"Yes," says the bird again and then he says, but now I can see his beak moving a little like lips and I think for a second that I might not be holding a bird on a stick but instead I might have something else in my hand.

"It's a wand," says Merle plainly.

Then my eyes clear a little bit, and it does in fact seem that I am holding a wand. It's a wand made of oak. Two serpents twirl around one another up its handle and the top is crowned with three feathers. One black, one grey, and one white.

"Those are the feathers of Math," says Merddin flatly, who now is no longer a goshawk, or a merlin rather, but an extremely grumpy man in his late sixties. But let's not tell him that just yet, because it might make him cranky. He may be rather in his late fifties, but if my calculations are correct, and because I am now holding the wind wand with the feathers of Math, I'm quite sure that they will be, well, we'll just leave it at grumpy old man.

"Sorry," I said to the old wizzard, "you've seemed to have caught me—"

"A bit off guard?"

"Yes," I said.

"With your pants down?" the wizzard asked glancing downward.

At that moment I remembered that I had just then been in a tree and in a most precarious situation. I nearly swatted the old man with the feathery wand in a quick attempt at covering my glory, before I realized I was back in full dress, armor and all!

"Please, watch how and where you swing that thing!" said the wizzard. "I am speaking of the wand and not your, glory, though in the future, you should mind the latter as you may better occupy yourself the most valiant knight in history, you know?"

I could feel the blood in my temples inflate my cheeks like two fresh apples. Then, I looked around.

It seemed that we were some distance down the road from the previous events. In fact, I could see the maiden quite some distance off from over the wizzard's shoulder. She was throwing up her arms in confusion among a throng of her relatives.

"I wouldn't concern myself," said the wizzard. "I am Merddin, but you knew that already."

I shook my head and looked at the wand timidly. Then, out of some errant impulse tried to put it into my sword's sheath and met with resistance as my sword was already there. Then I met with Merddin's ridicule which strangely made me start feeling a little more comfortable.

"Ah, ah. Lancelot. That goes into the wooden box with the rest of your symbols of mastery. And it's a shame I should have to remind you that no one else should touch it!"

I noticed that I did indeed have a wooden chest with the ogham sigils carved along its rim representing all four cardinal directions. Firewise, Waterward, Earthbound, and Windward.

"But where did it all come from?"

"Just give it a minute," said Merddin, "it takes a while to compile."

"And to be certain," I said, "we are still talking about the wand, and not my glory?" I said, thinking the wizzard was trying to get to a moral about things.

"Ah! You see. It's taking hold. I knew you would catch on. Soon you might remember everything."

I was wrapping the wind wand in a nice white piece of silk and placing it into the small trunk. The box was made in such a way that there were no hinges or seams, but when I'd lifted the top, it came straight away from the rest of itself, all while staying firmly attached to the saddle bag. Closing it was just as simple.

Over Merddin's shoulder I could still see the family milling about in confusion at our disappearance. "Are you certain that we are far enough away?" I began asking, but then I saw them passing something between the party. "Oh, I see."

"Yes. Wine," said the wizzard. "It definitely slows them down."

I remembered the odd experience in the tree and tried mashing a few ideas together in my mind to make sense of how I'd gone immediately from there to here but somehow, I just couldn't manage. Finally, I gave up on the endeavor and removed my breastplate and greaves, cinching them to the horse's harness then shook out my dark hair.

No wounds, all my limbs seemed to be in place. Merddin waited patiently while I assessed the situation.

"So, the business with the chicken wire?" I ventured, thinking it would be a good place to start.

At that, the tall man finally uncrossed his arms and paraded past my horse, blue robes swishing. His hat tried loosely to refrain from covering his eyes and his beard followed him from over his shoulder.

"All caught up then I presume," he said. He whirled around just past the hind end of my quite valiant white mare and sat on the cart, crossing his legs.

I certainly didn't feel that everything had been compiled yet. Quite frankly, I was unsure if anything ever would make sense again. But I wasn't through asking questions. I watched as the benevolent old sage began stuffing some yellow flowers into his pipe and thought it a good time to get some answers.

"Just how did you get your foot bound to that branch to begin with?" I asked.

"That is of no consequence," he said offhandedly, paying more attention to his pipe than to me. He shook out a match, "We're free, aren't we?"

I couldn't argue with that. But the how of it was still urking me. "And… I did that? Somehow set you free?"

Merddin made such an exasperation that I knew immediately that I had said something wrong. "You don't remember?!"

He sprang to his feet and marched directly to me nose to nose, he was taller than me by a whole hat. "I knew it!" he said pointing a finger up beside my ear. "Just when I thought you were coming around."

"Well," I said, "I assumed I untied the wire—"

"You did!" he said turning, "You did!" He took a huge puff from his pipe and went to sit again, looking into the bowl of the pipe and murmuring, "don't you do it, flame!"

His left eye was so large, I felt bad for the ember in the bottom of the pipe's bowl. Reluctantly, smoke started twirling up from it again and I relaxed a little. Then he looked back at me. "But you don't remember! Too much wine. You can't do it! Time gets too slow and you end up out in front of it."

I thought that might answer more questions than I realized. It had gotten kind of warped there for a minute. "That still doesn't explain how I got here," I said.

"Oh, that?" then said Merddin, "That was simple magic. Call it misdirection. Once that copper wire was removed it was no trouble at all. Troublesome stuff cooper. You can't enchant it, well, not the consecrated stuff anyhow."

"You mean to tell me; the chicken wire was keeping you from performing magic?" I asked, putting it all together.

"Well, don't be daft," said Merddin. "You can at least tell a simple binding spell when you see one, I presume. I mean, my foot was clearly bound to that tree Boy!"

He did have a point.

The gangly man stood proudly and stretched his back until it popped and then he leant forward clearly relieved, "Let's just say I had reasons along the same lines as your own for being stuck in that tree. Elaine's mother has a thing for birds, and I have an ongoing thing for Elaine's…"

In the spanse of one second, Merddin seemed to have forgotten I had been standing there and listening. He turned to me and seemed surprised all over again. "Now, what were we talking about just now?"

I started to tell him that I thought he may have gotten on with the wrong woman, but he interrupted me before my mouth could even form the words my brain was stringing together.

"How did we get here," he said.

I lifted a finger in protest, but he failed to acknowledge any authority over his own.

"First, the wand," he said. "Along with your other symbols of mastery. They have been keeping in a shop just up the way. I picked up on them when I came through Benwick. Yes, now It's coming back to me. The shopkeeper found your trunk washed up in Lionese and couldn't get it open according to the butcher who had tried his way at it with his cleaver to no avail." Merddin pointed to a nick in the darkened black willow of the magic box. "See there. I'll bet that's where the logger tried it with his axe when he next passed through Grinsbee." Merddin looked smug. "Three towns seen that box go through, no one could get in it. Enchanted willow, that."

He could tell I still remembered absolutely nothing.

"They come back to us. You have to remember that! Oh, don't worry, you will. Some things take longer than others." Merddin pulled out his own magic wand and smacked his palm with it saying, "your memories, for starters." He held up the crooked stick, "Our tools. This thing. Not the prettiest. But I can't get rid of it. I've tried!"

He whirled his wand and a broomstick peeked out from among the bushel lying on the cart. It timidly took a few steps out from the bundles, then gained a bit more confidence when I stopped shaking my head in disbelief.

"Well, saddle up," said the wizzard. "This manure is not going to shovel itself." Then he grabbed the broom and hiked up his blue robes sufficiently to shove it underneath.

I looked back at the damsel Elaine and her crew who were little more than ants on the horizon bustling about in their cheer.

"Don't look back my boy," said Merddin. "I think you were right. We should put some more distance between ourselves and the past. And I think it is fair to say that we've both learned which sex is the deadliest of the species."

Chapter Sixteen: Arthur and the Giant

After Hazeus loaded up disk four and it got spinning, the smoke cleared and Arthur's journey was picked up around the same time I was being found by Merddin.

King Arthur was taking up an early quest to establish himself as emperor of the free lands.

King Dionysus of Cornwall had offered his daughter Guinevere's hand in marriage to King Arthur if he were to defeat a Saxon Hoard, but upon his vow, Arthur had sworn to hold life above all else and that meant no taking life, especially many lives, unless for some holy or worshipful good, so instead, King Dionysus offered him an adventure to slay a giant.

A rather peculiar loophole, Arthur thought, and the blonde beauty that was up for grabs had no small weight in swaying the young boy king's decision to prove himself a fit and powerful leader.

While Arthur was no stranger to holy scripture, it was not going to be as easy as using a sling and casting the first stone to deliver a gift as large as a giant. As it turned out, Arthur's journey was one filled with trepidation, though mostly in the form of a clean conscience. His vow to Hazeus and to the Druid order, for that matter, weighed heavily on him.

As he urged his horse up the slopes of mount Saint Michael, the mare stumbled over uneven granite and broke a foreleg. This was just as Arthur had been hyping himself up to do brave and heavy battle. But as it were, the unfortunate accident had him looking his poor mare in the eye and considering putting her out of her misery.

As he stood there in the light rain, which was swiftly turning to sleet and soon to snow, his heated battle hungry heart found pity in the dark marble of his horse's gaze. For more than an hour he wrestled with the decision. Until her skin began to quiver. It was then he noticed his reflection in her eye and untied the bundle from her saddle and draped the large canvas over her to warm her.

Gently he did his best to splint her knee, and with a great effort got her to standing where he could help her hobble the last few miles up the mountain pass to town. Immediately within the city limits he found lodging and a stableman to house his injured horse for the night.

Upon the morn, and after a restless night considering the horse's fate, he went down to the stables to see if she had come along any better overnight. Alas, she hadn't and the stable hand recommended putting her down as she would never be good for work.

It was a bad omen for a newly minted king on a quest for glory, thought Arthur. But just then the stable hand's son arrived.

"What a beautiful mare!" said the boy, growing instantly fond of her, taking no notice of her splinted foreleg. Then seeing the king's armor among the floored harness and saddle, he said wide-eyed, "Are you a knight?"

"Just a cautious traveler, lad," Arthur said. "She took a bad fall west of town." He drew the boy's attention to the wound.

"She'll not do good for work, Eustace," said the stable hand firmly to his son.

"But she could breed," said Eustace to his father confidently.

The stable hand was shaking his head and folded his arms across his chest putting a thumb and forefinger under his chin. He massaged his cropped beard and creased chin between his fingers before seeming to come to a decision, "No. It's no good. We can hardly feed the one's we have, and we can't afford help."

"I'll take responsibility for her, Pa." The boy didn't wait for his father to object. "I'll groom her and exercise her and will work the back fields for oats. If I miss a single day, I will put her down myself."

Arthur and the man looked at one another exchanging mutual understanding. They each reminisced in the boy's passion and Arthur's soft expression gained the boy favor with his father. So, it stood that the young Eustace would hold himself responsible. Good thing, too. Because that mare would turn out to be a very important horse for the city of Brittany.

The stable hand and Arthur retired to the Inn and sat together for a meal while the boy tended to the mare. Arthur bid him well for his decent raising of the boy and confessed his love for the animal and his gaiety for the stroke of luck.

While he did not divulge the entire nature of his journey to the man, it was in the man's heart to offer Arthur an old pack mule in exchange for the lame horse so that Arthur could continue up the mountain. This act of homage brought Arthur to tell the man his true adventure and the man confessed that the boy's mother had been one of several women that a Giant named Fuzzick had seized as prisoner over the past two years to take back to his castle on Mount Saint Michael for a likely meal.

It had been the reason that the man was loathe to work the boy as he was still in the throes of a lingering depression. It had only been when the stable hand had seen that Eustace's love for the horse that hope had finally dawned for the father after the loss. Not for the father's own woe, but for his son's passing grief.

The weather broke by late noon and Arthur made his way to the lofty plateau of Mount Saint Michael and the Riton Giant of Cornwall. The peak was further still, but a plateau came into view with Arthur riding awkwardly upon the asses back, his armor roped to the hind end of the donkey and clanging like bells. He had much time to think of his humbling misfortune and rather comical arrival to the domain of the giant.

I hate to say that my reunification with my rod of wind might have had anything to do with Arthur's success during this quest, but it was rather coincidental that the God of wind was particularly busy that day.

His ass brayed as it clopped up and onto the landing of the rocky plateau and into the thick wind of the peaks. The twists of current grabbed Arthur's cloak and carried it up in twirls behind him with a voice he could almost hear. Indeed, it was a voice he was hearing. In fact, it was many voices. They were singing.

The voices were of the maidens imprisoned on a cliff that Arthur could see in the distance. A gap too great to jump separated them and seemed only able to be traversed by a great deal of climbing along the ridge. The ladies were huddled together around a fire, tending one another, but their greatest attention was on him, a fresh prospect at liberation. Some of the ladies were pointing, some jumping up and down with excitement, but only the sound of the gentle singing broke through the mighty gusts that swept through the chasm between them. The sight was such that it was no great surprise that Arthur didn't see the giant holding a great stone in hand behind him.

As it happened, and because Arthur could not hear a word that was being said, he did what was natural and prepared for the treacherous climb over to the prisoners. But when he bent down to check that his shoes were firmly fastened to his feet, a rock exploded above his head against another huge stock of boulders.

Furthermore, he was not expecting to meet with a beast of any intellect, but rather a man in bear skins four stone heavier than he.

Arthur stood up among the spray of chalky rubble and smacked his leather jerkin with the palm of his left hand.

"Now Fuzzick," he said greatly, while his ass, his donkey rather, sighed and carefully, though not without pains, clopped its way a few steps back down the way it had come to safer grounds. "You must know, before you would have a do with me that I am the new Emperor of Cornwall."

The giant, which did not in fact look anything like he had expected stood there with a sow-sized stone in his right hand held at the ready. More surprisingly, the giant spoke with a voice that came in a timber as thick as redwood; slow but indeed discernable.

"I will have you know, fresh emperor, that I threw the last stone with my left hand. If I let this stone fly, it will not be as apt to miss."

Arthur put his hands on his hips and with confidence said above the voices on the wind, "I assume that you are then, indeed right-handed?"

The giant stood poised. His great brown eyes did a circle in their sockets as his enormous brain worked out the answer. "That's correct," came the enormous woodwind instrument that was his vocal cords.

"Well," said the King, clearly outmatched by the giant's strength, but playing on the obvious humanity of the man inside. The 'man' in humanity says one great thing before a group of beautiful ladies. That one thing happens to be, "Play fair."[59] No man wants to be dishonored in front of the ladies.

"Well," said Arthur, "You clearly have me outmatched in size and strength. But I am willing to bet that I would outmatch your throw with my speed and have done with you by Excalibur before you reload your other fist."

The giant took a heaving breath and Arthur saw a grin come to his countenance with pitted teeth as large as thumbs. A straw-colored stack of hair was upon the ogre's head and the thing's breeches were fashioned of burlap potato sacks. It wore only a simple leather jerkin. "That's a bold statement," said the giant dryly. "I might be faster than I look."

The giant lifted the stone, but Arthur held up his hand, still refusing to unsheathe his own sword. "And I might be stronger," he said confidently while expecting to be imminently crushed.

The giant paused. There came no crashing of stone. Arthur cocked his head and looked at the large man through blonde locks. "You see," said Arthur seizing the moment, "I've vowed as emperor not to take life but to uphold sanctity and holiness rather." He saw the Giant's arm relax an inch and continued, "So, I am kind of at an impasse here."

---

[59] In the days after the battle with the giant Arthur recalled to his newly won betrothed, that indeed the song of 'Play Fair' was being sung on the wind.

"I should say so," said Fuzzick. "How would an emperor who cannot take life rescue a dozen women, much less defend a nation?"

Arthur looked across to the women on the ledge who had become silent during the two men's exchange. "Why the women, Fuzzick? The people of Brittany believe you've brought them here to eat them, you know? But I can see you've got quite a collection. Are you saving them for Beltane? There's enough here to feed a family of giants."

With this the giant dropped the stone in the dirt and put his hands upon his belly and began to laugh, first slowly, then with such great gusto Arthur thought he might just go on like that all day. Then the big man leaned against the boulder on his left and said, "What are you asking *me* for?"

The giant then pointed a finger across the divide and said, "You should be asking her. She's the one who enjoys the company."

At that Arthur noticed something peculiar about one of the prisoners. The ears of one of the ladies resembled the fins of a particular tench he'd grown rather familiar with around castle Tintagel's moat one morning. That one particular lady was at the fore of the others, her breast puffed out and her hands cupped to the sides of her mouth as if she were shouting something desperately to the entire universe.

But the wind had her whipped.

"You mean the—" started Arthur but Fuzzick cut him off.

"Choose your words carefully when you talk about Theresa," said the giant.

Arthur thought of how he could call a woman a fish in a more acceptable manner for a giant. He was running the thought through his brain when he decided that the particular fishstress in question had Fuzzick as whipped as the wind had her at the moment.

Luckily, before his brain gave up, the wind must have blocked enough of the Siren's wail from Fuzzick's giant-sized eardrums that he was thinking clearly for a moment. "She makes me do it," he said plainly.

The wind was so thick that little pebbles along the crevice were jumping like jacks, dancing their way out over the ledge.

Arthur raised his voice over the gusts, "So, why haven't you just climbed over there and clobbered her?"

"Can't climb," said Fuzzick, looking at his tender digits, "I have fat fingers."

"Then why not the rock? You seem to be a fair aim."

"Too messy. I was only trying to scare you before." Fuzzick sat down on a stone bench that Arthur had so far missed and took a hearty swig from an oaken barrel. After he had wiped the froth from his chin he said, "If you knew your history, you would have a different understanding of our kind." He raised the giant cup, "We live to party."[60]

The wind started dying down again, and Arthur could make out faint notes again in the air.

"Can't you hear her?" asked Fuzzick.

Arthur started to understand what was going on. "I can hear something, but I dare say that Lew Llaw Gwyffs is thanking me for those flowers I offered him this past Lugnassadh!" He then glanced down and noticed that the golden pipes of his youth associated

---

[60] Andre the Giant still holds the record for most beer consumed in one sitting

with the deity were in fact growing plentifully around him. "I don't mean to be rude, but if you'd excuse me for a moment."

Arthur then leant down and plucked a few of the golden rayless flowers from the ground and then stuck them firmly into his ears. The sound of the wind and the voices carried upon it immediately abated. This allowed him to focus.

Fuzzick was looking at him like he'd gone mad.

"I know you think I've gone mad," said Arthur.

Fuzzick's large lips moved with such silent animation that Arthur nearly took the earplugs out from pure habit, then he remembered he could read huge lips, it was just a slower cadence. Fuzzick had said, "Why are you yelling?"

Arthur stopped, his hands halfway to his ears and pointed at them instead. Then he leaned down and took another large bouquet of the golden pipes into his hands and held them up to the giant.

"For the lady," said Arthur a bit less vocally.

At this, the giant seemed to be more agreeable, though still surely confused by the king's strange actions. Then Arthur pointed toward the windy chasm and started making his way to the wall. "I'm just going to bring her these flowers," said Arthur trying to keep his voice at a more regular octave.

"I told you," said Fuzzick, "she loves company."

"Uh huh," said Arthur approaching the cliff's edge. He looked over at the deafening drop. Then he looked up again and saw a very nice set of handholds that looked made just for the job of crossing. So, he stuffed the bouquet of flowers in the seat of his pants and reached out while the wind was calm.

"Merddin," Arthur said to himself while he scaled the cliff wall, "you once told me that asking the beings of stone and earth to come out in the light was like inviting a fish to dinner on top of a mountain."

He stuck his leather shoe into a notch further along the wall and looked at the siren on the far ledge. Her eyes were white, and the fins behind her ears looked as if they were trying to catch a current in the wind.

"Flesh or fish, Merddin?" Arthur whispered as the Siren song started eating through even the thick polyps of the golden pipes.

He moved closer to her side.

"You can be nervous," Arthur reminded himself in Merddin's voice. "You can even be scared." He continued as he slid sideways over the chasm toward the beautiful woman in silver sequins. Or was that a tail? "But," he said, stepping on to the ledge where the dozen women were huddled in the back of the cleft of rock behind the singing beast. "Never let that affect your confidence."

And so, he hadn't. Standing there he was extremely confident as this thing, whatever it was, sang into his face, because this thing was smiling. But the smile was full of sharpened teeth outlining the ringed tunnel of a throat.

Arthur thrust out his bouquet of golden pipes and two fins reached out as if they were going to take them, but Arthur had his heart set on another woman already. So, with golden pipes in his ears and in his hands and love in his heart, he placed the bottom of his right foot between him and the golden-haired siren and kicked.

A bit later. Far, far below. There was a splash, as the giant's prize catch was finally returned to the sea.

Chapter Seventeen: Little John

I have done the decent thing and told you some of my backstory.

While Hazeus was privy to the following scene in the magiscope, he was not privy to my past sins. So, let's just keep that between you and I for now, shall we?

"Now, I can't tell you any details," started Merddin as the fog was clearing away for the scene, "because I don't remember if he's coming from the North or we're coming from the South."

Hazeus could see that Merddin had been riding on his horse backward for over a mile while explaining to a handsome knight named Lancelot that he was going to have to fight the Emperor of England to the death without anyone actually dying in the process.

"But you have already told me the details, Merddin. You've been going on about it for three whole days!"

"Have I then?" replied the wizzard, "Oh, confound it all. It gets this way when Nimue comes along. Balancing of the male and female forces and all of that."

"Yes, yes, you've explained that, too," said Lancelot, edging his horse up against a giant vine and gathering some rain in the cup of a huge leaf.

"Well, if you know everything, then you tell me since you're so smart," said Merddin, flinging his legs up and around just as his horse dipped, allowing the soaked geezer to turn his hips proper in the saddle and cross his arms in a sultry position.

"You've said that *if* I am to be the greatest and most noble knight in history then I must never lay with a woman."

Merddin looked halfway back at Lancelot who was drinking from the leaf and in no way disturbed by how upset the old man was. "Well?" muttered the wizzard.

"Well, what?" inquired the knight.

"Well, that's only part of it, it's not like I am a prude you know! There's a reason for it isn't there, or are you as stupid as you are handsome?"

Lancelot let the leaf fall back against the vine and leaned into the horn of his saddle. "Okay, old man. It's like this."

Merddin heeled his horse around and Cedric the raven came down and lit on the druid's shoulder. The whole scene suggested that this was going to be a really good failure on the knight's part.

Lancelot straightened up and brushed back his wet hair. The sun started to peek through the clouds now and he smiled confidently. "It's like this. You can't outrun a diet of sin you see. I may in fact be the best trained knight in the world, but I will never win a battle if I am not also the most humble, noble, and pure. Inside of me is this well of power, much like Mother Earth's aquifer. A type of steam is kindled there in the fire of Father Time's desire."

Cedric turned an obvious beak to Merddin and Merddin lifted his chin. Lancelot shook out the moisture from his hair and sat back in his saddle, he was relatively sure that the horse was even impressed.

"If I cultivate this proverbial steam," Lance continued, "This nectar of goodness, then I will prevail in all of my holy efforts. Because it is imbalance that grants authority over conscience. Conscience is the eye of our Father's and the wider open that their lids are on us, the more worship we will accumulate."

Lancelot had to stifle a welling smirk when he imagined the horse's jaw dropping to the forest floor. "In short," he said, "I ought to cultivate the gaze of my forefathers and bask in their protection, so that we won't have to do this all again… er again, again?"

Kind of a weak wrap-up thought Lancelot, but he felt that he understood it well enough. This being Merddin's second go round after the whole Thomas the doubter thing, left the old wizzard only mildly giddy, but not so much as to further inflate Lancelot's ego.

"Very good!" said the druid a bit shakily and then a bit more firmly, "Very good!" Then Merddin turned to the raven and said, "and I taught him all of that over the past few days, then?"

"Ah!" Lancelot interrupted. He was now biting into a peach, "Reminded me. You reminded me of all of that, over the last few days, in fact. Your words, druid! So, I dare say that it was me who had half a hand in it!" He then took another smug bite.

Merddin looked back to Cedric who SQUAWKED. Then he bundled up his beard, shoved it into his own mouth, and chewed.

Unrequited Love

While Hazeus was watching events unfold from the comfort of his bearskin rug, he could only know what the scene portrayed. While he was introduced to me as a character in the previous tale through the goings on inside of the magiscope, and oftentimes narrated by his mother or father, I am more personally involved in this coming tidbit. I only share my version of this story with you, the reader, because you are aware of my multiple incarnations.

Besides, without it, you would never understand the whole business of Lancelot's, my rather, lifelong infatuation with the queen. It should come as no surprise that reincarnation is not limited to Merddin and I alone.

"According to what you were telling me at lunch, we should come across Arthur near Brittany."

Cedric was now riding on my shoulder and Merddin was taking up the rear, quite in a mood.

"Mind the gravel here, Merddin," I said after my mount nearly lost its footing.

Just then, we came upon a fork in the road where the way leveled out a bit and started winding its way more evenly. When down below I spied some movement and reigned to a halt.

Through the saplings, I saw the sheen of a mare whose regal build and flowing mane brought me back to a past love. It was her!

Hazeus would never guess what was befalling me that day, as he did not possess the memories that were reassembling in that fresh brain of mine. What he saw in the magiscope were only the actions of a man obsessed with a horse. But it was more than that for me.

"That's her!" I said to Merddin quietly getting his attention with the back of my hand.

"Nonsense," he said. "Alicorns[61] wouldn't survive in this mess of a world!"

"But they would, Merddin! I am telling you that is Lady! I would recognize that backside from anywhere!"

Merddin let out a long audible sigh, "Now, don't go getting your loins back into a boil!"

"Look at her, Merle," said I, really getting a hold on my memories again, "Shouldn't we hold onto whatever magic possible we find this side of the veil?"

Merddin was twisting his beard around a finger trying to remain calm. His horse was doing a strange side-stepping action that made its rider look more nervous than he'd have liked. I was smiling and rather amused at his indecision, as that is always how things got when the old man was caught between right-doing and just plain fun. I was beginning to think he wouldn't respond when finally, he said, "I don't know."

"You don't know? You can't say you don't know. You know everything, you just don't want to try," I said, and then thought I shouldn't have insulted him in such a way. But, hey, what are brothers for.

Surprisingly, he kept his cool. He said flatly, "You decide. Quite frankly, what's it matter? But do remember, we are setting up this world to get on without magic for a while, you know."

"How would that help anything?"

"With the way this world is going, magic is just going to get in the way here. Chase after your horse if you want!

---

[61] A unicorn with wings and a horn with the ability to play music

But you're only using magic to trade in what you have for something better. Keep doing that and well, see where selfishness gets you."

"But she was mine to begin with!" I yelled as I spurred my stallion into action. "You can't blame me for wanting her back!"

Presently I was atop a white marble. A Boulonnais whose muscles heaved in response to my yearning. The mare was off like a shot as soon as the first young birch broke in protest at the flank of my steed. But I wasn't the only one yearning for her.

The heat was between the two horses, his strength and own magic burning for her.

I set my knees, keeping fast in the stirrups, and twice having to hold myself tight and low on the saddle's horn as he rounded narrow corners at a gallop. But then he had her at a pace and the track stretched out before us. She may be more agile, but we were strong and would definitely take her on the straight. The whip cracked in the air behind the stallion, and we found the top of our sprint, but still she pulled away!

The sound of her hooves remained a steady cadence but diminished and before another quarter mile she'd gained such a lead that she was disappearing over yon horizon. My stallion had thundered heavily to a stop and had begun stamping at the forest floor beside the road, turning its perfect carpet of green lichen over into rich divots of soil and commanding with its nostrils great swirls of pollen in the streaks of sunlight under the canopy when I heard Merddin chuckle.

"You almost had her," he said.

I was dumbfounded! It had been impossible that she pulled away. I thought back to the first time I had met Lady and won her by riding her through an exhausting series of life-threatening challenges. That had ended in her final defiant act of jumping off a cliff to end it all rather than be broken. Back then, I had surrendered at that last moment and compassion had won the day.

This was different. I couldn't even manage to get alongside her!

"You know," chuckled Merddin, "it's said that only a virgin can capture a unicorn."

"Don't give me that!" I said, "I've done it before in just such a state! Besides, she is lacking her horn altogether this time."

"It's magic," said he. "You can't expect to see her horn with the magic bleeding out from this place at every orifice."

I settled my mount and reigned him around to find Cedric perched atop a wooden sign. Its cross member indicated Brittany to the north along the well-worn road Lady had broken away to, while the word WOOD was charred into the mast of it with an arrow pointing west where a game trail disappeared into the forest.

The light would be failing soon, and from the direction of the game trail we could hear running water. It was a unanimous decision to find the stream and make camp for the evening.

"I will get that mare, Merddin."

He had begun his usual trick of ignoring me while simultaneously napping with his eyes open. Though, it was hard to tell after his hat had fallen over his eyes. What gave it away was how his feet were crossed at the ankles and propped up on his horse's head while his arms were crossed behind his own head in front of his bedroll. Archimedes would not have tolerated any other person trying this while riding.

The sound of the river had grown to a torrent by the time I found a suitable clearing to make a fire, but it was at that moment that Archimedes came to a halt and Merddin sat bolt upright demanding what all the commotion was.

At the far end of the clearing, where the river ran in rapids, was a large man in animal skins leaning on a six-foot fighting stick. His head and face which won the height of the staff by a whole neck was so covered in hair that only a large nose, two almond eyes, and a small crop of forehead[62] were visible.

I dismounted and noticed that behind the man was a large log which had fallen over the river. Beyond him could be seen tongues of flame reaching up from behind the far shrubs, and even over the roar of the water, the notes of a piccolo and the pleasant rhythm of drumbeat.

I glanced up at Merddin who was busy straightening his dunce's cap and generally trying to get his bearings. It's like that with him fresh from sleep. Always trying to remember where in the memory of his memories he is finding himself at the moment.

"Long days and pleasant nights," I said to the woodsman.

The relative giant spread his legs before the fallen tree as if we had come upon a troll bridge of sorts, but his face lit up like a cherub, the teeth a flash of white among the brown thicket of hair. "Is that Merddin?"

Merddin didn't seem to recollect.

I looked back at the man and then led my horse to a young ash jutting up from the tree line. "Well," I said,

---

[62] Perhaps, onehead or twohead would be more appropriate.

tying my mount to the tree, "if it's no insult to you, I've got firewood to collect."

"It's a free country."

"Is it now?" I asked. "Last I heard, Meldegrance was taxing the people extra for every male child they bore."

I started looting the wood line for available kindling while the large man was catching his breath from a laugh that spooked the blackbirds from the thicket.

"It's free on this side of the river by any account!"

Merddin finally seemed to be coming to. He slid off his mount from a sidesaddle position, minding his robes and marched straight up to the intimidating individual. He only lacked the height of the man by a few inches, even stooped over like he usually was, though his pointed hat rose above them both. Regardless, the wizzard resembled a blue racing stripe while standing in front of the giant as he only had a fifth of the girth.

The river guardian lifted his bo staff and struck the stone on which he stood. "I thought it was you!" he harked and tossed the staff into the grass, enveloping the old man in a bear hug and lifting him from the ground.

Merddin tolerated this, though Cedric squawked from the other bank, apparently unrestricted by tolls[63].

I tossed my bundle of kindling near to where an old fire had once been built and happened a bit closer to Merddin and the man. When Merddin's feet came back to earth he straightened his robes, and his friend plucked the hat from his head putting it back on straight for him and dusting off his shoulders.

"Now, John," I heard Merddin say, "you know that druids are slave to no man."

---

[63] Other than the tolling of church bells that is.

"Druids, no, of course not! But what of this one?" he pointed at me with indifference. "The last time I saw a man in armor, they were trying to marry off Maid Marion against her will!"

Merddin turned to me and smacked his lips, giving me a look that said he need not do me any more favors before turning away and saying, "This, is Lancelot. Destined to be the bravest, most famous, noble, and skilled knight in history." Then after a short pause he added, "Though not exactly in that order, or even all at the same time for that matter."

I shook my head when the stranger dropped his chin in acknowledgement and went back to picking up my sticks.

Rising above my disinterest the man remarked, "Is that right?"

I wasn't being suckered and continued gathering wood and depositing it on the previously scorched bit of earth.

"Well, you'd think he would have better manners!"

I stopped what I was doing. "I'm sorry, sir."

"Little John," he corrected.

"Little?" I straightened up, "Hazeus, I'd hate to see the big version."

"I ate him," he said rubbing his belly. Merddin sidled away, secretly smiling in my direction and Little John stepped forward and leant down to retrieve his stick. I reminded myself what brothers were for.

"It's free on this side of the river," said John reminding me.

"Not interested," I said. I wasn't taking the bait. "I'm perfectly fine over here. It doesn't seem to be costing me anything at the moment."

"You're wrong," said the giant stepping back to the end of the log. "It's costing you a ready-made fire and some decent company."

"I can make my own fire," I said still thinking about Lady. What I really wanted was to be left alone with my thoughts of her.

"We have elderberry wine."

That was too much for Merddin. "Lancelot, do stop being a baby!"

I dropped the sticks and walked to Merddin.

"There's elderberry wine," Merddin pleaded. "Besides Robin Wood is over there. If I remember correctly, he once helped Arthur and Kay rescue a maiden in the enchanted forest somewhere near Tintagel. Perhaps he can help you with Lady." He could see that I wasn't convinced. "It will be Beltane soon! I could do with a nice slice of red meat, and they have fresh boar, you can smell it!"

The smell was pretty enticing but, "Look at the size of him!" I said.

"Oh, don't worry about that! They fight fair. It's only customary you know. If he knocks you in the river, I will magic you into a salmon and you can leap to the other shore."

"I'm not planning on being beaten," I said. Then I looked over at the huge and jovial ruffian and gulped. He had what I thought was a horn of wine to his lips until it pealed out a battle tone on the wind.

Soon, the opposing forest came to life, and from the shrubs appeared a handful of woodsmen dressed in Lincoln green, and then a dozen other people crowded alongside the shore.

I looked at Merddin whose grin was so wide that his eyes and lips had disappeared among the beard and eyebrows.

I sighed. "The least you could do is get me a stick," I said.

Merddin was busy magicking me a quarter staff of white oak that was young and flexible but strong. Currently, it was still an uprooted tree doing somersaults in the clearing at the tip of his wand while I was facing Little John.

"You're not going to spar with that armor on I should hope!" he said. "If you go into the river, you'll sink like twelve stone!"

He had a point. I removed my greaves and fastened them with my breastplate and helm to Nicodemus and helped her settle down in the shade. I untied my left gauntlet from the saddle and walked back to the makeshift bridge.

"We don't have any gold," I said, "but that'll fetch some coin in Brittany." Then I tossed it at Little John's feet.

He smiled. "I told you, it's free on our side of the river. All you have to do is make it there. Lesson number one," he said strangely. "If you're going to be the most noble night in history, lies do not become you," and he struck at my bare head with his long staff, nearly offing me in one blow.

With no armor on, I moved twice as fast as ever and fortunately ducked the strike before my freshly minted quarter staff whooshed into my grip and I turned a glancing swing at John of my own, which he avoided by side stepping in a leap up onto the log and inching out over the water.

"I thought you said they fight fair!" I called in Merddin's direction, who was busy lighting his pipe with his fingertips now that the business of making my staff was over. "Took your time about it didn't you?" I said, aghast at his obvious enjoyment.

"I said fair," said Merddin as I cautiously advanced onto the log, "I meant well. They fight well! Now go on and have at him. I'm thirsty!" yelled the wizzard bringing a raucous from the opposing shore of woodsman.

I turned my attention back to little John who was now all smiles. I looked down at the rapids and remembered old Dap pushing me onto the wet river stones after an evening of drinking. John inched back further over the rushing white water below but continued taunting. "I know you have at least one golden sickle on your persons, so gold you have!"

"Well," I said footing it forward with my right, "I meant we have no gold that we can spare."

"Ha! Ain't that the truth of the world!" said John dropping down an octave as he swung his staff like a cricket bat, but I ducked again, and his staff met only air that I thought would throw him off balance and into the river. To my surprise, the large man pirouetted through the swing, and I missed him completely with my strike, losing balance of my own.

I was only saved by a healthy branch that was jutting out beside where I stood. I caught myself on it just as John's staff came down at my foreleg. I cartwheeled away off the branch and back onto the log with enough distance to time his next attack, but he paused.

"You're fast for a big man!" he said.

"That's funny," I said, "I was thinking vice versa of you!⁶⁴"

"So, you're not noble!" continued John, moving the staff into his left hand and taking a step toward me. Then

---

⁶⁴ I'm uncertain whether John's brain was fast enough to catch that play on words but Merddin definitely chuckled.

he lifted it above his head and began spinning it like the falling seedpod of a maple, "Lesson two!" His attack came from the left and I blocked it with my quarter staff, but as soon as the CRACK spread out into space his staff was on the other side of me, but I parried by releasing one half of my stick and turning my wrist over.

All the while John was dialoguing, "If you want to be the most skilled—" Along came another strike from above and I retreated enough to come down over his stick with my own in an attempt to unbalance him again. His staff was forced down onto the log but it wedged at a knothole and he used the leverage to push back out of the way of my counter. "—knight in the world, then you should always be sure you can win!"

I stepped inside of his staff where I would be too close for him to maneuver the weapon and took advantage of my shorter stick's range, bringing it down onto the top of his knuckles. "And the insect stings a bit!" John cried through a smile while shaking life back into his fingers, drawing laughter from the shoreline.

"You're wrong," I said loudly, now seeing my only opportunity. "No man is permitted to lay hands on a druid's symbols of mastery."

John's unibrow unfurled.

"That gold is off limits!" I leapt to the branch that had steadied me and dashed beyond little John using the collar of his tunic as a handhold. My feet found the opposite side of the log and I turned to sprint toward the other bank, but something clasped around my wrist like a vice.

"Ha!" cried John in triumph pulling me back like a yoyo and grabbing me by the waist from behind. He hoisted me up like a rag doll. "Your knight doesn't fight so well," said John playfully to Merddin as I tried prying his huge hands apart by ramming my quarter staff between them and myself.

"C'mon now," said John as I struggled, "I thought we were sharing lessons."

I still struggled in his grasp, his head too far back to butt with my own. He was amusing himself at this point. "Okay here's one, before you toss me in," I said.

The giant turned round to face his side of the river and gain an applause.

"The only three parts of the body permitted to draw blood from the druid…"

"Uh, huh," he said with a grunt looking down into the rapids below.

"The forehead," I said squirming.

"Uh, huh," he sidestepped toward the middle where the water would be deepest, and possibly less likely to kill me.

"The heart," I said taking a breath just in case.

"Uh, huh," he twisted for the toss.

"And the—" I brought the heel of my left foot up smartly into the final place that remained unmentioned, and the giant groaned, released his grip, and lost his balance all at once.

We both went for a swim.

Only a few meters downstream little John washed up onto a shallow shelf of stones and I atop of him. He was screaming for his life.

"I can't swim!" he wailed. "Mary and Hazeusephat, I'm drowning!"

"You're a sopping wet boar!" cried one of the ladies of the wood as she wadded out to us holding up her dresses. She was a big enough woman to grab John by the other arm and help hoist him up from the river and to his feet.

"You're embarrassing your son, John!" said the woman.

"Yes," I said steadying him. "And you were just about to teach me that lesson about being the bravest night in the world."

The big man stood still as moss covered stone, dripping from every tendril. The forest sound was still, flowing only with the water. Then he burst into a hearty grin and gave me a hug like I'd seen him administer to Merddin minutes earlier. "Bravery, you have my friend! I will tell you," he said putting me down then sloshing toward shore with one arm around his wife and the other around my shoulder. "Just leave the Druidry to Merddin, wouldya? He'd convert us all if he'd have it his way."

Merddin was waiting by Cedric on the bank, directing a couple of the merry men to bring hay across the bridge for the horses which would rest there for the night.

Robin of the wood and a Lady's curse

The Wood, beyond the troll bridge was indeed free. Beyond the scrub, it opened onto a massive round clearing. Which was odd in the midst of such a dense forest. A bonfire was raging, and merry men gathered round it in simple comfort. Most relaxed on stones or petrified logs, but some had strung up hammocks between stakes, as nothing grew in this strange space.

We still were in the embrace of the wood, as above the canopy was thick with oak leaves and branches so massive that men lounged among those as well.

"We call him Major," came the voice of a man who was all limbs. His hat was shaped like a paper boat and his beard was cut short and pointed. He was Anglo Saxon, that is blonde, though the ash and dirt might hide it in lesser light.

"The oak," he continued, "Major Oak. I haven't found an older tree. And I have done a lot of looking."

Little John patted the thin man's shoulder as he passed and Merddin and I came to stop before him and his wife. The man used a six-foot wooden hunting bow as a walking stick, though he indeed needed no aid. His other arm was involved in holding his darling's waist.

Merddin was face to face with him as he had him at the height, but I had to look up a bit, so I focused more casually on his wife.

"Robin," said Merle, at which point Robin freed his arm from the lady and engaged in a boisterous shake. The young woman took my moist hand and introduced herself as Marian. Her other hand gestured that I continue toward the fire and a waiting chair made of furs and sticks.

Merddin followed behind casually.

"Keep looking," said the druid. "This is merely Duir. I assure you there are Diaboeeth on the globe that far out age Major." The sounds of joyous hands clapping shoulders behind me said the men were very familiar.

Merle sensed this and said in my direction, "You'll remember Lance, give it time."

Whatever else was being said between Merddin and Robin became muddled when Marian sat me down and said, "So you saw her?"

I took the horn of wine being passed around the circle and looked to Marian. Fire twinkled in her curious eyes.

"The white mare," she said. "She can't be caught."

I was only shortly stunned before a handful of hunters from the circle began shouldering one another and laughing. Then raising cups in cheers of good contest.

"It's a running game since the King's wife was abducted in Cornwall."

"You mean by the giant?"

"That's right," she said.

Then from across the glade a high timbered voice said, "Word is the giant is being dealt with by the new emperor!"

There was chatter and I looked back into Marian's eyes.

"The giant has been being dealt with for years," she said, "but it's the new queen that's the problem if you ask me."

"Why do you say this?" I asked.

"Ever since Dionysus took on a new wife, we have had this untrappable mare in the wood. Rumor is that the new queen is so jealous of her stepdaughter's beauty and how it reminds her husband of his lost love, that she had her bewitched to spend the evenings and nights roaming the wild wood in such form as you've seen."

Marian looked into the dancing flames and let her gaze follow the sparks up to the natural opening in the leaves above where the heat escaped.

"So, you're suggesting that the mare is Dionysus's daughter?"

Marian nodded, "A prize who may only be won by the most highly worshipped knight of the day. A cruel bewitching as we know worship fluctuates with deeds."

Lancelot thought about Merddin's advice and then thought long about Lady.

His vision was interrupted by Robin. "The only way anyone is going to win Genny is by taking down that giant."

Merddin was having a reverent draught of elderberry wine, but then he licked his hairy lips and made a great smack with his gums drawing the immediate company's attention. "A giant now? I thought it was a legion Dionysus was exchanging for her hand?"

The wizard looked at me accusingly and I wondered what the implications of my chasing Lady may be having.

When the last fire beneath Major Oak had been reduced to cinders and the merry men were all dreaming, I found myself rising quietly to follow a neighing sound on the wind. I tiptoed between sleeping huntsmen and past Marian and Robin's tent, then hopped down from the log bridge where the smell of urine was thick, and Nicodemus was pawing the ground and swishing his tail.

As I reached a hand to calm him, I heard Lady's footfall, and like a ghost, her pale form floated past at an amble.

I knew it! Though I had been warned, I couldn't help but have one more try at her.

Quickly, I saddled my mount and walked him gently in her pursuit, though he was hardheaded. I wanted the jump on her. I had on no armor and thought that if she happened to recognize me as the once true and noble man of our yesterlives, then I might prevail.

So dumb, is me. Merddin had already deemed it a fool's errand. It may have been. But how was I supposed to know that deeds in one life can't outshine blunders in another or vice versa? In Arthur's time there wasn't any clearing of one's conscience by spouting off three prescribed hail Mary's or some such dribble. The only way to glory was through deed. And deeds were going to determine who Lady was allowed to love.

When we came upon her, she was at rest, munching on the fern. Nicodemus wanted to go right at her, but I had the sense to drive back his bit and hold him at an angry neutral march. She saw me.

Her head came up like a snake and I saw the unmistakable mark of her. A red patch between her neck and chest formed a star. Her human form's birthmark!

Then I confidently advanced a little, reaching out to her from a hundred paces off. I was certain she would recognize me as we sauntered closer, but I got the most unusual feeling that the road was getting longer. My hand still extended toward her dark and solid gaze, holding me tight beneath her lashes. But with every step whether left or right, another vine or branch would move in front of her as if the forest had come to life and were protecting her.

But why would she need protection from me? Can love like this be wrong? Can love truly drive something away?

Before I could answer my anguish, my stallion would be held no more and jumped forward toward her, clearly frustrated. Then he strutted in a full circle, his muscles tensing as he lifted his head proudly for the exhibition. Then, I became a passenger of his will as he bolted for her.

There was nothing I could do, so I watched from horseback as she turned and ran. This time the forest didn't change around us. There was no need. She wasn't looking at us anymore. She was off to Dionysis's castle, outrunning us at nothing more than a canter.

It took less than a mile for my mount to give up chase and relinquish control again. At which time I reigned him around, feeling rather irritated. "Aren't you even the least bit ashamed of yourself?"

I was met with resistance when trying to tug his head as to look him in the eye, which said enough.

"Just try that again and I'll have you castrated," I said, then felt guilty when he dropped his head. My head wasn't in any better place when I was caught in that tree. So, I patted his mane and trotted back the way we had come.

As we passed the stand of ferns on our left, I saw something cream colored draped upon one of the nodding stalks and reached down from the saddle to retrieve it. It was a handkerchief bearing an embroidered sigil. A red cross over a pink star.

I lifted the token and closed my eyes to inhale. Strawberry and hibiscus. Gripping the cloth tightly in my fist, I smiled.

Merddin stirred when I lay down beside him. "The ole factory senses are a glorious thing, no?"

Why am I never startled at his knowing exactly what I am up to?

I lied back against the bedroll and opened the handkerchief for him to see the sigil. His eyes were not open when I looked at him, but he always had the knack of peeking while no one was looking so I didn't find it futile.

"Hmmph!"

"Strawberry and hib—"

"Hibiscus. Yes, I know. And you're no better for it." The wizzard rolled over on his side opposite me and I thought he might be done but I was wrong. "If I could bottle up Nimue's scent, I could sell it for a fortune!"

"Really?" I said. "And you think anyone but you would be willing to pay top dollar?"

I could hear him munching on his beard.

"It's her!"

He spat his beard from his mouth and turned over so I could see him remove his hat, which meant he was fed up. "We've established that."

"All I have to do is take down the giant like Robin said!"

"Nonsense!" said Merle. "You were busy dancing when Marian finished the story. The offer of Genny's hand only stands for Arthur in place of the legion, as he has sworn an oath of no human bloodshed. Killing the giant would only ruin the rightful king's chances at her."

"Perhaps," I said sniffing the cloth. "But, if I killed that giant before Arthur got to him, and King Dionysus's ex-wife were still alive and imprisoned, I could return her to the king and nullify his second marriage, breaking the curse."

At that, Merddin largely composed himself and seemed to relax. He laid back, hugged his dunce's cap to his chest with his blanket and smiled blissfully.

"What?" I asked.

"Nothing," he said, blowing his eyebrows up out of his eyes like he always does before rest.

"Why would she not drop the curse if the first wife was returned? There would be no need in keeping Genny captive anymore."

He closed only his left eye, leaving one lingering open as if I had a second to figure it out before he was going to sleep.

"You think I don't deserve her!" I finally hissed.

Both eyes were open again and his pupils were slowly turning my way which meant I was getting warmer.

"You would!" I yelled in a whisper.

He popped up on an elbow and said, "Keep it down. You'll wake up the whole camp. It took a pound of skullcap and no little magic to get them all to sleep at once. Now you're interfering with my rest!"

"You would," I said a bit calmer, "Mister He-without-sin-throw-the-first-stone."

One of his eyebrows raised in both question and accusation all at once, "You are conveniently remembering things now, I see."

This time I rolled over and said, "I didn't see you throw one, either."

I was feeling pretty good about serving him his own medicine when I heard him blow his eyebrows again. Not believing he would nod off without the last word I dared a peek over my shoulder. Both eyes closed. So, I rolled flat to my back again and cradled the token to my chest.

One of Merle's eyes opened.

"I knew it!"

"Faith," said Merddin, "is something even I hate falling back on. But sometimes I must rely on it when memory doesn't serve."

"I don't get it."

"You want to go changing the whole course of history based on your faith that the new queen might have a change of heart toward Gwen after the old queen returns."

This time I raised one eyebrow.

"I'm just saying, in my experience, faith seems to work best for me, not you."

"What, Father Time only answers your prayers?"

"That," he said, "has nothing to do with it. It's just that I saw my life before I was born, so my guesses are educated."

"Why are you always pressuring me into being a righteous person? I can see exactly where this is going. You are going to suggest that if I want Genny then I should focus on being the most worshipped knight like is written in your dreams, er, your pre-dreams, or whatever."

He sighed, which was unusual to hear without him aiming to move one part of his body hair or another into a more comfortable position. So, I turned to him.

"Do you really want to know why I can see the future before I am born?"

"No." I said. "But I have a feeling you're going to tell me."

"It's relevant, or I wouldn't bother!" he blurted out defensively.

"Hey, keep it down or you'll waste that pound of skullcap and no small magic," I said.

He bunched his beard up in one fist to put in his mouth and I reached over and put a hand on his to stop him. He flattened it along his blanket and sighed again.

"Thank you," he said. "Now, this is why. Before I am born, I am pure. Without sin as you say. Power is granted to me in large quantity."

I thumped back into my bedroll and put my empty palm to my forehead.

"There you have it," he said and blew his eyebrows as if he were extended now and that was that. Time for bed.

I lay there in thought. Thinking was always better than outright telling him he was obviously correct. Perhaps, I could love again. But it was going to take a lifetime of effort. I smelled the token. What was greater effort than chastity? There had to be a better way to gain worship.

"You could start," came the voice of Merddin between whistling snores, "by not killing the emperor tomorrow when we meet him on the road."

Chapter Eighteen: Arthur and I meet

I may not have had the purity of spirit to catch Lady, but I knew I possessed faith in something else that others did not. I had faith in my physical body. It had always done what I told it to. It had taken everything I had thrown at it and everything anyone else had thrown at it for that matter. I had been bitten by venomous snakes, voluntarily ingested poisons just to see what they would do, had gotten a rash from one of the women I had slept with back in Gaul and it had gone away.

Yes, I could take a beating. I was the master of comebacks. I just didn't think I was setting myself up for another comeback the day I met Arthur.

Arthur was at the head of a procession winding its way down a mountain path just North of Brittany where we had met a young farm hand that claimed to be caring for the emperor's lame horse.

Behind him was a great wooden cart with a figure upon it draped in burlap rags and tied down with ropes. It was being pulled by a mule and aided by a group of scantily clad women. They would push the cart from behind when the ass had trouble over rocks and rises. Whatever was under the burlap rags wasn't moving.

"It's the giant!" I said to Merddin riding.

"Oh, ho, ho," began Merddin in the direction of Arthur who had just seemed to recognize him.

Arthur lifted his outstretched arms as if he could embrace the old wizzard from down there on the ground, "It's food! Enough to feed an army!"

Then, sure enough, Merle slid down from Archimedes and into Arthur's arms, though Arthur was the one who ended up engulfed in the old man's robes as Merddin stood head and shoulders above him.

One of the young women threw back the corner of the canvas to reveal the round orange edge of a giant pumpkin and the hazy ends of many bundles of wheat.

"Why are you drawing your sword?" cried Arthur as he came up from Merle's embrace.

"No!" I said pointing with the blade, "It's the giant!"

Fuzzick had just stepped out from behind the rocky outcrop and into view behind the caravan. His countenance was cheery, rather from years on the windswept mountain or ungodly gallons of wine. The giant's shaved face had big rosy cheeks.

"Relax, comrade. He's a friend."

At that, Fuzzick said something in such a low grumbling voice that I couldn't understand, and I assumed the thing was unintelligent.

"What's that he said?" shouted Arthur over his shoulder and the ladies went about talking amongst themselves.

I cut in while they were trying to figure it out. "Word is King Dionysus is willing to trade his daughter for that beast's head."

Fuzzick put a hand out toward the ladies as he lumbered past them, telling them to forget about it. Then as he stepped up behind Arthur he said very intelligibly, "I said we haven't made it town yet, and there are already people trying to kill me."

Arthur glanced from the giant to Merddin and then back to Fuzzick. "Well, we knew we were going to have to deal with that."

"Wait a minute," I said, reigning Nicodemus to a halt. "You're saying you are friends with this monster?"

"Hey," said Fuzzick.

"Hey," said Arthur.

"Do I really look that bad?" said the giant from under its mop of hair.

"Well," said Arthur, "you could use a bath and a fresh change of clothes."

Fuzzick shrugged, "I have a hard time finding things that fit."

Merddin looked up at me squirming in my saddle and said to me, "You're not going to start in about the girl again, are you?" He waved a hand at me, "Won't you come down from there? And put that sword away!"

I slid down and looked past Arthur and the giant at the group of women but saw Lady nowhere among them. Pointing up to Fuzzick with my sword I said, "You can't expect to walk that giant into Dionysus's castle and him hold true to his promise." I approached them and Arthur stepped between the giant and myself. I had him by a few inches in height and breadth and kept my sword pointed toward the massive being right over the King's shoulder.

Arthur didn't flinch. "I've made an oath to hold life above all other things."

I looked down into his eyes with a steady smile nearly forehead to forehead.

"He fears nothing!" came Merddin's voice from behind me and my smile faded as the heat rose in my cheeks.

The giant tried to contain a laugh but blew a raspberry by mistake and I dropped my sword hand to my side, the tip planting in the dirt pathetically. Arthur held his open right hand up, signaling Fuzzick to get control of himself.

"Now, that," said the King, "I think I can work with."

"His name is," began Merddin.

"Lancelot," I said still close enough to feel his breath.

"Well," he paused, "Lancelot." Extending an arm out behind him he said, "There are a dozen women here that haven't felt the touch of a good man for some time. Kiara is spoken for, as she is married to King Dionysus. Lydia is on her way to Brittany where her husband and son have feared her dead. But the other ladies…"

I bothered not a single glance and said nothing.

Arthur took a step to the side and looked to the ground, beginning to slowly pace back and forth. "Tell me." He looked back up at me a moment, "You think it better I deliver a dead man in thanks to a king than a strong man?"

I watched him.

"As an advocate for life, I appreciate the potential of all the kings of my land. They are valuable allies in that fight alone. When I show up with Fuzzick—" the king's eyes locked on mine again from under his thick eyebrows, "alive. Dionysus will see that diplomacy is sometimes mightier than all this sword and sorcery." He motioned to the armor hanging from his mule, and then to Merddin standing by Archimedes with his staff now in hand.

I glanced at them then back to Arthur where I could see Fuzzick was scratching his arse and footing a fist sized stone back and forth with his big toe in boredom.

"Am I wrong to think that preserving life is the greatest ambition?"

Just when he thought I would say nothing I said, "There is no greater ambition than the art of perfecting the soul."

He raised his eyebrows and his blue eyes showed deep understanding. His hands came from behind his back where they had been crossed. He drew in a great breath, stood tall and smiled wide saying, "What are the few brief years of life to that?" He touched my shoulder.

I still did not put my sword away. He looked down at it and then to his own side where his sword was belted on. He let go of my shoulder and began slowly drawing his sword out with his left hand.

I could see the round emblem with an equidistant cross decorating the pommel as it slid up.

Then Arthur reached across with his right hand, took the naked part of the blade and lifted it fully out with the handle up and held it aloft. "Faith, is what you speak of, Lancelot."

I knew the story of how Arthur became king but something else stirred in me when I saw that naked blade. Something familiar. A feeling of safety. "You have faith in symbols," I said before I knew it. "I have faith in my body."

"Hah!" said Merddin drawing both the king and I's attention. "I told you. Fears nothing! Not even disagreeing with his emperor."

"I never agreed to follow any man, besides my uncle Dap."

I heard Merle scoff at my statement, though I knew it was only for effect.

"You must be a druid!" said Arthur.

I looked briefly toward Merle and back again, "Something I am just finding out."

"But you carry a sword and know that it is blasphemy to bare a naked blade in the presence of one?"

"A rule I plan on amending."

Arthur and I looked at one another.

"I come only for Dionysus's daughter, nothing else."

"I am afraid this giant has already been won, and in turn so has the lady." Arthur then shook his head. "A druid is slave to no man," he quoted from the ancient ogham. "Yet, when I look at this one, I think that axiom should be amended to say, a druid is hard-headed."

At this Merddin laughed and Fuzzick stopped playing with his stone. "Would you amend the roots of your favorite tree? Would you amend the solar winds that led to life?" Merle pointed his stick and said, "You two are more alike than is easily seen."

Arthur started to turn slowly, "Tell me, a man who fears nothing, is a man who loves nothing. And a man who loves nothing, well, what joy can he have in his life?" He was walking toward the mule.

"Bravo!" Merddin called after him, "I thought, as my most apt pupil you might be able to teach him a lesson or two."

I looked back at Merddin and gave him a scornful look while rolling my eyes. He redirected my gaze back to what Arthur was doing.

Arthur was putting on his armor. "But" he said, "I may be wrong." One of the maidens hurried forward to help bolt on his chest plate. "I will tell you what," said he, as his torso was twisted this way and that, "You win the day, and I will yield my claim to Guinevere. But, if you should lose, you forget all this non-sense and perhaps consider finding pleasure in one of these maidens instead."

"But," I said, "it would be high treason to strike the emperor."

"You said it yourself; you have sworn fealty to none. Besides, I agree. For, I am also a druid, so we have time. You catch my meaning, I'm certain?"

I looked at the red dragon crest on his breast as he was pulling on his greaves. Stricken upon it was the holy cross.

"So be it heard," Merddin's voice came overall, "there will be no charge on Lancelot, despite the outcome."

I was wrestling with his logic as I approached Nicodemus and began donning my armor which was quite different than his, as mine had leather joints where his was polished steel.

Arthur motioned one lady to come and assist me, but I held a hand out. I preferred my armor, as it could move more freely, and I could secure it by myself. I had latches at the ribs that could be cinched down on my own, and my greaves were tightened by a single tug on an internal cord.

Arthur pulled Excalibur from its sheath and this time held it proper, tossing it gently and spinning it again and again, then looked down along its length. He had one eye closed (His helmet was faceless, so his visage clear) when he said, "I can't have you slaughtering Fuzzick."

At that the giant laughed.

"And besides," he warmed up by swinging Excalibur in a figure eight, "I haven't been in a fight over a girl since grade school." He chuckled matter-of-factly.

I approached him in a semi-circle. "I can't see how this will be fair when I already have the advantage." I snapped my face shield shut.

He circled with me, "What advantage is that?"

"Well," I said, "you've already exposed your weakness. You value life above all else. What danger is in it for me?"

"Ah," said the king, "I never said I didn't value my own." And then he struck me such a blow on the helm using the pommel of Excalibur I stumbled back and lost my footing. I heard a chorus from the ladies of both worry and admiration.

Fuzzick was just beginning to remark on Arthur's speed when I saw the flash of steel coming down at me from above and I rolled sideways in the dirt and took my feet. When I stood, I couldn't see him, but I heard the dirt shift behind me and I ducked in time for his strike to sail through the space where my head had been.

I pirouetted, one of Dap's legendary moves and quite impressive for a large man in armor at any rate. I brought my blade up beneath his armpit and the sound of my sword hitting his heavy plate rang like a bell. If I had taken such a blow my arm would no longer be attached, but he was well protected and only tottered a moment.

My next attack was a feint beneath his chin and then I reversed the swing to bring it down and full circle behind me and over the top of his head, but just as I squeezed my grip expecting a strong vibration, Excalibur was over his head and my sword catching in the cross guard.

He played the classic disarm counter, but I freed my handle willingly and turned behind him back-to-back watching my sword turn in the air above me where I reached up and caught it again by the handle, then ducking his full-bodied swing at neck level and countering with a clang to his back.

He stepped away and turned back to me while shouting jovially, "Excellent!"

"You asked me what joy I have in my life," I said side-stepping. Then I smiled and pushed my faceguard up so he could see. "Well, I live for this!"

"The things we live for, we will eventually die for," he said. Then he came for me again.

For more than half an hour we traded blows. Most glancing off one another's parry or block and then a handful of solid connects to plate armor. My rear end hit the dirt twice, both times while shuffling away from a relentless combination of strikes. Arthur once landed flat on his back when I unbalanced him with a buffet of upward swings. His convex armor saved him the embarrassment of being turtled as it naturally rolled him.

There was a gasp from the company and Fuzzick had stepped forward as if he were going to help the king, but Merddin held him fast behind his upraised staff.

To be honest I would have brought my sword down on him while he methodically regained his footing. What was mistaken as mercy was merely my being winded so terribly that I was afraid I would end up on top of him and we'd be rolling in the mud together like a couple of in season pigs.

I removed my helmet and tossed it over by Nicodemus. "I, almost, had you."

"You almost had me?" he pealed. "You almost had me? You can barely say the words!" He tossed his helm aside and came for me this time in a new flurry of diagonal swipes.

He was right about my breathing, and I compensated by simply stepping at ninety degrees with each swing, barely avoiding each cut by inches while conserving my breath. Then he did something unexpected. He hit me with the front of his breastplate. His whole body came forward into mine which was leaning into his next swing in anticipation. The combined forces knocked whatever breath I did have right out of me.

I stumbled back, gripped my sword in both hands and in one ditch effort feinted for his head and instead brought it down with all my might. Instead of the hollow sound of metal, there instead just came a crunch, and I realized my sword had cloven straight through his legging and lodged in his thigh. I could see Arthur looking at the spot in surprise, but I wasted no time with my last bit of air. I pulled it free and in another unforgiving and circling swing I came for him while he was falling to the ground.

My sword came down before all my crumbling weight at his naked head but when it found him, Excalibur was there. My sword broke on his superior edge, and I fell in the dirt beside the king gasping for a breath that felt as if it would never come. Then I heard something.

It was a King named Arthur and he was laughing.

After the battle and much turning of wrenches

"Did you figure out my riddle?" said Arthur as Merddin went about packing his wound with a poultice of herbs and then bandaging it. His ongoing laughter remained through the process and only reached higher octaves during the most painful parts of the operation. "You know, I haven't had that much fun since. Well, since forever. Hazeus Merddin, must it be so tight?"

I took a seat next to Arthur on the cart, ignoring his initial remark, "Why do you wear that symbol if you are the druid you claim to be?"

The question reigned in his radiant joviality, and he became quite thoughtful. He put a hand on my shoulder in a friendly gesture showing me genuine consideration of the question rather than defending himself hotly over what might be an accusation. "There are people of the church that think power resides in the symbol of the cross, and who am I to sully their faith in it?"

"But—"

"But I wear the symbol for the same reason I bear the red dragon. The dragon has long been the symbol of paganism, druidic belief, and I am but a man who can only be willing or unwilling to let the people find faith in their own ways."

"Why don't you just go ahead and put a monkey on there as well, and perhaps a moon and star like from the east? Soon there would be more symbology than crest or banner."

"As of now, I can influence only what I know to harbor a culture of inclusion. I can only be willing."

"Inclusion? If nothing is incorrect doesn't that mean that nothing can be correct either?"

"I am finding that exclusion is the enemy. If a culture is noble enough to advocate inclusion, then I will gladly adorn myself with their symbols." He inhaled, "When I spoke of faith, you said you had it in your body. I assume you thought I had faith in my sword or my cross." He looked for understanding in my eyes and when he saw none he said, "My God perhaps?"

My eyes lit up then.

"Ah," he said. "Then you would still be mistaken. What I have faith in—" just then the wizzard helped stand him up and he winced but then patted Merddin on the back, "Thank you, old friend. What I have faith in," he said again, "is men."

I thought about it while Fuzzick let the ladies each pull wheat stalks from his huge grip in a game of who gets to marry the losing knight.

"The riddle," Arthur said, "about time. When I said we would have enough of it…"

The riddle was easy. It was a druidic axiom and I recited it then. "Time is a man-made invention," I said. "As druids we are slave to no man, so time holds no sway over us."

He nodded and waved Merddin off, taking the weight of the wound and trying to walk without a limp. Merddin lit his pipe and walked to the rear of the cart to rummage under the canvas.

"I don't need slaves, Lancelot. What I need is men who are willing to listen to one another. Willing to sit at a round table. No head and no foot. Where all men are equal."

One of the young maidens squealed and the next beside her in the circle said, "I never win."

When we looked over, the giddy one was bouncing up and down holding up the winning straw and Fuzzick shrugged.

"It was the only fair way," he said.

Merddin arrived with a jug of wine, "Here son, it will ease some of the discomfort."

"Never touch the stuff," said Arthur.

"Moderation is what stands us apart from the lower realms of Abred." He pushed it into Arthur's hands. "Drink."

Arthur took the jug and raised it toward the commotion, "Seems you've been spoken for." Then he put it to his lips.

"What you're saying to me," I said uninterested, "is that you won because you had stronger faith?"

I couldn't quite understand what had happened in our fight. What was worse, I had no answer to how he bested me. Before he could answer I said, "I think your sword is magical. Perhaps you should have faith in it instead of men."

"Perhaps. But that is not why I bested you. My strength was more profound because I had faith in you, Lance."

But I was going to kill you! I protested in the privacy of my mind. Perhaps he could see that I had an internal struggle raging then. He held out the jug to me and I shook my head. If I drank that, then I might just change reality completely again.

"I am willing to volunteer my service," I said, thinking of Lady and how only the man of most worship could ever hold her heart.

"And I welcome it," said Arthur immediately but I cut him off before he could go on.

"But I want to be honest with you."

"Fair enough," said the king.

"Firstly, I will never love another but Lady, who seems to share a soul with your beloved Guinevere. But I swear I will, from this day forward, never lust for her or seek her desire unless she requests it of me. And if that ever occur, I cannot offer you any certainty that I would deny her."

I saw his eyes show doubt in me for a moment, but just a moment.

"And secondly, I must tell you that I swear my oath not to you, but to your higher endeavor and also, only because you have something I want." I thought again of Guinevere. Then I thought this was my first step on the road to worship and chaste. And if the time came that I could hold Lady again it would only be because I were holier than the man standing before me.

"And what exactly is that?" he asked confidently.

"Faith," I said, unsure if that were a lie. But if it were, it was going to be the last I would ever tell.

The knighting was unceremonious. It was spontaneous, and after it, both of us walked with a limp. Our business was concluded when Arthur put both of his hands on my shoulders and said, "Brother to brother, yours in life and death." Then, as I finished returning the gesture, he stabbed me in the thigh with his dagger.

"You've got to be kidding me!" cried Merddin, not wanting to poultice another wound.

The blow dropped me to my knees, and Arthur was drawing Excalibur in no threatening manner. "That should make us about even," he said. Then he brought the flat of the blade down on my shoulder, "Truth." The other shoulder, "Faith." Then he gently rested the blade on my upturned forehead and said, "Worship."

He put away his sword and offered his arm. I took his forearm in my hand, and he gripped my own, "Rise Sir," a tilt of the head, "Lancelot." Then he turned to the small procession of ladies, a wizzard, and one giant. "Knight of Camelot!"

No one cheered. But it was a nice gesture.

Looking back at things, it was wrong of me to let that horse chase Gwen. Though she had been subject to it a hundred times. I understood something after fighting Arthur. That Robin was right. There was only one way to catch Lady, and that was by taking down the giant. But the Giant wasn't Fuzzick. The giant was sin, and I of all men, brother to Merddin over lifetimes, knew I could conquer it. Of course, Merddin wouldn't be happy with the motives of my endeavor. So, I simply didn't tell him.

Chapter Nineteen: A Rise to Power

"And so it was," started Hazeus's mother in tandem with her own narrative coming from the scope, "Two wounded men, a cranky wizard, a happy giant, and many women, twined their way down the jagged mountain pass toward Brittany." Mother Earth's voice came from behind him as the final scene of disk four faded.

Hazeus craned his neck back in surprise, "Mother! How long have you been standing there?" His cheeks were glowing red.

"I watched the procession of naked ladies with you if that's what you mean," she said with a smile. Before her son could lament, she added, "I just love watching Arthur and Lance go at it!"

His mother seemed exceedingly chill.

"Is that a spaghetti sandwich?" he asked.

"Well, someone had eaten most of the pizza!"

He ran his tongue around his teeth to be sure there was no visible evidence in them.

"Don't judge," she said, turning and heading back through the kitchen. Her butt cheeks were peeking from under her nightgown, and she clearly was wearing no underwear. Then the light of dawn from the far window made it obvious she wore no under-anything.

"Ug," he said privately. "Mom?"

"Yes?" she was plucking a bag of chips from the bowl on top of the chifforobe.

"Did Dad call for rain last night?"

She hugged the chips. "Perhaps that is something you should ask him yourself?"

Hazeus sat up Indian style and leaned over to remove the fourth vinyl disc from the turntable. Paused, then considered rewinding it to the half-naked ladies again to put the image of his mother's silhouette out of his misery. But it wouldn't have done any good. Instead, he lifted disk five from the dwindling stack.

While he was pulling it from the paper sleeve, the magiscope rang. "Answer," said Hazeus and his father's face, eyes red and hair disheveled, appeared from the mists.

"Mom said you were asking if I called for rain?"

"Yeah," said Hazeus, "it was storming pretty bad last night, and I was just wondering—"

"Let me guess. Between disk two and disk three? Yeah, those are—" his dad's face was trying to get a better look at what disk he was holding. "Ah!" he exclaimed, "disk five? Okay, so you, what? Have two or three left?"

Hazeus looked down at the stack of three. "Yeah."

"You want me to give you a few more hours till dawn?"

His father had never asked him anything like that before. "A few more hours. What?" Then he looked out of the window where the light was already pouring through.

"Yeah. A few more hours so you can finish. You wanna play ball later, don't ya?" Father Time has a knack for reading people's minds, though he wouldn't call it that. "If you stop in the middle, you'll lose the thread."

Hazeus did wanna find out if the stable hand's wife was going to be returned to him, and King Dionysus's wife as well, for that matter. That would have to get awkward. Then, before he could even say that he guessed he was right, his dad snapped his fingers.

The room got a whole lot darker again.

"Ya know, Son," said Father Time on screen. "You're old enough now that you can make these kinds of decisions on your own."

Hazeus's face wrinkled up like he'd bitten into an unripe lemon and the juice had squirted him in both eyes simultaneously.

A hand came into the screen and turned his dad's face to the side, stroking his cheek. "Hang up that phone, Bobby," came the sound of his mother's voice from the other end.

"You got it, Boof," said his father, then quickly looked back out toward Hazeus and said, "I didn't call for rain, Son." Then the call ended.

Hazeus put down the MVD, stood up and crossed the living room past the maiden-shaped pillars[65] and into the hallway they stood before. The tapestries on either side of him flickered with the electric light of the sconces adorning the front door. To his left was the realistically woven image of a man bracing himself against a wave of silver and jewels beneath a golden shield. To his right was a wizard holding a flaming sword aloft.

He stepped onto the tile threshold and grabbed the brass handle to outside. He turned it and went through.

The air tonight, or was it this morning, was still. Curious thing too because Hazeus was looking on from the front porch and out toward the drop. A few wooden steps down from here was a trail that led right up to the precipice which had a three-foot iron fence as a barrier to accidental

---

[65] Why are statues of maidens always holding pottery and fruit?

disaster. Near the far side there was a lichgate to the open air that sported a sign which read 'Earned Your Wings Yet'.

At the other end of the fence line where it seemed to sprout from the hillside, there was a concrete marker as well. The inscription was nearly worn away but once clearly read, 'This barrier erected in memory of Omari who suffered a lethal fall from the bluffs while his nose was buried in the spine of a self-help book[66]'. Old news to Hazeus, he had learned a long time ago that reading had its hazards.

He was more interested in the strangely even pressure system he seemed to be inhabiting at the moment. Far above, there were dark clouds turning slowly, amid a shifting deep colored miasma of light. The brilliant light of the white hole was just a faint white glow at the center of the swirl.

He looked out over the edge and could see that down there were more dark clouds, like overinflated water balloons ready to burst. Yet they undulated easily against and around one another like single celled organisms dancing. What passed for a sunrise in Rootworld had to do with the pressure system cycling from hot to cool. The white hole did not move. It stayed just where it was supposed to be.

Hazeus stepped back and turned toward the house and began back up the trail in uneasy contemplation.

"Dad said *he* didn't call for—" Hazeus began absently. Then, he stopped before the porch steps, looked at the faint glow and impregnated clouds above.

"Rain," he said, staring up. The miasma continued doing its shadow dance in full spectrum. "Rain," he

---

[66] A study in attention and the pitfalls of gravity

said again more commandingly this time and closing his eyes. Then he flinched when something hit his cheek.

The sound of rice through a sieve came from the far treetops and he quickly took the steps before the tin roof started to thrum.

Hazeus gaped from the porch as the silver lines and fine spray filled the space and moved out beyond the iron pickets. He wondered what the people down on the surface would be thinking at this moment.

It was right about then that the teachers at the Rootworld academy of arts were having a very hard time explaining the validity of recently acknowledged career paths when the dawn suddenly disappeared.

There had always been meta-physics and alchemy, but now they were expected to teach beta-science, chemistry, and math.

One of the jocks in the back of the classroom was pointing out of the window at the clouds moving Firewise, "I think morning has been postponed Professor."

"Nonsense," said the professor. He'd heard of meteorology and in fact was not looking forward to that also being added to the studies at the academy, but he had no idea what actually made the cloud formations move perpetually toward the center sea. He was seventy-six and that was enough reason for him to argue.

He slammed the megalithic yard stick on the nearest desk, startling the glasses off the student sitting there. They fell to the floor and stared up at the ceiling with their painted-on eyeballs. Jacob snorted and his real eyes sprung open.

"If morning had been postponed, so would class," said the professor. "But, because we are all in attendance, morning obviously marches on. So, do please pay attention."

There was a murmur in the back of the room among the jocks. The professor thought he heard them mocking him, but ignored the unruly teens and began trying to solve the equation on the chalk board. When he saw there would be no hope in this, he turned and smacked his own desk with the stick.

"Now," he began, "for Zeus's sake, would anyone be so kind as to explain why the numbers in an equation are always mismatched?"

There was a snickering among the throng before a young man held his hand aloft with some effort, as it was impeded by the bulging muscles in his shoulders.

"Go ahead Lumps!" called one of the jocks from the back and the professor smacked his desk again, demanding silence.

"Please, Yusef," said the teacher, always receptive to an intelligible answer. Yusef was on all accounts, a nerd.

The jocks all relied so heavily on magic that they never learned any book smarts. Nor any street smarts for that matter. They also never learned any common sense. Nor any uncommon sense. They were good at sports though. Magic was powerful.

Kids like Yusef, who actually relied on their own strength to climb a flight of stairs for instance, and their own brain power to form complex sentences, for example, just couldn't cut the mustard against magic users. Smart though.

"Well, professor," said Yusef meekly. "I believe it has to do with the final result."

"How can two different numbers come up with something equal?" he protested. "And what is the meaning of *this*?" He pointed to the 'x' in parentheses. "This is not Mathematics students!"

Yusef covered his eyes.

"When you start adding letters to the mix it's called spelling!" he looked at Yusef who was shaking his head.

"Perhaps the jocks could help us out with this one?" He pointed his stick to the back of the room, where one of the jocks nervously pushed his glasses up on his nose. "Manny! Perhaps you could tell us what the meaning of this spell is?"

Manny canvased his peers for backup, but this wasn't the ball field. "Uh," he intoned. The sweat was beading up on his palms. He began to fidget. "Uh, yes. Uh. Now," he pushed his glasses back up again, "what was that spell for reading again?"

Just then the speaker above the door squawked in surprise, *"Attention students and teachers. Class has been postponed due to daylight savings arriving early this year. You should all be in bed, don't you know? The sun's not due for hours!"*

The professor slumped. "Fine," he said through a wheeze, "you're all dismissed."

Back on the mound, Hazeus had paused the new disk on the first scene where Arthur and Lancelot were limping their way into Brittany, prominent bandages on each man's thigh. "I can't believe Arthur stabbed him! I would never!" Hazeus said to himself as he moved toward the kitchen. He paused at the fridge and thought back. Then said to himself, "Well, there were the lizards. But I always brought them back."

"Come on, Arthur," he said quietly to himself, opening the fridge. "You can do it. It shouldn't take a martyr." There, in the door of the fridge, Hazeus saw the many varieties of beverage that his parents had been imbibing on this evening. He lifted an amber bottle with a white and red label halfway out of the stirrup and turned it. "Bed stripe?" then he read the tag line, "*Ja makin me crazy.*" He let it fall back into the plastic mold of the refrigerator door.

He closed the door and listened. He could hear nothing from his parents' bedroom. I mean, it *was* like four o' clock in the morning for the second time, after all! He looked at the island in the middle of the kitchen and then at the ornate cabinet doors below it. His eyes went side to side, and he dropped down on his haunches.

Slowly he pulled the little ivory knobs and the wooden doors popped out of their snug frames. Inside he found the good stuff. Big bottles of liquid courage. Well, that was what Tom used to call it. *TankofRay.* He twisted the top, careful not to clink it against the bottle next to it which was dark brown rather than clear. He sniffed. "Smells like, Christmas trees." He recapped it.

There was a tall purple bottle with a bleeding rosebud. Some creamy liqueur. *ToKillaRose.* He touched the lid of each but didn't dare try and lift the big ones. *JamesDean.* Yes. He'd seen dad mix that with diet Ecko over ice. Another clear bottle, *DeFinite.* He decides that absolutely had to be Vodka. Then he saw what was behind the bigger bottles up on a little shelf. A handful of tiny versions of each. He reached carefully back there and took a small replica of JamesDean, palmed it, and closed the door quietly.

Back in the living room, he looked at the frozen vision in the magiscope, twisted off the little black cap of the JamesDean, and drank it.

Immediately he felt guilt. But preceding that he felt fire in his throat. And then his nose. The guilt was going to have to wait until he'd run into the kitchen and grabbed a dishrag to wipe the magiscope and surrounding furniture free of whiskey droplets that had exploded out of his mouth and nose in a poorly timed cough. If it were his internal organs immediately rejecting the infusion, he wasn't prepared to admit it. However, as he polished the glass of the magiscope he could see his own eyes watering and realized his reflection may be more honest.

While looking into his own eyes, and then past him into Arthur's, the guilt came on hard. Did he just steal from his own father? Now something biological was happening to him. Things were getting swimmy, and he was feeling terrible about counting on Arthur to do what he had failed at. Was he really going to put him through it?

What was worse was when he thought about his dad offering him a drink one day. Now he would have to pretend he'd never had one! He'd not just robbed his dad of an airplane bottle of Dean, but a special bonding experience.

Things were grinding to a halt. He couldn't feel guilty fast enough to keep up with what was going on! He needed something to focus on before he lost it all together. Wait, what was that?

There in the magiscope, behind Arthur and Lancelot was something he hadn't noticed before and may not have hadn't he paused it just right. There was something in the woods, watching them. Right between the two but far into the background and standing in front of the tree line, was a green man with the feet and antlers of a deer.

He looked closer.

Did it just move? Hazeus turned to look for the controller, feeling very nervous. He wanted to turn off the thing all together. He got on his hands and knees and felt of the tousled quilt on the floor but found nothing. He turned back and mistakenly glanced at the orb again. The thing was gone!

"Uh oh," said Hazeus holding his hands up before the screen and watching as fur began sprouting out from the cuffs of his jacket.

Things were about to get weird.

Chapter Twenty: Arthur's Wildwood Coronation and Merddin's Disappearance

Now that Merddin had gotten Lancelot aligned with Arthur, he could start thinking about himself. But he had one more order of business before he went to meet his future, or was it his past? The older he got, the faster things flew by. In a loop like that, you could breeze right through the beginning and not even know it.

Stonehenge had that effect on him. The stones had stood such a great test of time that they seemed his closest mates. They were there when he came through, and if memory served correctly, they would be there when he went back. They had grown grey together.

Merddin was thinking about the living rock and how it not used to be so stubborn as he stood in the center of the stone circle. Once great gentle giants, now petrified in disbelief.

Anyone could claim leadership over the good people of Cornwall, he thought. It just took a shiny hat, and possibly a scepter, a good news article, and a few followers to spread the word. It's why the written word was so shunned by the Celts. Words carried power, though it was mostly the power of suggestion. And let's face it, people are gullible.

From his blue robes, Merddin produced a shiny artifact that caught the light of the full moon overhead.

She was running late.

He placed the small glass boat onto the altar.

It was well known among the Celtic Gods that a king could not truly be crowned, at least his crowning would not be taken seriously, until he had stood under the three rays of the summer solstice. A celebration that was not far off.

Merddin didn't have time for tardiness.

At the thought, a rift opened between two of the greatest trithalons, through which, Merddin could see a rowboat wedged into a distant shoreline among nodding cattails.

He never could get used to the sound of spacetime tearing.

Out stepped a luminous Dryad who bowed before him. The pearl on her tiara stood out beneath the rim of her hat but was no match for the milky white of her face.

She stepped through the rift, and it sealed shut with the sound of thunder.

"Vivianne," he said, "you're late."

She smiled unhurriedly, looked up to the old stone relic she had stepped out beside of, and put her hand gently to its surface.

Merddin watched as she ran it up along the ancient bones of the earth.

She licked her lips, which immediately turned a deep shade of pink.

Merddin shifted his robes, "I suppose you have it, then?"

She cocked her head to him and away from the stone. Her hand ran down the side of the velvety corset to her hip where it split as she walked toward him. Her other hand was removing something from her bosom. "What do you want with a gnarled old Mandragora root?"

"Don't play stupid. The boy needs to complete the hunt. He will never have true authority without Herne on his side."

Merddin's robes adjusted themselves this time as Vivianne twisted his beard around one of her fingers. "Yes," she said in a whisper, close to the wizzard's ear, "the very essence of the god of the hunt is contained in this mandrake root. It is one of only a few that we've cultivated these last years on Avalon. But I will require an essence in return."

Merddin eyed the glass boat on the altar. "I've brought the vessel," he said, suddenly nervous. "By the way, how is Mother Theresa getting along?"

Vivianne sighed and placed a palm on Merddin's chest. "I would say she fits right in if we hadn't had to craft all new furniture to harbor her physique."

Merddin chuckled.

"Your all she's talked about," she said.

Merddin blushed and then suddenly felt a whole lot better about his coming imprisonment. Well, that was the official story. Actually, he just needed a little time off.

"We'll be late if we don't get a move on," Vivianne said.

"You were the one who was late. Much longer and the moon will be waning."

"Well, we better get started. It's the time zones between here and Rootworld that always throw me off," she said removing her kimono. Vivianne reached to the shoulders of Merddin's robes and gripped them tightly in each hand. "Now, let's get that essence out of you!" She yanked the garment off of the old man, exposing his frail body beneath loosening skin. "Only one way to transfer power from a male to a female you know?" she said, stroking his upper arms and laying a gentle kiss on his old, tired muscles.

"I know," he said, "but I thought you wanted it in the vessel?"

"Oh," she said, "we'll get there." Then she pulled the frail man into her fiery embrace. "Now give me what I'm due!"

Merddin tried his best not to think of Mott.

A Celtic Vow

In order to gain station over the land, sea, and air, it took ceremony. In fact, it took fire. And that fire rested in the breast of Arthur who'd been born on Beltane. The ceremony had commenced and though no one besides the King's company were permitted past the great Tor stone, the Salisbury plain was peopled for a full kilometer, as it was said to stand in the first light upon the avenue was to be in lady luck's embrace for the coming year.

Fires were being re-stoked from the night before. Tents were being taken down. Sausages and blood pudding peddled. Acrobats performed; kites were flown. Banners of kingdoms who'd not supped together in decades stood as neighbors, their hosts greeting one another after a long night's journey to get the closest spots.

Fanfares woke no one, as the throng had long been standing in wait of the first summer sunrise. It was an annual spectacle, but this particular occurrence was not to be missed as it marked a union of Christian and Celt.

Merlyn knew well that only a man raised both in the Catholic Church but under the secret guidance of a Celt could earn and maintain minor authority over the old spirits. He had been spent of his magic and could only offer his student the key to his final victory.

It was within the same holy ring of bluestone at the Henge where Merddin had sacrificed his power, that Arthur gathered with eight of his closest comrades, so that they could again be knighted, and he could be crowned again before them. All for one, and one for all of England, Catholic and Celt alike.

The three rays of morning were breaking over the Tor and crawling up Excalibur's blade toward the pommel. Merddin had poised a wreath of Mistletoe and white berries above Arthur's head. Both men in their matching blue robes.

"Do you Arthur Pendragon, solemnly swear to uphold the Celtic truths passed down from the Isles of Anglesey and Avalon and to protect the three-fold utterance that parts the veil?"

Arthur moved to speak but was interrupted.

"Think long on it, as the onrush of religious intolerance is close at hand and there will be those who oppose you." The light had reached halfway up the steel. "Furthermore, will those who serve you stand fast behind your promise?"

One by one the knights knelt within the circle as a sign of declaration. Kai took his knee and the light moved. Borus and Gwain's knee met the earth and the ray of morning crept further still. Percy, Tristan, Galahad, Lancelot, and finally Kay bowed their heads.

"I do."

And the light of summer came full onto the altar where Excalibur lay breaking the white sunshine into a rainbow of color. Each huge doorway of stone illuminated with its own glow of brilliant hue. But one doorway stood brighter and lingered long after the sun had moved beyond the Tor. It was the gateway to the North, bathed in emerald, green.

Merddin held out a wrapped bundle to the newly minted King of Celts. "Now is the time, Arthur. You lack a final spell of making and it is clear whose authority you must earn for that! It is the forest god. He invites you to the hunt!"

Arthur took the bundle and embraced the wizzard, not knowing it may be the final time.

Merddin reveled but a moment then urgently pushed the king out to arm's length, "Now go, before the gateway closes!"

The king and his knights had taken their oaths, and the rays of morning stretched out across the plain as Arthur approached the glowing gateway. There, in the green grass, just before he stepped through the portal, he could boldly see the earthy divots left by the hooves of the forest God Herne.

Chapter Twenty-One: Morgan Visits Mim

Only a few had not set out to the Salisbury flats for the official crowning. King Lot's wife, Morgaine, was one of them. She was paying a visit to Catherine's cathedral in the city's absence.

The taste of Catholic hierarchy was like rust in her mouth. Morgaine's hair spilled like black paint down her shoulders as she raised her arms overhead before crossing through the picket gate.

"Nid Dim on Dew, Nid Dew on D Dim," and the mist erupted from the ground, shadowing the church under the veil of Rootworld.

The true form revealed itself.

Imperfections in the white marble became dark moldy lines of strangling creeper vine. Roots grew up through the cement of the front steps, bulbous fruits threatening to erupt from their tendrils.

'Truth," she said under her breath and took a step into the lychgate.

The taste in Morgaine's mouth turned bitter as she pecked her way between the nodules on nimble feet. Bitter she could deal with. At least she could swallow bitter. The milk of the maiden's slipper and the root of the elephant's ear had both been bitter when she'd concocted a draught of debridement for Patricia back in Orkney. When it comes to marriages, debridement had less to do with cleaning, and more to do with having a clean slate. It was little chores like that which had kept her in practice since she had left Avalon after a disagreement with her mother, Igraine. She was set on showing her mother that she could get on without her.

She reached out and took the handle of the door. Here was real power. She'd felt it as soon as that red ruby of mars had exploded at the drawing. She'd been watching remotely, on the surface of her mirror pool, below the castle of Orkney. It was easy to spy on King Arthur. She had shared a connection to him, in many ways, since Igraine tutored her in the ways of the sight. Rootworldly power was like the opposing poles of a magnet, as were all things Rootworldly. In Rootworld, like attracts likes. The king had power; it's no wonder he was the first thing she always saw after a drop of her blood struck a still liquid surface.

The ripples had spread out after enveloping the single crimson drop from her fist. A drum beat on the surface of time space. Then, there he was, the boy King. His blonde locks in a moist tangle, falling back from his face, blue eyes looking up to the blade he held aloft when the gem burst. A powerful relic he held above, but something with as much power had fallen to the Earth and began its descent. As above, so below. There's always a leak; always a balance of power. A mars ruby doesn't just explode unless it is overpowered. Any decent witch knows as much.

She entered.

Arthur Goes on the Wild Hunt

Arthur was not happy.

He had been accustomed to bearskin rugs by a ready-made fire. Now he was going to have to build his own.

Gwen had been most outspoken about his loyalty to the Celtic traditions. In short, she had not been present at his summer ceremony and certainly was going to be more unpleasant now that he would be home late.

By the look of things, he was already quite a number of hours tardy because the moment he had stepped through the portal on the Salisbury plain he found himself in a dark wood with no return portal.

More wind found its way through the forest there than light of any sort. A full moon, that revealed itself briefly through the windswept canopy was his only solace. Darkening clouds were threatening, but at least it was the same evening!

Arthur removed his sickle from under his robe. Though he would have traditionally worn it exposed. It still lacked a proper ruby. In some ways, the sickle was a far more useful tool than Excalibur. He untied the cord, removed the birch cork from its tip and held the blade up, peering through the void. There was not enough light to use a fire ruby anyhow, he was going to have to improvise.

He went about the arduous task of gathering kindling and peat moss which was no small effort for the terrain was treacherous. Pitfalls and steep angles, littered with boulders. There was a flat stretch of land atop what appeared to be a fallen stone wall. It was here that he deposited his faggot, judged an area a bit larger than his height and started clearing away the marsh wort with his sickle. He felt like a farmer harvesting the grain!

Once he was certain he had cleared enough room to avoid burning down the forest, he began collecting stones. He lifted the first fist-sized stone and tossed it up playfully, thinking of old Murdack. Then he lugged twelve to the circle, cradled in his robes, and dumped them into a pile. Close by was an unfortunate oak which had been split down the middle by lightning. Half lay protruding over a precipice. From inside of the split, Arthur pulled a small slab of the wood suitable for a fireboard.

A branch of dry fir could serve as a spindle, so he sharpened the end and used his sickle's cording to fashion a bow from a crooked live oak branch. He considered his position as he tried to figure his cardinal directions. Perhaps he was on Snowdonia? If it were so, he was fortunate that it was summer, or he may have frozen to death before he got his fire going. "Think," Arthur said aloud, his words getting lost in a gust.

He was starting to think that he had missed the lesson on how to tell what direction you were facing when you can't see the stars, have no light to judge your shadow on, and have just been transported to a mountain possibly hundreds of miles away! He spread the stones out with no real purpose and started working on making a little makeshift bird's nest out of his kindling.

He was regretting the fact that he had neglected his fire sickle since his kingship and was doubting seriously his ability to call the fire, even if he had happened to possess a good ruby of mars. "Authority," he mumbled under his breath and pulled his robe tighter at the neck. His authority over fire was his birthright, technically. He had had no real tribulation to gain it. He had simply been good at it.

He looked at his bundle of moss, wood shavings, pine needles and dry peat, satisfied. Then he put it loosely on the fireboard and looked around from his haunches. That was it, he thought. The moss. Vegetation and moss have a tendency to grow on the northernmost side of the trees! He put his fire-making implements on top of the little nest to keep the wind from taking it, then got up and began a survey of the surrounding vegetation. He scraped a line down the thickest patches of lichen covered tree trunks. There seemed to be an obvious collaboration between the plant life and his intentions. He reminded himself that plants are simply very slow animals.

Using this consensus, he judged the placement of his northernmost stone. Then he put the other cardinal stones in their proper quadrants, filling out the rest of the circle clockwise.

Removing the bundle from his robe, Arthur thought about the hoof prints he'd seen at the portal's edge and sized the forest god up to about eight feet. He had heard stories of the heavy footfall of Herne being reported around late-night campfires. Those alone would chill a believer to the bone.

Merddin had once remarked about the shocking look of the mandrake root, but he was still disgusted when he folded back the linen.

There had been sweet potatoes that had misshapen figures. Perhaps resembling a face or other more obscene body parts at one time or another throughout his journeys. Borus once saved a particular legume that had a rather amazing pair of knockers, for example. And Mott had been reputed to grow her stock from only the most well-endowed of the malformed ground veggies.

But this? This was uncanny! He held what may pass for a malformed and petrified fetus. Swaddled there like a babe. Round little cheeks both north and south. The former flanking a most grizzly visage and the latter extruding opposite of a sprouting penis. Legs and arms ending in spindly taproots of exactly five digits each. And atop the head of the sickening thing was a perfect heart of antlers.

The king realized he was grimacing, when from only paces away, he heard the clap of hooves upon stone. Before he realized, the pine branch that he'd stripped of needles was in his hand, ready to fend off some awful minotaur. Then the wind dropped, and he found himself standing in silent stillness. He recalled when his teacher had invoked the four elemental realms from his childhood. What had he said back then that had left Arthur so confused? Then it came back to him as if it were only yesterday.

"Stone glade in dark wood," he'd said. Merddin holding aloft his stone of Fal. "Pine branch in warrior hand…"

Arthur sighed at the memory and was greeted with a cloud of steam on the chill air. "He knew," said Arthur coming back to himself. He looked out from the circle among the dark wood, trembling. But then more words came back to him.

"Where there is no imagination, there is no fear."

With that, Arthur used the broken end of the branch and scraped a rough circle around the circumference of his stones. "Y Gwir!" he forced out, closing the loop.

"Now," said Arthur, "let's see the truth." Then he got down on all fours and started working with the bow while the God of wind seemed to be showing him some favor[67].

Why was it this was called the wild hunt? Arthur wondered while warming his hands on the fairly impressive fire. It would be a short-lived inferno, what, with only four decent hardwood logs[68]. They were already piled on and well on their way to joining the rest of the glowing embers.

Lifting the mandrake and looking around, he could see that the wind had returned. "I guess I haven't grown completely out of magic after all," he said, enjoying the stillness of his protective circle. Then as he looked down at the grizzly, antlered little cherub, he said, "What secrets do you hold?"

Merddin had often recounted tales of his own hunts. Bringing him up to believe that it was simply a matter of survival. The entirety of Newais mountain, where the wizzard called home, had been taken under Merddin's authority from such seasonal hunts. The whole process had been thus.

The druid places an offering to some entity in a difficult or treacherous piece of terrain and challenges that entity to some friendly sport. Then if the offering is missing

---

[67] It's always nice to have the wind at your back and it seemed Lleu lau gwyffs was his most favorable entity of late.

[68] You can only fit so much fuel inside a protective circle.

on the next morning the challenge is presumed accepted. Burning the root of a mandrake[69] symbolizes the start of the hunt. Once commenced, the druid is to try and return home from the agreed upon location before sunrise. In short, the stories of his tutor brought him to believe that he were to be the hunted.

It had always seemed a simple thing to Arthur, but according to Merddin's accounts, the business was always uncertain. Again, Merddin could trip over his own beard, while talking to himself absently, and had a knack for burning his own fingertips on matches. So, the king had always chalked up the old man's difficulty in following a familiar trail home to his senility. However wise he was.

Merddin's brain resembled an overactive thunder cloud at times. Lots of ball lightning going on in there, but still, a terribly thick cloud. As if the universe could hear Arthur's thoughts, a chain of orange lightning rolled above the canopy of the forest. Illuminating the interstitials of the treetops systematically from what he had determined to be east to west.

He glanced from the treetops back down to the ugly root just as the thunderclap came, forcing his head down into his shoulders like a retreating turtle.

Arthur had no clue as to where he was. Even if he were on Snowdonia, he had no clue as to where he should be headed[70]. Well, as with most things Druidic, perhaps the inhalation of whatever smoke this root produced would cause some delirium and he'd be done with this challenge after some well-administered black willow in the morning.

---

[69] The root of the may apple can be substituted depending on your geographic location.
[70] Downhill was sounding most promising.

The thing about not knowing whether you were in Rootworld or not was that you could never really find any comfort in knowing whether the whole dying thing was permanent. It was something he'd still not worked out completely.

How does one tell if they are dreaming? He went to put his wrist in his mouth for a good bite but paused, remembering that there was a time he had once found himself awake, whilst thinking he was asleep[71]. Another time he had found himself asleep while thinking he was awake. Though Gweniviere was polite enough to snatch the reigns of his horse who had traveled unaided the final fifteen miles of a very tiring journey. It was the ground inside of the outer walls that had actually woken him abruptly.

He got down on his knees and picked up his sickle from the fireside, turning the last two logs to support one another and blew at their bases until the coals were good and red. A goodly flame was born at the apex again. "Well," he said with one final look at the gnarled little figurine, "back across the seas of Annwyn with you." And he tossed the doll-like root on the fire.

There was a squeal that matched the cherub's pinched facial features perfectly as the thinnest taproots twisted in at protest. Before five seconds had passed, the shoulders of the little poppet curled in and the effigy's countenance seemed to reflect the hellish torture. It began shrinking into an implosion of sap which dripped onto the coals.

---

[71] Merddin had referred to that time as being born.

Arthur peddled back, crab walking to the edge of the circle on his palms as the smoke started pluming up. Something familiar was happening.

The smoke was filling an invisible vessel and it reminded him of something he'd witnessed back in a cave as a teenager. But this wasn't the form of a man! And his teacher was not here to guide him if he spoke out of turn.

The black smoke was thickest at the tips of the antlers but soon coalesced its way down finding no retreat. The being was in the middle of a massive yawn, as if it were trying to catch enough breath to its brain as to fully understand what was taking place. When its muscular limbs, which were covered with the smoky shadow of fur, and its cloven feet were filled out, the thing knuckled its eye sockets.

Then it looked briefly at Arthur cowering there. Then turned, and fled.

Its antlers and then forehead collided with the invisible wall of the protective circle and its whole form went shapeless like a wispy train wreck. The thick black shade reformed itself gradually, seemed to consider, and then lowered its horns and tried again. Again, it malformed the specter.

A grey smoke was also filling the space of the orb now. The essence obviously spent, but the burning sap was making the area quite unbearable to a living being who fancied breathing.

The half deer thing turned its head to look under its arm at Arthur. It was obviously Herne the hunted, and not happy that it had twice now failed to exit. Arthur could read lips, but these were somewhat of a muzzle made of smoke, and besides, an idiot would know that this look was an accusation and if whomsoever it were aimed at would be terribly lucky if the look was followed up by a threat, giving the receiver another minute or two to consider the life he had lived thus far before perishing.

"Sorry?" Arthur offered timidly. He was trembling, fearing this was already game over, as having summoned his aggressor right into a cell with himself. Yet, he crab-walked a foot closer as the smoke grew into a palpable thickness. Then, as quick as a snake, he struck with his right foot and kicked the eastern most stone out of place.

The orb deflated. Wisps of smoke being taken up in turning eddies by the whipping wind and misty rain of the unprotected landscape.

Arthur heard the crunch of wood and coal and watched the sparks of his murdered fire rise up along the whirlwinds. All of the elements seemed hostile. A cloven hoof must have picked up some of the tarry oil from the fire because, there, leading away from Arthur's broken circle, were five embossed remnants of the forest god's feet, and they were still rimmed in flame. As luck would have it, they were leading away from where lightning had just struck in the swaying marsh wort behind him.

A branch came down across the glen with a line of fire running its length where the lightning had struck.

Arthur turned abruptly, "You would still humble me, even as king, old man?" he wailed to a Merddin who wasn't there. He got the band from his fire bow and wound it back round the sickle handle, tied the sickle to his belt, and stuck a piece of charred wood chip on the tip so the blasted thing wouldn't swing and re-open the old scar in his thigh for the umpteenth time.

Down on the ridge below he could see the dark shade of Kernunnos, the forest god. He was looking back over his shoulder at Arthur and beckoned with a hand that left dark grey tendrils trailing behind. Fire bloomed behind Arthur. He looked down to where Herne had disappeared on his right. Heat rises, he thought. The fire would trap him like a rat if he climbed toward the peak! Down it was, then. After the horned god of the wood.

What if, Arthur thought, as he edged around a cypress that was growing treacherously near the cliff edge, Merddin was misleading me for all of those years? It does seem a coincidence that I have no home to run too, and instead seem to be chasing after the challenger rather than the other way around. Even stranger are the many names of Kernunnos, Forest God, and among them, Herne the Hunted!

Why can't things come straight forward from the blasted wizzard for just once?

He'd regained another foot of precipice at this point and was feeling like he was back on Mount Saint Michael. How did Herne traverse this, he wondered. And just as he'd thought it, he saw the satyr. Still a solid cloud of ebony, but on all other accounts real, jump free from the wood and scale the cliff below as easily and impossibly as any billy goat. Pebbles slid from under its clopping feet as it went, and its fingers left tracks in the soil around roots it used to climb.

Arthur wasn't going to get down that way. Above, the fire was raging, and ash and soot were coming down in great grey and black flakes, sometimes animated with flickering orange and red rims. He gauged his options as he skirted the cliff face along the fragile shelf. The fire was moving quickly along the ridge above, he was only ahead of it by mere meters. Below, where Herne had disappeared into, was a green and lush hollow. But just ahead was only more fuel for the inferno, he could only keep on and hope to find a more climbable way down to the hollow. He kept side-stepping along.

When the plateau opened back up again, he could see the severity of the threat. It had indeed swept up the side of the mountain. Whirlwinds of flame rolled along the ridge as the wind shifted direction. It was as if Belinos was stoking the fire with his very breath!

The drop made a crescent shape above the hollow. He was traversing the rim of a giant stone bowl, desperate to find any possible way to outrun the living fire. His only option was to go back onto the ledge and try and ride out the carnage. At least he wouldn't be cooked alive there. But, as the thought struck, a pine folded over and fell to rest; a burning barrier back from whence he'd come.

There was another ridge. It was perhaps twenty feet below but looked like nothing more than a cliffside prison. He would be stranded there, but at least it was an escape. He untied his belt and sickle. Took off his robe and laid it on the sandstone thinking of cutting it into lengths to tie together. He peered over the edge again, shirtless. Then a gust of wind came so fierce and sudden that he found himself grabbing for his blue robe as it was lifted up and circled on a thermal. He reached out for it hopelessly as it was carried out over the expanse and watched as it spiraled down into the forest below.

Arthur was fighting the forest and losing. He took a deep breath, closed his eyes, and listened to the pop and crackle of the burning wood. When he opened his eyes and looked to the only way forward, he inhaled and said, "No more fighting." Then he retrieved his sickle and stepped between two pines whose branches were already dancing in circles on thermal updrafts.

"I am a child of fire," Arthur said, hearing a great commotion come from behind the thicket on his left. Where is the fire telling me to go?

Before he could answer, a buck came crashing through the brambles and made a mighty leap over a fallen log. Behind it came two does, cutting a path in much the same direction. Snuffling from under the brush then came an armadillo, scuttling on its tiny legs in a desperate attempt to flee the heat.

Would he only possess such agility or small form as to move beneath these interwoven nets of foliage! He joined the movement and did his best to follow the game trail left by the deer. Climbing over the fallen trees and cutting vines with his sickle. Still the fire gained, and he could only watch as birds, and little mammals passed him by, unable to offer any help besides a general direction in which to flee. In desperation, he began cutting back toward the center bluffs in case he may have to resort to hanging on the ledge, but soon he was tangled in hawthorn and vine.

He turned his naked back to the thorns and covered his head, still not able to break the net of thorn and leaf. The fire closed.

A crack of thunder accompanied a great flash of lightning and in a space of seconds, Arthur's hopeless visage was upturned to a torrential fall of rain. The drops streaked down his bloodied back. The rainfall was not dousing the flame, but it was holding! Another armadillo moved wetly between Arthur's legs, part way swimming through the mud. Arthur wished Merddin were here to magic him into such an animal! But that was it, wasn't it?

He closed his eyes and felt the rain running over his skin and imagined the lesson all over again. The story of the noble born.

In the beginning God had started all living creatures with the same choice. Each fetus would begin as the very same zygote, just a pink little shrimp of meat containing in it all the possibility of life. Each living thing was permitted to request any number of gifts from their loving and good god before they began their time.

The bird's had asked for the gift of flight, so in turn God made his appendages grow into wings. The mole said it would like to be able to dig easily. So, God made its forelimbs and paws stout as to navigate the subterranean earth. The fishes humbly asked for the ability to swim without burden, so God fashioned their bottom appendages into a tail and gave them gills. Of course, these are the simplest examples. Other animals like the penguin were more greedy and asked for a complex gift, or many different gifts and so got transformations to withstand the cold and was given webbed feet for swimming. The badger for

instance, listening all the while to the other creatures'
requests, and coming directly after the mole and porcupine,
asked for both the ability to dig and protection from
predators. And on it went like this until it came to the man
who solved the riddle and requested no gift, as he was
grateful to have the opportunity of life to start. With that,
God granted him dominion over all the rest and the ability
to learn from each.

Arthur opened his eyes and watching after another armadillo disappeared through the hole where the mud was now rushing through, and he dropped down on all fours and became like a salamander. Bellying his way along through the torrential river of mud and under the hawthorn.

And then, down an earthen slide where he tuned onto his back, reached out with his sickle to stop the ever-speeding slippery descent. Failed, then lashed out on the other side. Still failed to gain purchase. Then saw under a bright flash of lightning, the dark opening to a cave beneath the washed-out roots of a cypress. Before the sound of thunder came, he was thrust into pitch blackness and the roll of the heavy drum followed behind him all the way down the cold stone throat of the earth.

Chapter Twenty-Two: Were in the Wolf am I?

Arthur opened his eyes on a sparkling emerald glade. He had been ejected onto the soft grass and log rolled several times before ending supine and spread armed, staring up at the fireflies winking in and out. When he turned his head, he was greeted with the source of the light that laid on the glen like a blanket. A line of torches ran along both sides of a garden where a stone bench sat occupied with the strangest arrangement of creatures he had ever seen.

The forest god Herne sat on the bench, a recently muddied armadillo in his arms. He was just finishing cleaning up the beady eyed rodent with the cuff of his rather strange tunic. The lapel had the letters BTHS and on the back of the colorful apparel was a large number forty-two.

"There you are little guy," said the hunted, releasing the armadillo to the forest floor where it jovially waddled away. Then dusting its palms off, the goat-legged, antlered, man stood up from the bench and said, "I know what this must look like."

"Really," said Arthur, rising to his elbows and back peddling as the god stepped forward on cloven hooves.

Kernunnos paused and held a hand down, bending its oddly jointed legs to shorten his towering form, "Oh, come on. Even the little ones need their feet washed once in a while."

Arthur paused. He looked past the deep fissures of the grey fingerprints before his eyes. Beyond the hairy knuckles and red fur erupting from the wrists of a high school team jacket[72]. Up to the white teeth inside of the grinning muzzle and across the bridge of the black tipped nose to the eyes.

There was compassion in them.

"Shall I get a bowl and some water, so you see me truer?" asked Kernunnos. "I think you're brighter than that. What you really need is a shower. Perhaps, when you get the mud out of your eyes…"

Arthur's muddy eyes betrayed his disbelief, but he reached up and let his old friend take his child sized hand. "Hazeus?"

Herne held out an arm and Arthur followed its direction to the edge of the glade where a clear waterfall broke through the canopy above. Beside it was the cave he'd entered so violently from.

"But, how?" Arthur asked, peeling his breeches from out of his backside with a sucking sound.

"Hey, it surprised me, too," said Herne. "I come in many forms, apparently."

"And," said Arthur, lifting the corner of Herne's jacket with two fingers, "what are you wearing?"

"Oh, this?" said Hazeus, down at Arthur gripping the lapels. They were walking toward the falls. "Dad got it for me. He's a basketball fan." Then seeing Arthur understood

---

[72] Whatever that was, or would be.

absolutely nothing of what he was talking about he added, "It's a team sport. You know, a lot like war, but without all the killing and such."

"Ah."

"Anyhow, he won my high school championship."

Arthur put an arm in the cool water, welcome after his ordeal, "Sounds like a lot for you to live up to?"

"Ah, it was no big deal. According to Mom he was using his powers right up until the end when he decided teamwork makes the dream work and all. I never played. More of a baseball guy myself."

Arthur dipped his hair back into the falls and started scrubbing, "Well, he could have gotten you one that fit!"

"Ya know," said Hazeus, "It's really pinching under the pits. But I don't think I'm getting outta this thing, I grew into and then straight out of it all in under a minute."

Arthur was pressing the water out of his leather breeches the best he could. "Ya know, if you wanted to chat with me, you could have done it in the circle."

"In what circle?"

"Up on the mountain? Where I summoned you."

Hazeus had already taken a few steps back toward the bench but turned, "Oh! You think…"

"What?"

He snorted, "You think," then he pointed and open mouthed laughed, "you think you summoned *me*?" Then he started walking, or whatever you call what two legged goats do, toward the benches again.

"What?" said Arthur, trailing. "What's so funny? I nearly died chasing you down that confounded mountain!"

"Wasn't me," said Hazeus.

"Oh?" said Arthur, catching up to walk alongside, "So, I suppose it was some other antlered and hooved smoke shade I was following?"

They reached the bench and Hazeus sat down, reaching beneath it and tossing the blue bundle to Arthur who barely caught it from surprise.

"Came down from the trees shortly after I drank dad's whiskey and found myself here."

Arthur held it up by the shoulders and started pulling it over his head. "That still doesn't explain—"

"Wild hunt, right?" asked Hazeus, crossing his legs. He could see that it was. "Yeah, mandrake root on the fire, lots of sour smelling smoke?"

"Yeah, so?"

"Well, this is why you don't trap yourself in an enclosed space with noxious fumes."

"Ha! Says you who drank your father's spirits! Besides, I thought you only had a mother. So, what is this, the actual God you're going on about, I assume."

"Mary was my surrogate. I think by now you should know how procreation is achieved," said Hazeus. "I really shouldn't have partaken of my father's spirits. It was wrong of me. But at least I know it doesn't agree with me now! It seems to have shifted the time-space continuum or something. Last thing I remember was you and Lancelot making your way toward Brittany after your fight and then…"

"You mean you blacked out?"

"Pffft!" his muzzle fluttered in indignation. "I didn't black out! I was just preoccupied with being transformed into a weregoat, or whatever you call this thing!" Hazeus looked thoughtful. "Hey, did the wives ever get returned to their proper husbands?"

"What do you mean?"

"You know, the stableman who had his wife kidnapped, and his son which was depressed."

"Ah, yes, happily!" said Arthur. "And he even has my old horse running again, word is."

"Amazing," said Hazeus with an inadvertent snort. "What about Dionysis's wife?"

"Well, that was an awkward matter."

"I thought it might be."

"But you know what? Kiara is a tough woman. She wasn't going to stand for any sorcery in her house. There might have been a problem had Fuzzick not recognized the king's now furiously jealous second wife. But he did. And let's just say she had a fishy relationship with a siren I knew for too long. And I only knew her for a few minutes. The king put her out upon the giant's word. Ha! And just think how Lance was initially so set in his judgment of Fuzzick."

Hazeus's eyes were getting kind of glassy. "Nice," he said absently, then he whispered, "In fact, I do recall… something."

Arthur was looking at Hazeus who was looking at the armadillo snuffling around the base of a torch nearby. "What?" blurted Arthur, snapping him to.

"Uh oh, I think it might be wearing off."

"What, the spell?"

"Oh, you're still on about that? No! The buzz, man!"

"Regardless, you can't leave yet! By whatever means you've landed here, you're supposed to answer three questions!"

"You always do that after you already asked a handful of them! Besides, the hunt is about gaining authority, or didn't anyone explain that?"

"Well, if I have authority then you must do as I ask! So, please what is it you've recalled?"

"Hey, I thought we were friends, no need to be threatening."

Arthur looked ashamed.

"I'm just getting one over on ya! I will tell you what I remember seeing, and you can even ask me the question you were nearly burning to ask. That is, if this holds out."

He looked thoughtful then. "Say, wouldn't happen to be any oxychana sage about?"

Arthur glanced around the glen and shrugged.

"Morning glory?"

"Search me," said Arthur.

"Poppy would work in a pinch," said the Satyr rummaging through his tight jacket pockets and coming up empty. "Shoulda nipped more than one bottle of the good stuff. Anyway, you should know, you're not going to see me, er, see Me, erddin again—"

Arthur thought he was acting a little weird.

"—until he's released from captivity. As long as we're speaking of the act of procreation, there was a scene in the magiscope I kind of recall right there before everything went all swimmy of Merddin and Vivianne, well... Let's just say his essence has been retained and he's going to need some time to recharge."

"What is a magiscope?" asked Arthur.

"Oh, just forget I said it," Hazeus waved a calloused palm absently. "I'd just advise keeping your palen tan[73] away from Stonehenge before room service is able to tend to things in order to avoid embarrassment."

"Okay," said Arthur, rearranging the compartments in his brain to make way for more terms that he clearly wasn't ready to understand yet. "So that just leaves the most

---

[73] A blown orb of blue glass containing a black candle. For all intended purposes; a black light.

pressing question. What is the third spell of making, then?" asked Arthur plainly. "And please, no riddles!"

"You do have to take the fun out of things, don't you?" said Hazeus sighing.

"The third spell is personal, Arthur." At this Hazeus coughed, and then he hacked, and then he wretched like he would vomit and then, a hairball came out of his mouth and into his great palm.

Arthur had begun to strike the big guy on the back until he saw the spray of mucus at which point, he leaned away to avoid getting gobbed on.

"Why is your face all mashed up like that?" asked Hazeus as if nothing were out of the ordinary.

"No reason," said Arthur trying his best to relax while the Goat god wiped wet hair from around the spherical mass. Arthur was starting to see the shine of red beneath.

"You just have to have the right ingredients for real magic. Well," said Hazeus, "and you've got to know the thing's proper name that you want to conjure. And I mean in the old Welsh." Hazeus was now polishing a perfect red ruby of mars with the fur at his wrist.

Arthur was staring at it in disbelief.

Hazeus sat back casually and inspected his work. "A lot of these priests and magicians nowadays walk around demanding this and that like they know somebody. But, if you truly know someone, you will call them by their real name. Just try calling your mother or father dude or bro, instead of Mom and Dad and you'll see what I mean."

At that, Arthur thought about his late father and Hazeus could briefly see that he may have stung him with the jest.

"Here," said Hazeus, handing him the flawless ruby. "Chin up."

Arthur took it. Tossed it up in the air once and snatched it sideways in his grip again with a bright smile. "So, what you're telling me is all that hacking and clucking you were doing was this here rubies true name?"

"It's from Mars!" said Hazeus, "Alien language that one."

"And the ingredients?" asked Arthur reluctantly.

"Well, I'd tell you what I had for breakfast, but—"

"Nope!" said Arthur with a palm up, "that's quite okay."

Then Arthur went trying to fit the stubborn ruby into the void of the blade but something was keeping it from a perfect fit.

"Here," said Hazeus, "Let me see."

"You know," said Arthur, "It is written that a druid's symbols of mastery should never be handled by another man."

Herne put out his earthy hands. "And what's it say about old friends?"

Arthur considered this and placed both ruby and sickle into the Forest God's outstretched palms.

Holding the sickle between his thumb and first two fingers, Herne plucked the ashen cork from the tip and then pinched the tiny ruby between the solid fingernails of his left thumb and two middle fingers like a vice. He then cut away a sliver of the stone with expert skill. His eyes darted to the shard in his palm. "Take that," he said. "I know a certain someone who would appreciate it."

Arthur did. Then he watched as Herne placed the main ruby into the slot of the golden sickle and twisted it with such might that the tool bit into the ruby, becoming one with it.

"I still can't believe you stabbed Lancelot!" said Hazeus, handing him his completed symbol of Mastery. "How did that feel?"

"You know," said Arthur. "I had forgotten all about that. But since you mentioned it. It felt good!" Then he laughed a windy chuckle. "Do you have any idea how long I worried about that sin ruining my rise to worship?"

Herne slapped his great hairy thighs and said, "I knew you had a conscience!"

"Yeah, but then I thought about how some guy once died to forgive us of all of that and suddenly, I was right back on track. I mean what's meant to be is meant to be. I can either use you as my martyr or your father as an excuse as he is apparently omnipotent. So why not draw a little blood once in a century or two?" Arthur then laughed nervously when Hazeus seemed to be enjoying the charade a little too much.

They shared an awkward silence which was only broken when Hazeus said, "Well then." Then stood up from the bench looking a bit doggish and pointing to Arthur's belt line. "Guess you outta tie her on there and let me take a look at ya."

So, Arthur did. He straightened up his robes, hung his new trophy in plain sight from his waist cord and stood before him on the bench's concrete slab. "You said, last time we met, that one day we would again meet as brothers."

"Ah," said Herne proudly grasping both shoulders of the complete druid king. "And we shall. I just have to finish the rest of the movie."

"What's a movie?" Arthur asked.

Hazeus held up a leather-bound book that Arthur recognized as The Tome of Ages, "Like a book but with moving pictures."

"Ah," said Arthur uncomfortably, moving in the direction Hazeus was beckoning. But just as the king stepped from the concrete slab, the sickle swung on its cord and wouldn't you know it, the tip caught him in the old wound tearing the flesh open and letting the blood run for the umpteenth time.

The king disappeared from the glen with a flash and Hazeus smiled. "That does feel good," he said. Then taking a few thoughtful steps, he said to himself, "Yeah, Dad probably meant for that to happen."

Arthur was standing under the northern trithalon in front of a mile-wide congregation. His sickle hanging at his side and blood trickling down his thigh. Under his breath and through gritted teeth, he said silently to either gods or sickles everywhere, "You son of a brachet!"

Then he waved to the masses and smiled as naturally as possible.

Chapter Twenty-Three: Bircham's Disarray

It was no secret that Mother Theresa was the tie that binds when it came to the monastery and its operation, but if it had been a secret, then the cat was out of the bag. This time, the cat was a mountain lion which had more or less taken up residence under the Friar and Abbott's pulpit. This turned all the gossip from the color of the friar's frock to the color of their sunburned faces. As the congregation was now being held out in the garden.

The altar was but a linen-covered tree stump. A sight that Merddin would have been proud to see, had he not disappeared after the King's trial by fire up on the Henge.

Friar Charles was keeping the mountain lion relatively happy by throwing scraps into the chapel once an evening and re-barricading the heavy wooden doors.

"Are you just going to continue feeding that feline?" asked the Abbott, sneaking up behind the friar who had his ear to the doors.

Startled, friar Charles straightened his robes and stood up before the chapel entrance. On the top step he was a hat taller than the friar. Well, at least one of the friars less honorary hats.

"Someone has to do something, Abbott!" said the friar over the sound of a clawed beast enjoying the night's leftovers. "She's a lady. We can't just let her starve."

The Abbott stood in pallid consideration as the commotion continued and then waned. "Hmm," he said putting his chin between his finger and his thumb. "It has been quite some time since we've boarded a proper pussy."

Friar Charles at once interjected, "Oh I wouldn't say that Mott is the most feminine Nun we've ever boarded, but I wouldn't downright deny that she is a—"

"What on earth are you saying, Friar? I was talking about the litter of orphaned bobcats that the boys adopted last spring. Get your head out of the gutter would you!"

"Yes, of course Abbot."

"But, speaking of Mott..." Both monks took a good look around at the monastery.

The sheep had taken over. One was chewing on the English ivy that Mott had planted specifically to cover the cracks along the trellis wall. Five were taking turns jumping over a bale of hay, and that had put Friar Geleskby to sleep in the manger where he'd been feeding them. Another was eating his hair.

Two of the altar boys had been sparring with wooden swords and now one was bent over the adobe wall and being spanked by the other with the flat side of the blade. A sheep watched with doleful eyes.

Abbot looked down at the friar's frock and decided to himself that it was neither gold nor blue. No, it had become just plain brown.

Just then Murdack crossed the menagerie to deal with the two boys, but as he did, the ties on his breast plate snapped and his armor fell to the ground. And wasn't the sign above the entryway a bit crooked?

While the fuming Murdack collected himself, the two monks looked back at each other embarrassingly.

"Perhaps, this place could use a woman's touch?" said the Abbott.

"Shall I let her out then, Sir?"

"God's no, Charles! I mean Mott you idiot. Get me Mott!"

Mim and Morgan's pact in the Cathedral

"Ah! Quite a powerful witch!" said Madam Mim. She was covered head-to-toe in a tattered black cloak that was spotted with the white droppings of the blackbirds which roosted in the rafters. Atop the podium, which had replaced the pulpit hiding opposite the veil, was a vulture picking at the stringy remains of some unfortunate animal.

The former weevil turned woman was poised to drop an old boot into a bubbling cauldron. Her gnarled hand still resembled the little weevil claws Morgan had seen in her vision. The tiny thing was half-transmogrified and now more human than bug; Fed from the faith and goodness of the prayers and pleas of the churchgoers happening on the opposing plane.

She dropped the boot into the miasma of belching fluids and began circling the wooden ladle with both hands. Her eye peeked out from under the hood. It was a round black bead, resembling the vulture's in every way. Mim dipped a finger into the stew and sucked the grime from its tip. "Gives it kick!" she said and then cackled.

The vulture squawked its own joyous laughter.

"Shut up you!" cawed Mim, and the bird lowered its wings and covered its head with its primaries.

Morgan's nose crinkled in disgust, and she briefly considered if this had been a mistake.

"I know who you are," said the crone. "You're Arthur's sister."

The pile of rags scooped out a ladle of muck and poured it in a wooden bowl then threw it onto a table where it clattered and slid to stop. The vulture came out of hiding and eyed the stew until a pointed finger went up; a gesture filled with threats. The birds head ducked back under its wing.

Then the hag tottered around the large black vessel as if one leg were shorter than the other and came toward Morgan. Her nose was a large triangle with a hump on the bridge. It protruded from the hood as she approached.

Her finger came up inquisitively before Morgan's perfectly virgin-skinned face. Morgan's eyes were like a tiger's eye stone, her hair straight and black. Eyebrows thin and high, accenting deep eye sockets rimmed with blue. Her neck was long, and the cavity at her throat a round fissure where the old hag began her slowly raising gaze.

Mim's breathing was labored as she sized up young Morgan.

Her body was like an hourglass. Frail and succulent limbs hung perfectly down her sides, held back at the shoulders proudly. A pert little frown shaped from darkly colored lips. The young woman was standing erect and straight headed but her pupils were cast down on Mim in inane curiosity.

Mim's sharpened fingernail touched the young witch's bottom lip and pulled it down enough to see her teeth behind them. Morgan tilted her head, not retreating from this sensual gesture.

Morgan closed her eyes, perhaps to escape in a memory of a past lover, and the fingernail fell from her bottom lip, the lip popping closed and leaving the slightest taste of blood in her mouth. Now the finger was in the neckline of her black bodice and the witch bent a knuckle to dive under the cloth and slide the back of the nail across a white breast.

The hag's tongue was lulling from her mouth as she watched small firm bumps form under the thin black material. Her nail was brushing the hidden pink flesh when the vulture's head came out of hiding again to take a peek.

Suddenly, Mim removed her finger and returned her tongue to her mouth. Morgan opened her eyes exhaling lustily. Mim laughed under her breath, her mouth revealing rotten teeth and the crumbled skin of her face bearing deep green lines of mold within the folds of her jowls. She smiled and shifted her dusty cloaks in giddiness.

She did a little dance from foot to foot and turned a pirouette. Then grabbed the bottom of her cloak and hiked it up, showing the wet and matted tangle of pubic hair to Morgan, and turned again raising the garment over her pale and putrid backside where she shook it in morbid temptation at the girl.

Morgan did not move and neither showed interest nor disgust.

"You think you can have this pussy?" Yelled the crone. Dashing her cloak side to side in a dancing jest and then skipping up the steps of the dark church. "She comes for power," sang Mim rhythmically. "She lusts for more. She touches skin and becomes a whore. She seeks to bring out what's within!"

Now Mim stopped and became rather serious. She pointed that finger again. "The only way is the greatest sin." She said and twirled on a heel, a magic whirl of glitter and dust enclosing the tattered old sorceress.

From the whirlwind of color, she could hear the woman's voice changing. "You watch him from afar. You want his power. You want his inheritance. You need—" said the whirlwind subsiding, "—his essence."

Then the colorful stars and dust fell away and there stood another entity in the dark church. It was a muscular, young, and naked man. And atop his head was a crown of gold.

Morgan's eyebrows shuddered but she stayed stoic and cold. Bringing her shoulders even further back in protest of the ill trick.

The false Arthur walked down the steps toward her. His shoulders back. His stature also tall and firm both in body and loins. Morgan's eyes dared a glance down at the pulsing member when he was only feet from her. A small bead of liquid forming at the tip.

She tried to breathe but it came out audibly as Mim encircled her with her arms pressing the member against the young Morgan's soft belly. Morgan's arms came up and around her brother's arms in a mentally strong and willing way and then she felt the back of her dress come undone. It fell, slipping slowly over her erect nipples and then falling to the floor in a heap.

Her thighs were sweating when Mim squatted down and slid the moist undergarment from Morgan's hips. Morgan's knees became weak. She put her hands around the head of the fake King cradling his ears beneath the crown as she felt a rough licking muscle press into and caress her tender inner pieces. She put a hand back to catch herself against the steps and lowered herself to them opening her legs, but the king was standing again, and his member was truly pulsing up and down.

"Now," said Mim in a King's most confident voice, "let's get his essence into you."

And a thick warm liquid shot from the member onto her belly and between her breasts, then she could not resist the terrible sin any longer. She took it into her mouth and drew long deep draughts in ecstasy. Her own loins pouring forth onto the stone steps of the evil cathedral.

Mim lapped up these sacred fluids with her own tongue while the young woman was petrified in ecstasy. And when they were devoured and began mingling with the inner workings of the witch, the young woman's eyes turned from that of a tiger's to those of a raven.

While Morgan slept, Mim readied her magic mirror and devised her plan.

Interlude

Hazeus had just stepped out from a nice cold shower.

There had been so much fur that he thrice had to scoop out the drain and sling it into the ivory-colored waste basket by the toilet where it magically flashed into non-existence.

He was beginning to wonder if the things he threw into waste baskets didn't actually end up somewhere else in the universe. The law of opposites was one of those big ones, wasn't it? He wasn't so sure anymore after the whole rain thing.

He dried his hair and was thankful that he didn't have to navigate around a pair of antlers, then he twisted the rest of the towel around his head and put on his bath robe. He could see a multitude of Fat Alberts printed on the green robe while flossing his teeth in the mirror. Just to be sure he didn't still have fangs of any sort, he peered a little closer, and then used some mouthwash for good measure.

He slid the bathroom door closed and passed under a bust of medusa made of faux stone while he sauntered toward the living room, absent mindedly twisting the corner of the towel in one ear. Then he stopped and looked at the spread of mvds on the floor. He had been through six. The previous album's artwork was a bit risqué, and the content didn't disappoint. That was if what he was looking for was the good stuff his father had been warning him about.

But incest? Hazeus was kind of glad it was all over with and was hoping that it wouldn't get any worse than that. At least he'd not yet had to witness men killing one another. He felt a little better now while drying off. What had it meant when Arthur woke up alone?

The previous mvd had ended with Arthur's waking up after an intimate dream of him making love to a dark-haired woman on the steps of a cathedral. It was a scene that came after a lengthy recounting of Guinevere and Lancelot on a night ride through Sherwood Forest when they stopped and stayed with Robin and Miriam. It was an innocent excursion and pure happenchance. But Arthur waking alone after an intimate dream of a woman that was the total opposite of his wife's golden complexion could have meant a number of things.

Was the king tired of the same old same old every night? Was it a vision brought on through guilt because of his absence in his mother and sister's lives? Whatever it had been, something had changed. Whether the King had recognized the woman in his dream as his elder sister Morgan, or not, was left untold, but now Hazeus was starting to think the king may have had some inkling because if Lance had spent the night with the queen (another piece of the puzzle that had been left untold) then something in the King's heart must have made room for another man to become more holy.

Hazeus had watched as Arthur descend the steps down into the catholic hall at Glastonbury Abby, a red shawl across his shoulders. It seemed he had given up calling on the old wizzard Merddin and now was turning his faith to a statue Hazeus knew the semblance of all too well. It was his adoptive mother! Holding little Hazeus in her arms before the manager. Cast from marble, set into the recess of the chapel beneath a stained-glass window; gilded to resemble the scene of the peace dove delivering a fig branch over water.

The king knelt before the holy mother. The hem of his red train catching the yellow light coming through the sun painted glass. The dust made the isle between the empty pews less empty. Up went the king's arms, and for a moment Hazeus thought he was going to again try and invoke the three-fold-utterance which should drop the veil, but there instead came a sigh. And the tired king made first the sign of three rays and then crossed himself and prayed.

Shortly after, on the eve of Lughnasadh, a laden donkey had arrived at Camelot carrying a weary messenger. Word was that Mott was eagerly being requested to return from her extended vacation on Avalon. With Merddin on sabbatical, the only way to reach her would be by way of ferry, and there was only one person Arthur knew might still hold the power to raise the mists. Besides, it had been far too long since he had seen his sister and mother if not for dreams.

The hill at Camel was turning into a kingdom. Albeit temporarily devoid of the king. Arthur was relatively confident enough leaving the company in the hands of Lancelot[74] and Kay, and now that he was accepted on both religious fronts there was even less to threaten the peace. So currently he was headed to the Isle of Avalon to retrieve Mott before Bircham's fell into complete disarray.

And that is where Hazeus had struck the pause button.

---

[74] Okay, we all know the story, but let's focus on Arthur here okay.

"What's that book?" said Father Time and Hazeus nearly spat the popsicle he was currently putting into his mouth out completely.

"Sorry!" said his dad, leaning down and lifting the Tome of Ages up from beside the stack of Mvds. "Looks like you."

"Uh, yeah," said Hazeus untwining the towel from his hair, as to not make his dad feel he were taking too many liberties. I mean, lately he had been watching something he definitely should not be watching, changing the weather, vegging out on his parent's dime, and drinking his father's liquor! But, if he even thought of that last one, there was going to be Bran to pay, so he just tried and act as normal as possible. "I kinda took that back from the past, I mean, that's allowed right? I can see how the future might mess things up, but from the past?"

Father time stood there. He opened the Tome of Ages, thumbed a couple of pages, nodded and 'hmpphed'.

His Dad dropped the book back on the bearskin rug where it made a soft thump. "I never said it wasn't," said Father Time.

"I turned into a satyr dad!"

"A satyr? Oh, you mean a roebuck. You don't know your history," he said. "But you'll get there. Regardless, I am proud of you, son! You didn't freak out?"

"What?" said Hazeus, the word accented with a heavy roll of thunder. At which his father reached out with his right arm and caught a candle that had overturned and rolled from the shelf. Hazeus ignored the deft act, "You knew it would happen?"

"Well, I had hoped," said Father Time placing the candle back on the shelf. "But you never really know these days. Anyway, that's great! I bet it was the scene with the half-naked maidens that finally did it?"

"Dad!"

"Well, sorry Son, but I thought that your mother would have said something. She was up with you afterward."

"No, she was only interested in watching Arthur and Lancelot go at it."

"I see," said his dad tapping the remnant stumps of this latest hour's antlers. "That explains why she woke me up."

"I guess that also explains why you're only wearing a loincloth," said Hazeus trying not to wonder what had happened to the rest of the poor koala[75] that adorned his father's waistline.

His Dad winked.

"Eww," said Hazeus. "I'm just saying, I could have at least won a series in baseball or something for my transformation."

"What, traversing time and space isn't enough for you then? Kids, I tell ya." Father Time looked at his son, "You think finding yourself as a roebuck is alarming? Well,

---

[75] He failed, and remembered the cute cozies his mom and dad had been using earlier that evening to keep their beer cold.

you've come of age, Son. Just wait until you meet the hounds of hell."

"The what?"

"Oh, don't worry too much about it, you're still young. Gotta lot of life left in ya. Besides, heck of a motivational cue, that."

Hazeus was starting to think he'd sprung the trap called growing up. He was feeling too far out of his depth and kinda wished he could go back in time. But that trick was elusive and seemed to be happening of its own accord.

"Could always be worse," said Father Time, breaking his reverie, "my old Da strapped a slab of raw meat to my leg during my first go round the calendar. He just told me it was called training!"

Chapter Twenty-Four: Retrieving Mott

The prow of a flat boat slowly emerged through the mists in the magiscope. Dampness swirled up in little rivulets along Arthur's temples. Temples set beneath a light golden crown and propped above cheeks laden in the golden down of an emerging beard.

An oarsmen silently poled the little skiff through the mists. The drip and ploop of the reed ever present, interrupted only by the tolling of the bells on Glastonbury Tor.

A cloaked figure, who knew that Avalon was more than an island absent from maps, sat at the bow readying herself. She had not parted the mist to Avalon since her argument with Igraine, but she was confident that the shades of sea and air followed her command.

It wasn't following stars or moving the fog that mattered. Avalon had only been accessible to those with proper authority. And the authority needed to enter there wasn't simply the friendship of the elements. It was something more. It had to do with the balance of the spirit.

Morgaine had been teetering along a filament of light and dark. Though Mim had granted her the second spell of making, and the comfort of sure power welled within, her repressed self was unsure that Arthur could ever forgive her for betraying him. He could never find out!

She couldn't live without her brother's love.

Now, he sits behind her, a grown man. With bitter shame, she thought of when they were but knee-high sprouts and when he had thought of her with so much love. Before now, not a single bitter thing could move her, but this memory had the strength of a thousand key limes.

Before Arthur had been taken in by the brothers at Tintagel, she had been his everything. Even now as she peeked from under her hood and looked back into the pale blue eyes of the king, she could remember the day they were separated.

Morgaine and Arthur's Upbringing and Separation

The time before their separation was the most magical and happy time of Morgaine's life. But it was the morning of the separation she still coveted. Strange how the most powerful emotions are the scariest ones. Or the most shameful, as Mim had put it. Only after Mim had shown her the events played out on the surface of her magic mirror would Morgaine know the truth behind her brother's right to the throne.

Merlin had been King Uther's advisor when Igraine, Morgaine's mother, was married to Gorlois. Her memory of Gorlois, her true father, was one that had been swept away with the many emotions of loss and gain. But it surfaced in the silver of Mim's mirror while she supped on the vulgar stew for dinner.

She remembered the night her father's body was delivered to the keep, struck down in war. She recalled the spiral of confusion it had brought her mother.

Igraine had not accepted the fact that he was dead. The guards had granted him entry that evening from the battlefield for a much-needed respite with his wife. Then later watched as he left to return on the road northwest back toward the battle at the river Usk.

The entire camp flared with controversy when Gorlois's body was delivered back less than an hour after his departure by horse drawn carriage. His lifeless body was there, and Igraine was full with the life of Morgaine's little brother within her.

In time, people would rumor the pregnancy magic. And in Mim's magic mirror, Morgaine saw that indeed, it was.

According to what Morgaine saw in the mirror, while Mim wrung her hands in delight, Arthur's conception had been the result of King Uther sneaking into Igraine's chambers disguised as Gorlois. A disguise only accomplished by the feats of Merddin, Mim's nemesis. The Druid had used the charm of making in exchange that Uther promised him any child resulting from the night.

In that way Uther had secured victory over Gorlois's land and his wife in a single strategic maneuver. Then, in time, Morgaine's little brother would be born, and the pain of her father's death would be swept away.

It was a pain that was only put on hold until the day that both of them came of age. She would take young Arthur on horseback through the city gates and into the fields where they could witness the villagers reaping the grain. They would play along the creeks together, building dams to net brim and bring home to Uther and Igraine.

It was difficult for Morgaine, at first, when Uther took over the household. She was no ordinary child. She possessed the sight; a gift passed down through the bloodline of Avalon priestesses. And though, Igraine was of the old religion, it was Vivianne, Morgaine's aunt that was the high priestess.

Morgaine suspected that magic had been involved in Arthur's conception so was for a long time indifferent to Uther. When the indifference finally passed their relationship became more of a friendship than a custodial one. Constantly she was bombarded by visions. She had seen when Arthur had fallen from the fence and was nearly trampled by the sows. She had known that the Saxons had landed on the shore even before Uther rode out to greet them. But she never saw the separation from her beloved little brother coming.

It was only a matter of time before Viviane would be taking her to the Isle of Avalon for her training. She remembered thinking about it as she watched young Arthur playing with a wooden soldier, no older than the age of seven. But wouldn't he be able to come along?

No longer than she let the thought cross her mind she had heard her aunt's familiar voice down by the fire. And there was another voice, the Abbott from the monastery down the hill.

"I'm here on Merlyn's charge to collect on an offer you made long ago," said the Abbott.

Morgaine encircled her little brother with her arms when he put his toy soldier down and peered through the upstairs railing to see what was going on. They watched and listened together; her only hope harbored in their being born away together.

"Morgaine has the sight. She needs to be trained as a priestess."

Igraine was in tears. She was imploring that Uther do something to prevent Viviane from taking both of her children away. But Uther knew the consequences of turning back on a promise made that was bound by magic and when he weakly debated with the lady of the lake, Morgaine silently thanked him for intentionally being coy.

"Would you have Morgaine raised behind the walls of a convent, Sister? Even you could not possibly stand being bound up in the new religion while knowing you were born for more," said Viviane.

"At least she would be safe in a convent," argued Uther, with no real conviction.

Viviane was quick to answer. "Safe but never satisfied! How can anyone be safe if not by their own strength?" She looked to Igraine who was clasping Uther's arm and trembling.

"Would you see your daughter relinquish all her spiritual authority and spend a lifetime begging for strength from her knees? Is that the Avalon bloodline?"

Viviane was standing upright. Her eyes shooting arrows at Morgaine's parents. Not a sound was uttered from either one. Just gentle sobs, lost in Uther's cape. Then Morgaine saw Viviane nod to the Abbott. And as the man ushered in some servants, she met her mother's eyes.

From the top of the steps, she felt her mother pass her what little strength she had left. Morgaine pulled her little brother back behind the baluster and urged him to pack his things.

The following morning Morgaine and Arthur set out behind the Abbott and Lady of the Lake into the misty morning, enjoying one another's company on a fresh new adventure. Little did they know that it would be the last time crossing the clopping drawbridge together.

As the horses pushed on toward the crossroads, the children were keen on the talk between the two adults whose jerkins and gowns they clutched from behind. It was becoming more and more distressful.

"She's old enough to understand," said Vivianne.

"But Arthur is young, he won't like it."

"Oh, stop with that prattish nonsense, he's a dragon! He's been promised!" The Lady of the Lake reigned her mount around and it reared up, cowing the mare on which the boys rode.

Morgan's eyes were wide at the respect this woman demanded, and she clutched to her to prevent from tumbling backward off the horse.

When the black stallion's hooves came to a restful state under its tightly braided main of arched and commanded muscle, the Abbott spoke from a bowed head, hiding behind an upraised praying palm. "I'm simply being compassionate for the boy, my lady."

Viviane looked down upon the friar with cold power. "The boy has no time for compassion!" At this she saw the tears roiling behind Arthur's lids.

Morgan could sense her brother's dismay. She could feel the tumult threatening to break those dams, disguised smartly behind pretty lashes. She could hold it no more!

Morgan leapt from the horse, feeling the Lady grabbing at the back of her robe but not having the strength in grip to stay her. She ran to Arthur, and he reached his arms to her and bawled like when she'd rode upon him in the pen. Though this was no fear of injury but a loss more bitter still.

She couldn't take it. Maybe he would endure because he was a boy. But she hadn't raised him under the harsh fist of boyhood, so she wasn't certain. She didn't know if just being born a male made you truly stronger. The only strength she fostered in them was for them both and that was from their real father's absence.

Her heart was breaking, and she only had one feeble thing to grasp on to now. Hope. A word. A thought. An intangible thing! Her love for Arthur could also not be seen, but it was felt so strongly, and she would hold onto that thought up through her teen years. And that thought would grow in her and remain a thorn in her side that would fester, just as any question left unanswered eventually does.

"Don't go, Morgan!" railed Arthur.

She clutching him, and him wrapping his legs and arms around her. A grip she knew too well. He wasn't going to let off unless Uther tickled him into a savage laughter, first.

But their false father was not there, only the two cold strangers wrenching them apart.

"No!" Arthur screamed. "No!No!No!"

But the Abbott was holding him about the waist, and when Vivianne took Morgan, it stood too much for Arthur's grip. The red-faced boy reigned ineffectual blows down on the Abbott's forearms. Writhing in his grip.

Morgan was crying helplessly, but allowing herself to be led away without restraint, gauging the lady's strife against her own. Oddly, she felt empathy in Vivianne's grip. When a woman[76] should be worried about their horse, Vivianne had both hands engaged in Morgan's emotions, one leading and one drawing symbols on the wind. Wooing her away and letting Arthur take the pain.

The Abbott knew nothing of the sight but was well versed in empathy. He just waved helplessly at the women and said, "Away with you! Before the boy dies of distress!"

Then the girls were mounted and riding away. Arthur swaddled in the heavily sweating Abbott's arms, two siblings' eyes connected by a silver thread of misery, broken by a turn in the roadway that avoided a drooping yew tree that both kids would forever associate with loss.

---

[76] Even a knight

Morgaine and Arthur's Reunion

Their reunion at Camelot had been rushed as Percival was busy recounting his findings on his quest for the grail. A charge voluntarily taken up by the lad when word had come that the Pope was siding with the Roman Catholics and declaring that the old religion was idol worship and that they should be converted or purged from the land. His hope was that securing a holy relic might gain them favor and help sway the Pope's decision of siding wholly with the Romans, preventing unnecessary warfare.

All those present for Percival's tale were utterly rapt. It went on late into the afternoon, and only after a late lunch was Arthur able to usher Morgaine in from her place at the rear of the audience. Then, her welcome was a public one, next to the round table.

A glass had been raised in thanks for Morgan's recently divulged pregnancy and a much-awaited heir to Lot's household.

This brief reunion did not, however, deter them from racing their horses at the head of the procession toward Glastonbury like the two young siblings of yesteryears. Of course, much to the dismay of his meager retinue who possessed far less able mounts. But they had laughed, and recounted adventures along the route, yet there had been no time for more lengthy private exchange.

Avalon

"Sister?" called Arthur, presently from his seat in the drifting vessel.

Only a slight turn of a shrouded head offered any registration below those upturned arms.

"Is something the matter? The duke never portrayed you as one slow to act." He leaned back against the oarsmen, whose face seemed too skinny for the living. There wasn't any humor in the downcast glance of that countenance.

Her little brother's blood-bound tact pierced her to the core, souring her sin. She cinched on a powerful emotion that came careening away from her light sphere. Snatched it from the misty air, a blue purple twist of energy, unidentifiable until it was cast, and she decided quickly rather she should be angry or humored.

She chose the present and smiled, opening her palm, and spreading her arms above her head in a halo, exhaling and calling down the three-fold-utterance. The tolling bells of the Abbey fell away mid cast and the mists parted. The King sat up staring through to a vividly colorful landscape.

Morgan was smiling, but a tear ran down a pale cheek, now slightly roused from the sun.

"I never thought I would see something as beautiful," said Arthur steadying himself while he took his feet. But he was looking at her.

His sister blushed and removed her hood, looking back over her shoulder at him. She had turned from the effervescent rainbow of the mountain stream which emptied itself in the bay they were approaching and was seating herself at the prow. Her cheeks were full-on pink.

"I love you, sister," said Arthur, captivated by the moment. He stepped forward and knelt before her, taking her hand and dropping his head into her lap.

The oarsmen looked away.

Arthur brought his face up from the soft linen and met her eyes, not holding back in his admonition. "I have missed thee. Not a night has passed that I have not called upon your strength and compassion."

But in her eyes, he didn't find solace. There was not even empathy there, and feeling he had overstepped on a relationship that had long been rent asunder, he gathered his robe and sat back at the stern.

The seashells beneath the sea foam at the water's edge gave a pink hue to the shores of Avalon where the skiff was currently being hoisted up onto the sand by two bald-headed maidens dressed in red. Each of their foreheads were adorned with a blue crescent moon. Not of the deep inked symbol like Vivianne's who stood further up the shore on a velvet carpet which had been deposited there hurriedly on their approach, but a shining temporary stamp that glistened in the light.

Arthur made to lighten the load by disembarking but Morgan stayed him. "They will find it an insult if you try and help," she said.

"Y gwiyr yn ebyn y byd," said Arthur to the maidens, a respectable greeting in the Celtic dialect.

"They won't answer you," Morgan said tersely, "they've taken a vow of silence to the Mother."

Arthur tried not to seem chastised but obliged. The boat was moored properly and another maiden, her head hooded, came down the sand and offered her hand to Morgan.

"The veil has lifted," said the woman, whom Morgan seemed familiar, "nothing else need be said."

Morgaine allowed the assistance of her old acquaintance, but when her feet hit the sand she responded, "I am here only at my brother's behest. I have done nothing for the Mother."

The robed maiden turned from Morgan at that, ignored Morgan's retreat up the bank, then turned to Arthur offering him the same pale hand with silver fingernails.

"Is Igraine among you?" asked the King without reserve.

The maiden inclined her hooded head and helped Arthur from the skiff, "She is," said she, "but I have ill tidings as your mother has been in rapid decline. The lady has been at her bedside frequently these last two moons."

Arthur's heart sank and his distress was furthered by the sight of his sister in a heated argument which was muted by the wind. Her scorn was met with Vivianne's cold countenance who stood there like a block of marble until Morgan turned and stormed up the trail.

Arthur felt out of place in his royal garb. Though his gold and red was a welcome adornment on the isle of women, he felt that he was not representing the blue of Anglesey like he had so sworn. He found himself, for the first time, feeling that the world was sweeping him up with its changing tidal current.

"She looked upset," said Arthur to the Lady of the Lake.

"The moon is waxing full, many of the maidens are in such ill repose." They stood there, eye to eye, neither with an urge to first surrender one another's gaze. They were two chess pieces. Both with no choice of failure in their charge. "I am sorry for your mother," said the Lady, finally.

Some color came into her face, and even the empathy that Morgan had lacked waxed on her visage. Arthur softened at this, and the two chiseled characters found one another human once again. He took her hands, and she kissed him on the cheek. "And your tutor," she said to him. "He has told me to assure you that he is well and safe, and to send his love."

The King couldn't decide what question to present first to the Lady of the Lake, nor which was more appropriate so he offered his hand. She turned and began leading him up the trail toward the menagerie and quaffed his confusion by producing an answer in old fashion manner. Via premonition.

"I cannot see where he is," she said on account of Merddin. "It is closed to me. As for Igraine, she came to us in the second trimester of pregnancy…"

She gauged Arthur's reaction before continuing, "It isn't safe to carry to term so late in years, but she insisted."

"You could see her fate?"

A pause then, and the Lady inclined her head solemnly, "She would not take any debridement concoction." Vivianne stopped Arthur as they approached a translucent tent in the garden. Morgan's outline could be seen within, standing at the bedside of her mother. "Arthur," said Vivianne, "there is evil afoot. Morgan could not have raised the veil without assistance. I am leery to consider that assistance came of her mother's dying wish to heal whatever rift still lay between them. But we can hope."

Arthur moved to enter the tent and Vivianne grabbed his elbow. He looked back to her. "Be careful," she said.

Inside, Igraine lay surrounded by tight bundles of juniper and vervain. She was covered with a light blanket and rested atop a feather bed. A grey aura of damp sweat surrounded her. Morgan stood with her hands on the bedside but refused to reach out and hold her mother's hand.

Igraine only looked up at her through deep eyes, not ready to waste any words on apologies just yet. Arthur took Igraine's hand, and she gave up the staring contest with her daughter, smiling at him. "My son," she said, making it plain that she was under great effort of speaking. "Would you please?" she said pointing her other frail hand at a small open phial.

He reached over and lifted it gingerly to her lips so she might sip.

"Black willow," said Morgan plainly, "a mild analgesic."

Their mother drank and then lay back a moment. Arthur watched as color began returning to her cheeks and then she opened her eyes again. He was surprised to see they were much clearer now. "You see," said Igraine, "that is where we always hit a roadblock."

Arthur looked at Morgan who returned his glance with a cold and disinterested glare.

"You had only to say what you saw in the well, Morgan. Why lie about your abilities?"

"I said just what I saw," said Morgan. "Would you like to hear the truth again? The truth is I saw nothing! Vivianne only wanted me to see something so that she could pantomime her next magic act."

Igraine laughed suddenly.

"What?" asked Morgan, surprised.

"It was the same with me once," she told Morgan. "I saw parlor tricks when I was with the younger priestesses until I realized that my magic came easier."

Morgan crossed her arms. "What does that mean?"

"You were so worried about what Vivianne wanted you to see, that you didn't consider what you wanted… or perhaps, did not want to see."

"Oh, I didn't care what Vivianne wanted me to see, Mother! I just wasn't going to lie and say I saw anything so that she could somehow twist things and manipulate people into making whatever it was I said come true!" Morgan audibly huffed. "That's what she does! Her ego is so huge she will change reality to make it seem as if she possesses some real power! All the while she just sneers inward and thinks of what great liars and fools, we all are while we play her game!"

When Morgan's anger was spent, Igraine sighed. Then she said, "Scrying is not something that resembles a waking dream. Scrying is simply admitting what your desire or fear is. Whether it was Vivianne's magic, a world manipulated by hormones, or your own ingrained will, would it matter? There is more to magic than the ingredients, Morgaine."

Igraine released Arthur's hand and took her daughter's wrist. Morgan allowed this, sensing her mother's strength fading again. Her mother then took Morgan's hand and pressed her thumb nail hard into Morgan's palm. When she returned her hand to Arthur's, Morgan could see that a crescent moon had been left behind in her fist. Just the blood brought to the surface by the pressure of the thumbnail. But it was the perfect crescent of the Mother.

"There is magic," said Igraine wearily, "in you."

Then Morgan clasped the hand to her own breast as if she were holding an unbearably hot brand. She took one more look at her mother and rushed past Arthur into the open garden.

Arthur stood to go after her, but Igraine held tight to his wrist. "No," she said forcibly, then relaxed again, "it will be well with her."

Arthur knelt back down at the bedside.

"I have something I must give to you," she said. Then, from around her neck she removed a fine gold chain. When she produced its charm that lay hidden beneath the neck of her gown, Arthur could see that it was a ring. She held it up for him to survey.

Two dragons wound round a center emerald of green. One was crafted of a silver alloy shimmering with a white outline, and the other was forged from gold, whose tail completed the underside and majority of the artifact. That dragon was rimmed with a rose color. "Inside," whispered Igraine.

Arthur took the ring and tilted it toward the candelabra as to better read the inscription. "*Vermatrix*," he read aloud.

And then his mother closed her eyes and took a long deep breath. "Yes," she said seeming to be reveling in a memory from long ago. Arthur felt she was letting go and turned his head to the entrance as if to shout for Vivianne, but Vivianne was already standing there.

"Is there nothing else we can do?" he asked her.

Viviane shook her head and pointed to where a mist was gathering at the hem of the tent flaps, "It's the dragon's breath. Her time is near."

Arthur stood up and then leaned down, kissing his mother's lips for the last time. As he pulled away, she whispered, "More to it than ingredients, Son."

Then the mist crawled over the bed and the smell of flowers would be reported across the island.

Chapter Twenty-Five: A Solemn Departure

It was the morning after his mother's passing and Mott was not being very agreeable. Arthur had Viviane request that two donkeys and a length of rope be brought so that he could back up his threat of pulling the door from its hinges, would Mott not abide their wishes. The maidens had been trying to convince her to come out of the den since late last evening.

"You may need to remove the door just to get her out willingly," said Vivianne to the King before waving off a second serving girl in the last five minutes who'd approached with a cask of wine on her head and a wheel of cheese under arm.

Arthur rubbed his chin and raised an eyebrow at Viviane, "Couldn't you just magic her out of there or something?"

"And make this easy on you?" Viviane belayed the jest, and took the rope from Arthur's hands, "Here, I will tie this to the handle." She went about the duty as the donkeys watched with curiosity. "Strong willed, this one! Nothing's been easy with her. Everything manual labor. She simply refuses to believe."

Arthur let out some of the line so she could get a good knot on the handle. The rope seemed to mind her rather well, since it tied itself like a snake might under a charmer's spell.

"You'd think one would flee from the disciplinary and downcast disapproval of one's peers, but thick skin, this one! She has no shame, I tell you! Broke her vow of silence within seven minutes, and that was only because we were short a maiden and couldn't keep up with slicing enough bread to keep her mouth occupied, otherwise." Viviane returned to Arthur who was looking rather proud, she thought.

"And don't get me started on her makeover," she continued. "Ursala said she threatened to curdle what's in her udders, whatever that means, if she so much as touched a hair on her chin." Viviane ignored Arthur's sly grin, "So, we've been dealing with that."

"Sounds like Mott," said Arthur.

Arthur signaled to the two silent priestesses, and they slapped their respective asses on the asses.

"Then there was the furniture we had to convert—" Viviane was just getting warmed up when a giant *Floomp* went up and the wooden door came away in a plume of hay dust which swirled down and then back up again from the roof. Then from the dark interior of the dugout den, came a voice Arthur thought no man should ever have to admit that he'd missed.

"By the Mother Mary, I swear I won't set foot on that skiff until I've tidied up this mess you call a den! It does no good to be leaving a place worse off than you'd found it and I'll not have these fairy folk saying Mott didn't carry her own. Now where's those girls with the cheese and wine? I'll be needing my strength if I'm gonna make heads or tails of it."

Arthur waved the sun-soaked motes of dust from his field of vision and clamored toward the doorway where his one adoptive Mother Theresa was waddling toward him up a staircase beyond the shorn away portal. Her baby blue pants bloused at the knee with lace edgings, possibly fashioned from an ornate tablecloth. Her bodice was white, besides the many speckled plum stains which were congruent with a good hearty laugh while having a mouth full of wine.

There was a maiden behind her trying to tighten and tie her corset with much difficulty as each time she tugged, Mott's bossom[77] bloomed up in front of her own face, and she immediately stuffed it back down again, ruining the attempt.

"Ma'am please, if only a moment!" the girl said while being dragged along like a plow.

"Oh Dear," said Mott when the dust had cleared sufficiently to make out Arthur and Viviane.

He thought she looked ten years younger, but that could have been either powder and blush, or simply the rosy cheeks of a most content lush. Well deserved, he thought.

"What's happened?" asked Mott seriously. "Don't tell me your tutor has gone and decided to cut my vacation short! We had a deal you know!" said Mott, swinging a ballet slipper in one hand to make the point heard. Then as the slipper drooped pathetically, she saw Excalibur at Arthur's side and seemed to notice he had a beard filling out.

He watched as slow understanding dawned. Then Mott's bosom swelled with pride and the serving girl behind Mott proclaimed, "Aha!" and stepped away dusting her palms together having tied a satisfactory knot.

Arthur reached out and took the slipper.

Then, Mott realizing she was going to have to stick her neck out or drown in her own breasts, she reached up and hugged Arthur's neck. When she was back at arm's length she said, "Has it been that long then?"

"Longer," said Arthur laughing. "Time tends to move a bit differently in Rootworld."

---

[77] When one writes about bosoms such as Mott's they are often inclined to believe that the word bosom deserve two s's.

Mott considered this while Viviane muttered something about having tried teaching her about time on half a dozen occasions in Basic Forces 101. Then she said, "As it should then, what with all the fairy glamour and what not."

Viviane's exasperation at the statement was palpable.

"So, how's the old man?" Mott asked.

Arthur and Viviane looked at one another. Then, Arthur just came right out with it all.

That evening a pyre was built and the soul of a beloved mother and sister to all present, was cast back across the seas of Annwyn. Morgan watched from the valley alone until the fires were gone and the full moon was blotted out from its apex over the sea. The rains came then, washing away the remnants of one upon this plain and marking the beginnings of others. She cradled the soft convex of her abdomen.

"So, you're telling me that Bircham's is a downright mess? I've only been gone…" Mott thought about this as she was being helped onto the boat the next morning. Another boat had already arrived and was wobbling unsteadily out onto the lake which carried her luggage. Somehow, she had laid claim to a variety of the island's luxuries and had decided she could not live without them. "How long have I been gone exactly?"

"Six months," said Viviane in tandem with Arthur saying, "Four years."

"Felt like longer to me," said Viviane absently. Arthur shrugged.

"So, which is it?" asked Mott.

"Well, a lot has happened," said he, "you won't have Borus to blame as he and Gwain have been at Camelot all this time, more or less in service of the kingdom. Kay moved in from castle Tintagel and—" Mott plopped down on the cross member at the stern and the two bald maidens seized the sides of the boat as it threatened to tilt entirely over. It seemed to settle after it sunk six inches only to be halted by the sandy bottom. The oarsman standing behind her looked ten years more bedraggled and had only stayed dry by leaning heavily on his pole and grabbing onto Mott's shoulder for support.

"Well," continued Arthur, "I'm married."

Mott's mouth went agape and before he could consider that she may not have received word, he realized she was looking over his shoulder where a priestess had seemingly materialized out of thin air and was now folding an ornate cape of blue and gold bearing many occult symbols.

"In light of such tradition, we won't let you depart without accepting a late gift on that account," said Vivianne.

Morgan was just then coming down the trail with a tail of young girls. She looked in a cheerful mood among the children and was entertaining each of their inquiries in turn. But she paused when she saw Viviane handing Arthur the two relics.

"The cloak of Paden," said she. "It hides otherworld entities from mortal eyes, and here," she said, unfurling a blue and yellow sleeve of finely woven fabric. She held it in both hands so Arthur could see its entirety. "The sheath from Lugh of the Long Arm's lance, retrieved after the Battle of Magh Tuireadh on the plains of Mayo. Cover Excalibur's scabbard with it and you will never suffer a mortal blow."

The sleeve was ornamented with the little yellow flowers of his youth. The rayless golden pipes. He took the items, conscious now of the giddy little chatter of ignored children behind them. They had begun talking over one another during Morgan's secret bout of jealousy.

"Viviane, always the most generous relative," Morgan said, leaving the girls behind.

"Indeed," said Arthur, "thank you for your hospitality." Then looking at Mott and back to Viviane he said, "and your patience."

"Thank the goddess," she said to them both.

Morgan took Viviane's left hand and kissed it, regardless of her inner turmoil, then climbed aboard unassisted. Her right hand remained tucked inside of her cloak.

When Arthur stepped into the vessel the oarsman prevented the king from taking his place in the center and struck a note on the cross member of the prow with his stick by where Morgan sat. The King obliged, yet still, after the huffs and guffaws of six scantily clad maidens guiding the skiff out onto the water, the King and his sister felt considerably taller than those occupants in the rear.

"So, will we be meeting your lovely wife?" asked Mott, trying to get comfortable in her old habit, which had been cleaned and starched, so was in desperate need of a good roll in the hay with a certain wizzard, whether he was present or not[78].

"Nay, ma' am. We're straight away to Tintagel. Word is, there is an animal making her home in the church and she must have a litter of kittens in there

---

[78] That should loosen it back up a bit. If not, a round of wrestling with Murdack may suffice.

with the way she's protecting it. Friar Charles says the monks are getting sunspots on their scalps and the summer heat is withering away the delegation, though I think he more or less means the weekly proffer."

"On about money again, then, is he?" says Mott. "I tell the Abbot each season he'd better give away his earnings else he drink them to his own demise!"

Arthur looked out into the mists that were gathering thickly now as they moved away from the island. He was thinking of the ensuing threat from the Romans and his meeting with Hazeus when just then he came up with an idea.

"That's it, Mott!" said Arthur.

"Well, of course it is, I've been saying it for years," said she with her nose up, still addressing her smocked habit. Then she paused. "What's it exactly?"

"You're a genius!" he said.

Morgan stood and raised her left hand above her head. When she dropped it, the mists fell away and the toll of the bells at Glastonbury came skating across the rippling lake toward them. But something was wrong with Morgan. She still stood there in a trance.

Mott was opening her mouth to speak when Morgan collapsed, caught in Arthur's arms. Her face was upturned and pale, and she was quivering. He could feel that she was taking no breath. "Morgan!" he cried.

Just then she convulsed, and her eyes shot open. The irises were as blue as they had been in their loving youth. A strange vision among the veined and pallid skin of her lifeless face. And then she spoke. "The moon will wane and wax and you will die by your own blood and your own blade."

Her eyes clapped shut and her body went limp.

"Oh dear," said Mott.

"She's burning up!" said Arthur, pulling her right hand from within her cloak. The sinews had the fingers locked in the semblance of a raven's claw and the veins were like bright red wax.

He reached a hand into the lake and splashed some water on his sister's face. It stirred her.

Morgan shot up like a mongoose and then back pedaled into Arthur's lap. Her hand seemed to be easing its tension as she was gripping an invisible ball with it over and over. She looked up to him and the color had returned to her face. "What happened?" she said, looking about sheepishly.

"You had a fit, Dear," said Mott. And Arthur met her uneasy gaze across the deck, thinking of how Viviane had told him to be careful.

Respite at Glastonbury

They took respite at Glastonbury abbey, where the nuns were happy to feed them and let them rest. Morgan was wrapped in a shawl and was napping on a cot in the main hall where Arthur and Mott sat at a table eating. He was telling her his plan to check the Roman's seemingly unending desire for more.

"Aren't you worried that any one of those inebriated people bearing weapons might just do something stupid?" Mott was asking.

"Oh, I'm counting on it!" said the King. "I've made a vow to maintain the peace through bloodless means and I plan on keeping it."

"Yeah, but I mean, like what if someone accidentally gets hurt?" said Mott, biting into a muffin and landing on a particularly tough piece of bran. "Ow." she said, thumbing her tooth.

Arthur held up Lugh of the Long Arm's sheath like it should be an obvious answer then began fitting it over the end of his scabbard.

"Let me see that!" said Mott taking it from him and the scabbard. "I'll not sit here filling my gob hole while you are going about trying to save the kingdom and fit your own tools, you being king and all." She looked sidelong at him as she dressed it up properly.

"I got the idea from what you two told me about Dad. His men drinking that tainted water from the enemy's encampment—"

She finished it proper and handed it to him.

"—well, and that time Merddin took me to Dragon's Isle after dosing me with magic tea."

Morgan lay there in the shadow of the shawl, one beady little raven's eye staring out while Mim listened through her, vowing not to let the girl break free again. Not even for a brief moment, Mim said to herself.

Mott returns to Tintagel and the Romans try and strong arm her

The road between Bodmin and Wells had been riddled with peddlers of Roman wares, and in the town centers of each city, there was obvious Roman influence. Arthur and Morgan agreed about the unease they felt at the church in Wells when they stopped to offer a bundle of golden pipes at the altar[79]. They were doing so in heed of Lughnasadh and their safe passage through the veil during his season.

When the church was vacated under the guise of giving the King and his entourage their privacy, Arthur declared uneasily, "My meaning was not to displace anyone, only to share your house of worship."

There were custodians with brooms of pussy willow, each side of the pulpit, hiding in the dark shadow of the oddly spotless chapel. Besides those hiding, there were only a few priests with the roman cross on their cloak, who held censures and were brimming with the energy of directing the boys to sweep up any messes a vagrant might put down among their holy shrine.

"If a single flower be removed from this altar before sunset, may it be by the wrath of Lugh of the Long Arm as well to the distaste of your King," said Arthur when it had become overly obvious.

---

[79] Which also happened to be the feet of the crucified Hazeus.

At that, the priests fell back with their censers and disappeared altogether from between the rows of polished pews.

By the time the trio was nearing Bircham's order and Mott's abode, Arthur and Morgan had heard all about her opinion on how there was a certain balance between cleanliness and godliness. In short, she believed that God himself shouldn't be pushed from a chapel with a broom!

Arthur had reigned his horse around at the entrance of St Materiana's to skew Mott from forcing them to stay for dinner.

"Oh, don't you worry," said Mott, waving some of the speckled faced boys from the welcome party over and directing them to start unloading her first donkey. "There's like to be a lot of cleaning up around here before I'd dare to invite royalty to order. Though I'd not deny you what morsel we might have at present."

"Oh, no Mum," said Arthur, "The fairy isle has stolen time from us again and the Roman presence is thicker than I had foreseen. I must get Morgaine back to Orkney, but we will fare better once we stop in Camelot. Come and visit! I must repay the many years of love and hospitality at the hands of Mott and *her* order at Bircham's."

Just then Friar Charles was striding up from the courtyard and witnessed Mott swell with pride at Arthur's remark. His mustache drooped heavily on both sides at his taking the compliment as some royal decree.

Arthur and Morgan started off with a wave just as Mott noticed the friar deflating on her left. "Oh, grow a pair, Charles!" she said. "I'm just the maid!"

Friar Charles's lips turned into a squiggly line until they could figure out which way to turn, then just like that, he hugged her. "We're glad you're back, Mum."

Mott did a pretty good job acting like Charles wasn't a total mess, but internally she was burning for the feel of a good ole rolling pin. She waved from his considerable embrace as her party ambled their way down toward Camelot and past a particular yew tree that the siblings both shared a distant scar with. Strangely, Arthur was the only one who seemed to notice.

Chapter Twenty-Six: Mott Cleans Up

Tommy took Mott by the thumb, just as she was coming to a boil. At this, she looked down at the lad over the arc of her hairy chin with stern eyes. The boy stood his ground with a peevish smile behind hopeful eyes.

Mott thought of a much younger Arthur and relented. She excused herself from Charles's vice and turned toward the courtyard which she had been intentionally averting her eyes from.

It was like being dunked into a barrel of cold water after a fantastic night of high jinks.

In short, it was abominable!

"Where is Murdack?" cried Mott, marching into Bircham's, not letting the crooked sign over the entrance lintel escape her evil eye.

"Don't you worry, Charles," said Mott, "I'm not angry. I just would like to have a word with him."

"Well, perhaps," said Charles wringing his hands together and trying his best to keep up with Mott as she paced down the stone steps, "You should leave the frying pan with me."

"Well, you did say he was in the kitchen!" said Mott, stopping abruptly and pointing back at him with the iron skillet. "I'll leave it with you first if that's how you'd have it."

"No, Mum," said the friar, wondering if anyone would notice the sudden color change of his frock to include a bit of yellow.

"You shouldn't have tried hiding them from me, Charles!"

"We were just putting em in the closest to keep them safe for you until you returned."

"All of them?'

"Well, we were organizing," said Charles nervously, coming up from under his defensive position as Mott's face had softened a bit.

"Hmmph!" declared the woman before hiking up her habit and continuing her march down to the kitchen. "Organization? I've seen tornadoes organize a farm more properly than you've kept my house!"

Charles thought of telling her that she knew how much of a whirlwind little Tommy can be but thought better of it.

Mott paused at the bottom of the steps when she saw Murdack.

He was shin-deep in water and covered in soap suds, currently trying to unplug the grate leading to the moat. His butt crack was peeking at her from a considerably soiled pair of leather breeches that had shrunk to the point he may never have off with them unless someone cut him out of the work clothes.

"Damn it all!" said the man, his face level with the muck that his arm was buried to the shoulder in. A large hairball was turning slowly in the water and making its way toward his northern cheeks as everything whirlpooled toward the clogged exit.

Mott realized that this was a return trip for the hairball when Murdack blew the clod through pursed lips to keep it at bay again.

"Confounded feline!" Murdack said hoisting his bottom again and working his arm at the plug.

Charles had caught up with Mott and stood on the last dry step beside her. He was about to call to Murdack when Mott's eyes did that thing that said, he would suffer a rather uncomfortable knock to the nether regions if he thought twice about it.

"I'd give a week's libations for a single trick of Merddin's right now to clean up all this mess!" he barked before finally retreating as the hairball struck his lips. He stood up and had a dry wretch before turning to the shadow that was blocking the entrance and his working light, then he saw the two of them watching him.

"I'm going to hold you to that," said Mott. Then, hiking up her habit she waded out into the water with Murdack and reached up past his head. Murdack didn't seem to even possess the energy to flinch, which was his natural response to such actions involving Mott[80]. She took a rusty polearm from a nail behind him. The straight blade was twisted in a

---

[80] That told Mott everything she needed to know about how hard the chap had been working in her absence.

way that suggested it wouldn't be the first time it would be misused.

She turned the handle over in her hand, came as close to Murdack's face to hers as possible without kissing him, and jammed the blade down into the muck next to his feet. This time he flinched[81].

When the halberd was pulled back up from the pool it had a giant mass of hair wound round it and the whole room became a swirling maelstrom.

All three of them stood there until the last of the water had found its way to the drain and the slurp of a full stone cavity emptied into the moat with a burp.

Murdack's thick red mustache did a little dance before he said, "Hmmph!"

"Now," said Mott, "I'd hope you were smart enough to be keeping the firewood off the floor." She was shooting daggers from her eyes at the iron mantel that held a goodly bundle of wood at chest level and then down at the considerably larger collection of waterlogged kindling along the floor.

"Of course, we'd do that much," said Murdack bristling. "We keep the extra up high in case of flood."

She walked over and blew the dust from the topmost logs. She reckoned there was about four years' worth accumulated there. Or six months' depending on if you were going by Avalonian time. "Leave it to a man. Nothing rotated! If it were dairy, it'd all be sour! I'd bet two silver

---

[81] This told her there was still life left in the man and in turn blood to squeeze from the turnip.

nickels that if it weren't all just washed away, there'd be termite dust on yonder floor to prove your daftness."

Mott lifted her frying pan and this time both men automatically ducked as she gave a wide gesture indicating the entire kitchen, "Use what dry wood we have and stoke the fires in these stoves. She'll be dry before we know it, I've got other things to tend to, it seems." She slammed the iron skillet onto the nearest wood burning stove. "And I'm hungry!" she added.

"Attend to?" dared Murdack, "You mean my armor?"

"No, you imbecile," said Friar Charles, "she means to wash my frock! I haven't heard a decent argument over its color for far too long."

Mott threw up her hands. "And I bet three gold quarters that every last attendant agrees the frock is gold and white during next communion!" she wailed.

Both men suddenly looked lost in their own skin as they hadn't expected this from the nun.

Murdack spoke first, "Don't you have rules against gambling and such?"

Then the friar, "I think the Isle's done put some devil in her."

"Oh," said Mott, "There ain't no Romans around! Take it or leave it."

The sound of the great wooden door at the top of the stairs came down and all three of them turned to see the Abbott standing there in his robes. In contrast, his robes were the most acceptable version of clean Mott had seen since arriving. This, however, did not impress Mott, she knew the glamour behind the magic and was more impressed by the half-dozen or so altar boys that had likely become rather adept with a washboard in her absence than with the sword and shield.

"I'll take double or nothing!" said the Abbott. "What a sight for sore eyes."

Mott shifted her weight from one saddle bag to the other. She put a hand on her hip and rolled her tongue across her upper teeth to accentuate her beauty mark. The Abbott's expression remained as if carved from stone. His face drawn into a pout; his eyeballs set in their lowest declinations like eggs in a basket.

Mott sashayed up the steps toward him, flipping her veil down over her face so that she could hide her own poker face. He made no reaction when she raised a finger. The Abbott had either become a master of the bluff in her absence, or he was in fact telling the truth.

"We'll see," said Murdack sidling over toward Charles, "Puck always says Black and Blue, and I've always said he's just guessing."

Slowly, Mott dropped her finger back to her side and studied the walnut-colored eyes staring back at her. Then she turned her head to the side and pointed to her veiled cheek.

The Abbott wrapped his arms around Mott, doing his best to grip the opposing fingers by the tips, but failed for having so short of limbs, then decided it was probably best as he was thinking of lifting the lady in his arms, which would have ended badly for them both, so he gave up the endeavor and settled for lifting her veil and turning her face and planting a smooch right on the smacker.

Friar Charles and Brother Murdack both waited in astonishment as the two red-faced participants outlasted the long sucking noise which accompanied the kiss, only for the Abbott to forcibly remove his face from Mott's at the great protest of each of their facial hair which tried futilely and awkwardly to belay the separation.

"Well," said Mott, smacking her lips, and smoothing her habit in a way that said the lusty fires of angst had been dutifully quaffed. "I am happy… to be home."

As Mott emerged from the cellars and came into the light of the courtyard with the Abbott by her side, some of the younger lads were poking their heads up from behind the feeding troughs among the pigs to sneak a look. "No more bastard sons from the druids I take it?"

"No."

"No daughters of Avalon?"

"No."

Mott's habit was swishing this way and that as she swung it side to side with both hands as she walked. A habit that she picked up on Avalon while wearing a dress. A habit that she would well be known for in the future, as there was never a more powerful figure than Mott in the habit of swishing her habit side to side in full march! "Shame, that," said she. "Now, take me to the hussy."

Hazeus gets a bad feeling

Hazeus was getting a bad feeling about the congregation approaching Bircham's monastery. Though Mott was there to clean up the mess that had ensued during her absence, he wasn't sure it was going to be enough to stand against the mess that was beginning to take shape across the totality of the video disc series he'd been watching.

He wasn't ready for blood. In fact, Hazeus didn't think he would ever be ready for blood. What good god would ever be ready for blood?

He was asking himself this question and remembering feeling so trapped over there on the globe when his adoptive mother had been urging him to just have another drink and relax. He wanted to, no, he needed to fit in over there. But something had been telling him to tear off the band aid, and that what was happening was wrong. It looked fun, but it was wrong. He thought about one of his father's sayings, 'Just because everyone in the world believes something to be true, doesn't mean that it necessarily is.'

With the thought, a great white light suddenly came across the kitchen blinds and filled the living room. Bathing Hazeus, the magiscope, and everything inside in a dipole and then unipole color of white. The beam of light refocused, moved around the room at a much more concentrated point then retracted from inside of the house back out of the window, where Hazeus chased it like a cat after a laser pointer.

He ran over to the window and split the blinds with his fingers and watched as the light shrunk like a tractor beam into a saucer shaped disc in the sky. Then there was a flash of light and a fissure opened out in the direction of the white hole before the craft blinked out of existence among the sound of a sonic boom.

As there was no way his parents didn't hear or see that huge phenomenon, Hazeus sat there in silence, expecting his father to burst from the bedroom and accuse him of setting off a bomb[82], but nothing stirred. Nothing made a noise. Nothing except the little ticking and popping of the needle bouncing along the final disc of the magiscope video disc player in the other room.

The strange Morse-like code beckoned him back toward the screen with great reluctance.

---

[82] Much like when he was little and his dad brought him home an alchemists set.

Chapter Twenty-Seven: The Knights of Arthur

King Arthur was leaning on his gauntleted knuckles at the round table with a letter bearing the seal of Romulus Augustulus spread open before him. The knights looked on.

"So, they think we owe them taxes," said the King.

"Taxes?" asked Gwain.

"That's ridiculous," said Kay, "for what?"

"What else?" said Arthur.

Lancelot tapped his finger on the great wooden table. "What do men constantly lay claim to but have no right to own?"

Arthur smiled thoughtfully through a filled-out beard, "Well said, Lancelot. Land is something that was made by God and is owned by God. It should be free to all men."

"Then tell him that!" said Gwain.

"He refuses a personal audience," said Arthur. "Won't stand for reason. One might assume he is already disillusioned as to where the true throne of God lies. For, it is under no man's ass but rather in his heart."

The room thundered as each knight rapped their knuckles on the table in salute to the statement. Once the commotion softened King Arthur asked, "What's the one thing the Romans want more than anything else?"

"Money?" asked Kay.

"No, well, we all want money, but for what?"

"Jewels!" shouted Lancelot.

"Food!" yelled Borus.

"Women!" yelled Kay, taking second liberties.

"Power," said a cupbearer from the corner of the room.

Arthur shook a finger at that. "Close, but not quite."

"Wine?" ventured Gwain.

"Now, you're talking!" said Arthur. "I wager that inebriation is what stands in the place of reason to the blood thirsty." He looked to each of his brothers and then said, "I once asked myself how thin the veil could get before dying became permanent, I think the Romans need such a lesson. Gather all the mistletoe that has white berries that you can find," said the king. "We're going to give them exactly what they want."

Mott turns the Romans Away

"She's been in there for twenty minutes," said Charles to the Abbott.

"She knows what she's doing," said the Abbott sitting heavily down on the steps outside. "You wouldn't think word would have spread so fast," he said, motioning toward the crowd that was gathering under the crooked entrance sign.

Friar Charles stood up and looked out beyond the wall and over the heads of the crowd, "I don't think they're waiting to see what Mott does with the cougar, Abbott."

There was stirring in the crowd and then a fanfare that crescendoed and was cut short. Out beyond the dusty garb of the monastery knowns, was a delegation approaching, all dressed in rich red velvet.

Friar Charles and the Abbott were standing just inside Bircham's entry arch where twelve Roman soldiers were at parade rest. A thirteenth was front and center, holding out an unfurled proclamation.

Murdack was riding up on horseback trying to look threatening and was doing a rather good job of it as his old armor was twice the size of any one set of the Roman's, however his was held together by failing twine and his visor clapped with every pace of his horse's gallop. When he steadied his mount, just inside the courtyard, and turned his helm round the right way he was a noted force to be reckoned with.

"By decree of the Roman Catholic Vestige and the Pope and Romulus Augustulus, all hedonistic and Celtic activity is hereby disbanded in places of worship," began Sir Ector, captain of the small Roman company.

"Nonsense," piped up Murdack. "How then can we ever enjoy communion?"

The announcement came to a brief pause. Sir Ector lowered the decree and looked at the rabble with a brow furled beneath a raised silver visor. "What," asked Ector, pointing to the makeshift altar in the courtyard, "is that?"

The rabble all turned to look.

"Well, that's our temporary pulpit, that is," said friar Charles quite unsure what the offense was.

"You're worshipping the lord under the light of the Sun? Having no headwear? While the church stands empty and unused?"

The rabble looked confused.

"Well, it's not totally empty," said friar Charles. "The two ladies are in there working out their differences." At this, a commotion came from within the church sounding much like two cats in heat. This was followed by a hiss, the clatter of some copper artifacts, and then a loud meow.

The rabble collectively cringed, and the company of Romans went from parade rest to ready positions, spears fixed into the small bites that were missing from each of their shields.

Sir Ector placed a hand on his broad sword and had taken one step back toward his company. "Now," said Ector in a wavering voice. "I know," voice wavering even more, "you harbor that druid Merddin within this convent at times, and if ye be holding out for him, it will be the Christ's fate for the lot of you!"

Murdack couldn't believe that Ector bellied the courage to finish that sentence, as it had been quite some time since testosterone were allowed to run rampant at St Materiana's. Perhaps things we're changing?

At that moment, the cathedral doors flew open. A plume of yellow air came from within. Only a lady of Mott's standing could ever have withstood the smell of Ammonia that burst forth. She descended the steps alone.

In her hand was the scarf which usually comprised the majority of her hat and veil, but now was hanging loosely from her fist and seemed to be cradling something in its folds.

Mott then did the last thing that any man or unit of men would want Mott to do. She performed her habit in her habit. That closed half the distance to where Ector stood beneath the sign of St Bircham's.

"Now, madam!" said Ector at an unsteady timbre.

"Don't you, now madam me, you gluttonous, hedonistic, and intolerant bully! I've said it before the light of God and I've said it before the dark of day. Not priest, nor friar, nor boy become Sire, not even the Pope himself will ever hold their title over my head!"

"I don't know what you're planning on doing with that sling, mada—I mean, ma'am," stammered Ector.

Murdack backed his horse away and the entire rabble seemed to sigh and fade back into the courtyard, a bit away from the Romans who were apparently in mortal danger, though no one of them knew exactly from what[83].

Then Mott whirled her scarf above her head and just before she released her index finger from the fabric said, "You don't come here after wizzard, priest, nor tutor, unless you are looking to learn a lesson in intolerance!"

The bolt flew. Ector ducked from sheer reflex though he was in no real danger of being injured. Then looked back up again at Mott who was standing there smiling in a way that made him think twice before declaring any certain victory.

Above his head the round shot connected with the sign over Bircham's, and the last remaining nail gave up its purchase. A plume of green leaf sprayed out over the company and the sign came tumbling down on to Ector and the first rank. Who then went down smack into the dirt.

The rabble all clapped and started cheering much to Murdack's dismay. Murdack, being the only one in actual armor and on horseback, seemed also to be the only one really worried about retaliation from the company of Roman soldiers. Who could blame him?

Behind his visor, Murdack broke out in a cold sweat. Despite his better judgement he reached down and drew his sword. But the scabbard came with it. Then trying to shake off the scabbard from the sword the horse took his motion to begin a charge and reared to go. Back he pitched in the

---

[83] What it was was six feet of religious habit with a skin tag strategically placed on her chin.

saddle and inadvertently pulling on the reigns, made his horse stand up on its hind legs. At this the children cheered.

The Romans were unimpressed and were tossing the old driftwood from off their person in an attempt to gain their feet, now madder than ever. When then, from the chapel, there came a rush of orange and tan fur. It was fore shadowed by platter-sized paws. The large cat stopped in the courtyard and glowered at the company brandishing all of that red and silver.

Then it was all out in the open and Ector understood quite well what was going to happen. His company was a china shop, and there stood the bull. Well, he actually realized that his company was about to have a crash course in long distance defensive running.

With a flash, the men turned tail and clamored down the hill from the monastery, rolling one over another, the frenzied feline batting the tin men around like balls of string.

And Murdack trying to figure out why everything was suddenly so dark.

Of course, this was remedied when the Abbott chided his horse and helped the man down from the saddle, righting his helm.

"How on Earth did you do that?" cried Friar Charles.

Mott smiled. "Catnip."

Chapter Twenty-Eight: It's Lancelot again, only now, Arthur awakens to Treachery

"Sorry, Sire," I said, rousing the King. "It's your sister, Sir. She's left upon horseback. Gwain and Borus pursue her."

"What's the problem man? She's no prisoner here."

I confess that my eyes registered serious unease. "It's your scabbard, Lord. She has stripped it of its sleeve." I gave him a chance to consider. When he stirred from bed, I meant to lessen the blow of it all, "I can only think she might—"

"Enough, Lance!" said Arthur pulling on his pauldrons. "Ready my horse."

"You can take Merddin's," said I. "Archimedes stands ready outside to outpace any globe-born steed. But Arthur," I felt that Death himself were watching. "There's more."

"Well, out with it, brother!" said Arthur donning his cape, "she will be halfway to Rome."

"She won't have to go that far, Sire. There's word the Tor stone at Glastonbury Abbey has been pulled down by Ector and his men in preparation of Roman governance. All the druidic artifacts have been removed from the grounds."

"The stone?" asked Arthur as if physically struck. "It was erected in the mother's name, for God's sake!"

"The pope had Ector publicly resurrect it in the name of Hazeus at the foot of the hill."

"The Pope is in Glastonbury?"

"Nay," said I, "he's on his way back. Likely to Rome seeking the protection of Romulus. Ector met with resistance at Tintagel and now has gathered what forces remain and is forming along the shores of Anglesey."

"Why? It's nothing but old men and young boys in training out there."

"In the words belayed, 'To cut off the head of the serpent where it nests,'" I said, and then helped Arthur with his sword and sickle. "Shall I take a force to defend?"

Arthur lifted the circlet of gold from his nightstand and placed it gingerly on his brow, "No. By my life, this will remain a bloodless war. Men have a right to go to their graves preaching their own truths." He reached out and took my hand and shook it. "This is no country for old men. The Arch Druids knew that. Let us hope that what little we have done to prepare will give them time to work their magic."

"Then I shall come with you."

"Stay, Lance," said he. "Watch over Genny. Mark it. Much will change this day. Yet we can hope that what must be changed be limited to perspective."

I knew precisely where Guinevere was, Glastonbury, but not because she was ashamed of the affair between us as legend often concurs. Though I will admit, in that moment, I worried Arthur was indeed the more worshipful man. I could see it. I felt that I would go to Glastonbury, and she would turn from me to repentance if she could not have Arhtur. Alas, that is not what happened.

She was touring the new catholic churches after being rededicated to Hazeus and purged of the heathen offerings. We both knew this had been coming and often spoke of it in secret. It had been terrible not to tell Arthur what was befalling the holy sites, but to me it was negligible and to Genny it was a victory to her faith.

I could only watch as Arthur gathered the ingredients from an herb box at the foot of his bed. A pouch of palm resin, and some iron shavings. I remembered enough at this point to know what he was about. He glanced back at me on the way out the door, downed the phial of mistletoe draught and was gone.

It was here our paths would finally divert, he in the favor of the spirit, and I of the flesh. In layman's terms, he was on his way to Rootworld when he brushed past me, and I was destined for the Globe.

Both were one at this point, if you haven't been following along. Kind of like a seed matures and unfolds, as the roots reach down into the soil and the sprout reaches up toward the light. The globe was breaking the surface of the universal ground, and the veil of reality which connected the two was becoming more fragile with every moment. It gets that way when gods and men are making decisions. Right up until the very end, there is a lot of grey area.

Merddin and I both could tell that somewhere there was a god who was growing a conscience and a big head to go right along with it. Things like that happen every time we are apart for too long.

Because of this strange dividing of realities that was about to occur, things were experienced quite differently depending on each person's perspective and which particular world they were going to end up in.

Those who were bound for the Globe, where gluttony would prevail and set them back a few million years spiritually and technologically, would see a classic form of warfare and conquering by the Roman Catholic Church. There would be bloodshed and the poor druids who decided to tough it out on that side of reality would have to go into hiding as the culdees[84].

Despite popular belief, the hardest part of surviving the next two millennia until the continental convergence and re-discovery of magic would be staying sober, as it would be a very long road teaching a world of drunks just exactly how water was once turned into wine. They were going to have to understand things like science, and physics first, before they could ever get a grasp on metaphysics or magic again. Yes, the culdees were going to be the true heroes of the Globe when it came right down to it, so don't feel bad for them, they knew what they were signing up for. That is, *Merddin and I* knew exactly what we were signing up for. Only, it's taken this long to remember again. Fancy that!

Gwen was worth it, plus she needed someone after Arthur's disappearance. Of course, she was part of the crowd who believed that Hazeus would be returning one day and all that stuff. Constantly and eventually, in later

---

[84] A sect of Arch Druids who desguised themselves as Arch Bishops and integrated with the Catholic rules and laws to survive while secretly passing on their knowledge

life, after she began drinking more, she would remind me how we would see Arthur again in heaven after we died.

I put up with that into our seventies. Gwen was a good person; it was just that the church became her voice and her intolerance of other beliefs blinded her from ever seeing truth. You have to let a girl down easy, ya know? As a druid, and a friend to Arthur, I am not one to pass judgement on anyone's faith. I believe she did return to Arthur in another universe all her own. And one day she will return to me, and I can have my Alicorn back proper again!

It all goes with the times, as a lot of weird happenings were taking place across the globe while Arthur gave chase to Morgan and considered the casting of the third and final spell of making.

Fuzzick had all of a sudden gone on a dry spell and gotten a shave and a haircut. Firedrakes were losing their wings and becoming komodo dragons. Water nymphs seemed undecided if they should turn into fish or mammal and that led to sightings of mermaids before they finally settled on becoming seahorses. The platypus and dodo bird suddenly appeared.

The veil was wavering in the winds of change while Hazeus's father lay in bed with his wife, playing with a fidget toy. It was an orb with a triangle on top. Father time would twist the triangle and it would descend into the orb leaving only a tiny point sticking out from the top of the sphere. He would twist the orb the other way round and the pyramid would pop back up again on top of the ball.

"Yep, I remember my first world," said Father time, reminiscing. He twisted the fidget toy again into itself.

Mother Earth fingered the few little strands of hair on his chest as they lay. She used to be able to make him go roebuck just by doing so. "Oh, go on. You do not!" she said.

The fidget toy popped its little pyramid hat back out again on top. "I do!" He scratched his temple absently. The smoke in the room still hadn't been totally diffused by the filter queen. Then, Bobby looked at Boof and saw her looking at him. "Oh, alright," he said, "well, that's *your* job inn't it? I live it, and you remember it?"

"We make a good team."

Bobby twisted the toy back and forth a couple times. She played with his chest hair some more.

"Ya know," she said, catching his attention again, "some women around the office say their relationships are more like them small gods."

"Yeah, how's that?" asked Bobby, the air finally clearing and the filter queen's electric whir dying away.

"The husband does the dismembering of things and the wife does the remembering…"

The top of the fidget spinner snapped off in Bobby's hand and he held up the two pieces, which they both looked at quizzically. "Would you look at that," said Father Time.

Mother Earth stopped playing with his chest hair and took the two halves of the fidget toy in each hand. "Well, look at that. I guess they don't make things like they used to," she said, finally getting a rise out of him, and she tossed the two halves on the bedside table and said, "I'll fix it later."

Chapter Twenty-Nine: Changing Worlds

Arthur was going to catch his sister. Besides being on Archimedes, Merddin's magic horse, the landscape was literally changing.

In the days before Arthur, all the continents had been connected as one huge mass known popularly today as Pangea. But when the veil was rent asunder, simultaneously when Father Time broke his fidget toy, Hazeus finally realized he was in control, and when Arthur decided he knew where he belonged, that all changed.

The event, on the globe side of things, came to be known as the casting down of the tower of babel. On the Rootworld side of things it was the raising of the tower of Nimrod, or at least that's what Hazeus's father told him later in life when they finally got together for that drinking event he'd felt so bad about ruining early on.

It took a lot less time to travel from Tintagel to Anglesey when the waters were all gathered together in one place. And that's direct from the Tome of Ages. Nowadays, there's St George's channel there mucking things up. So much for a few hours by horseback.

Essentially, what happened was, the great pyramid which once stood high above God's great garden of Eden was twisted down into the center of the Globe, forcing the one great land mass to divide into the continents known today. This of course had the adverse effect of people speaking different dialects. Albeit mostly because they were brewing different types of fire waters at varying proofs. In short, some countries would be slower learners than others based on their brand of whiskey.

And if you've got an ear for languages, or a babel fish on hand, you've probably already figured out that the mechanism we use to interpret language is just based on speed and cadence. Everyone is actually speaking the same language, it's just that people are inebriated at different saturations, so logically some speak really slow, and some speak way too fast. Dialectically, well, let's just say, as long as body language doesn't change too much. We shouldn't have a problem keeping up now that magic is about to show up again.

The currently known Giza is just the tip of the once great pyramid of the Globe, everyone's getting along through handheld devices translating English into proper English and merrily finding out that drugs are bad. Drinking is bad. And that Hazeus is not coming back but rather waiting on everyone else to sober up and get with the program.

Hazeus is currently sitting comfortably watching as King Arthur races up a hill on horseback armed with the third spell of making. Arthur is feeling a lot like I did chasing Lady. Serves him right for stabbing me!

The Great Chase

The landscape is shifting because Father time is messing with his fidget toy. So as Arthur thunders after Morgan on Archimedes the land is stretching out like chewing gum before him. Every time he spurs her on, again the land seems to grow. He is oblivious to the Gods. He is oblivious to the one God. He is in a moment where he is all alone with the power of his thoughts. Every suggestion wrinkles time. A concentrated thought might just slice reality to pieces. He is worried only about catching his sister and asking her why. But the landscape shifts again and he is on top of a mountain, just then jutted from a stable sea that his horse had run atop with no fear.

He stops.

He climbs from Archimedes and casts his personal set of twelve stones into a circle on the plateau. He walks in a circle spreading the iron shavings and chanting, "Cum saxum saxorum!"

Down he throws the palm resin, and he raises his sickle so that the light hits it through the shifting clouds he has just willed to split perfectly. A white ray strikes the ruby of mars in the blade and a red ray finds the mound of dragon's blood resin where it begins to boil and spark, then smoke.

"In dersum montum apperundum!"

He uses the sickle and carves the semblance of the dragon's eye into the sandstone that is shifting colors at his feet.

"Morgaine," he calls to the whispering time, then he sees her coming down from horseback, just up a small white hill. She walks toward him with her arms out as he is drawing Excalibur.

"Give me the sword, Arthur," she says.

Archimedes sidesteps unsteadily when she nears, but Arthur hardly notices. She enters his protective circle wearing Lugh's sleeve on her left arm. She puts her hands around Arthur's own grip, and he relents, ever faithful in mankind. She takes Excalibur and Arthur kneels before her. She raises the sword by the pommel. A cross member in each hand with the blade pointed down, the whole thing above the downcast head of her brother. The wind becomes nothing but colors. Pastels that darken into a bruise.

Arthur begins to wash her feet with a bowl that has just appeared from the ether. He looks up at her and smiles. She still has the beady little eyes of the raven, and he says, "I have been the sword in the stone."

Then she brings the blade down through Arthur's body. Brings it down through his chest and through his heart. And leans upon it heavily with a satisfying yet terrifying scream, forcing the blade down through him. And down into the earth… and also deep into the body of the dragon.

Arthur's whisper is overcome by her ecstasy, and she never hears him say, "Vermatrix."

Merddin returns

"Where were you Merddin?"

Arthur's head lay in the blue fabric of Merddin's robes, inwoven with the many occult symbols he remembers from his youth. He was staring up at the peaceful face of his mentor just like when he was a kid and would listen to him read in the afternoons. But this time, though still steely blue, they both had tired old eyes.

"I was always there, Bear cub."

"But love has lost. Violence and greed is having its way with things. I thought I was strong enough. I tried to summon the dragon."

Merddin smiled but said nothing. He just stared down at the tired and dying king, the bright light of the sun coming from over his shoulder. They may have been under a shifting forest canopy or still on top of a mountain. The colors were all just glare over shrouds, mostly from the dream state, but also from real tears.

Arthur thought he saw a glint form in Merddin's eye, but it disappeared when the old man smiled, "There is no try." Arthur briefly joined in a chuckle until a pain shot through his chest. "Try and relax," said the Wizzard laying a hand upon where the wound should be.

The pain subsided and Arhtur said, "I should have cast the final spell of making and closed the rift forever, men and women have become cold and gluttonous. They have no respect for life, not even their own."

Merddin's cheeks softened at hearing Arthur speak this way. Never had he heard such negativity cross the lips of the jovial and faithful boy king of pure heart. He sighed and whispered a few words in an ancient dialect then he said, "Perhaps you *should* cast it, but not because man is evil."

Arthur was shaken by that; he had always been warned against doing such a thing as even Merddin himself dared not experiment with such an unknown power. "But mankind would be forever lost!" The king suddenly rasped, revealing his greatest fear in one go.

"Even with your own sword driven through your heart by your own sister it still fails to be divided." The old druid shook his head in disbelief. "Conscience is the eye of God in the heart of man, my son. Never stop following it."

Merddin could see that old look in Arthur's eyes that pleaded for a straight answer. "Being lost," said Merddin to his student, "and losing, are far different things. For one is but a matter of time, and may be remedied in such, while the other is a truth. Wasn't it successes that brought your original ruby, and its true replacement? Deceit is what brought the false one, and that was only through fear of discipline. Well, I say you've brought your own lesson to a head."

Arthur stirred. "You knew?"

"Boys will be curious and learn at their own pace. What is important to remember at this point is that Love is the truth, as long as you carry it with you. Your sister loves you, it is not her that you should be calling the dragon to. I would wager it has something to do with my old counterpart, Mim."

"Mim?"

"Yes, and now you know the name, Boy. And have already cast the ingredients…"

The pain came soaring back through Arthur's chest. "Wait!" he cried grabbing at Merddin's sleeve. "Will I see you again?"

Then, as time started again, he lost Merddin in a smile, "Sooner than you think, Bear cub. And as I am moving backward, you may be the one doing the teaching!"

Then he was back, and realized the arms he was in were his sister's, and she was shedding tears.

Chapter Thirty:
All Good Stories End with Dragons

Sylvia had saved room for the main course.

Taliesin hadn't even dropped his wand before she heard her ancient name come booming through the waterfall.

"Well, that was fast," said Taliesin.

Sylvia, huffed. Then she darted back her neck like she were an arrow fixed and being pulled back on a well-strung yew bow. "I suppose he will have to do," she said. "Would you mind?"

"What?" said Tal. "Really, you could use the bath." She eyed the clothes pin still firmly on his nose and rolled her eye. "Oh, okay," said Tal, "I know how you hate cold showers." And he circled his wand overhead.

She shot forward like a train on living pistons which were her four clawed and armored limbs. The giant body and then tail following her thin but powerful neck like any perfect machine. Out she went under the rainbow coming from the refracted light of the falls which had been magically lifted like the dress of a giant ballerina. And then up and up straight along the edges of mound Meritites and toward the great white hole above Rootworld.

Vermatrix Eats the Weevil

There was a ripple in the colored wind which had gone dark as pitch.

Morgan's eyes tried dilating to let in more light but the raven's eyes had gone and her own weren't yet back up to the task. Her brother's head was cradled in her lap, Excalibur's handle protruding from his chest while he lay supine across the triscale design of the great dragon's eye in the sandstone. His blood was filling the etchings he had just earlier made himself.

"Arthur?" says Morgaine, "My Love. My sweet baby brother! What have I done?"

Arthur reaches up and grips her elbow. It is decorated with the golden pipes of Lugh. Morgan is crying, but she follows his hand and places her hand upon his, helping his fingers to get hold of the fabric there and begin peeling it from her forearm. Then she looks into those true-blue eyes, his golden beard only slightly spoiled by the faintest drop of blood at the corner of his mouth.

"Do you forgive me, brother?" she asks, beginning to slip the sheath onto his arm.

Arthur knows she was bewitched and only shakes his head uncertainly, but her eyes close gently and her head also shakes. The tear strikes Arthur's cheek and rolls down and off into his hair with his own. She places his hand on her round belly.

He gasps. The pain through his heart a searing hot kettle, screaming like Merddin's old teapot used to do. He strikes it with an imaginary wooden spoon and says in in his mind, "Now you just stop that!"

Then he opens his eyes and says to her, "It was my fault. It was me. It wasn't a dream."

She says, "I will name him Mordred."

The tears come between them, and the winds shift. Then the pain comes again. The teapot screams and just as he is about to hit it with the spoon again, he sees Merddin's face. So does Morgan. They both see him enchanting Uther, and Gorlois dying, they remember everything together. And Merddin says to them both, "It… was… Mim."

Then Arthur screams as the last rivulet of blood in the dragon's eye design is impregnated and Lugh's sleeve is slid fully into place, "MIM!"

Mim's Fucked

Mim stood watching in her cauldron, waiting for the O of victory to form as a scream on Morgan's lips. But the clouds above her and Arthur suddenly lit up and from far up there was a sound like a thousand hunting dogs and then a great shadow drifted above the swirling pale miasma in the sky. But then it paled and waned away.

What were they doing, exactly?

Things in the dark cathedral, now having been moved by a clumsy large god to a rather remote section of the world, were silent. The rumbling had stopped and Morgan's sobbing from the cauldron seemed to be dialing away like the volume was being dropped on an old tube tv. One large bubble ballooned and then popped, sending muck splashing across the image she was now only lightly paying attention to.

Mim's attention was now on the ceiling.

Two large chunks of marble came thundering down from above her as Sylvia's great talons pierced the moldy and vein-covered roof. In a moment, it was shorn away and the serenity that was before was obliterated when the whipping wind and rains filled the space around her.

Mim's cloaks, now soaked with the chaos, flapped furiously like the tails of euglena, and her toothless mouth was agape when the giant dragon's jaws entered the perverted house of God and clasped over her.

Mim had no chance to transform, because her first tactic in battles with other magical beings had always been to go dragon first. And that just so happened to be already taken.

Chapter Thirty-One: Ector Takes Druid Isle

Although Gwen and I had set off to experience the more real side of things, and Arthur was in the midst of the change itself, the druids bound for Rootworld experienced a more G-rated version of events.

What can I say, Hazeus's Mom and Dad don't like blood either. So, in the magiscope, Hazeus watched as Arthur's plans were coming to fruition.

Bran's well was located in the most sacred of nemetons on Anglesey. It was widely believed that the only way of finding it was through lifting the veil. But that was a misconception. Like a game of telephone, the rumor had passed from druid to bard to merchant and eventually to the owner of the inn where Ector and his band held up the night before they mounted their offensive[85] on Druid's Isle.

Quite frankly, the Romans, from the Emperor to the Pope, were discovering that evil deeds were best accomplished in a state of self-deniability. This evening, the imbibing had been considerable since the armed Romans were already dreading their charge to rid the fairy isle of magic by any means.

Ector had been raised well. He knew better than to fight with girls. The fact that their upcoming opponents were all to be male offered him no consolation since all of them were apt to be wearing dresses. It was a shameful errand, and he would need a cloudy head to carry it through. They all would.

---

[85] The druids were bound to take offense at the demand to bow down to Catholic dogma at the edge of a sword

Regardless, the rumor had bounced between enough ears that hearsay had become local truth. Along with that rumor was also delivered the local standard of protocols when it came to feeding and lodging roman soldiers. They were to be served from the specially prepared casks and barrels of Arthur's Camelot.

The Arch Druids of the Isle of Man, in whose hands were held the last hope of the Anglo-Saxon Celtic rights to free expression, believed no such rumors about Bran's well and that wasn't due to their higher education. It was simply because they were following the map.

During the morning offensive, the Armored Romans were having quite a time keeping up with the old men in bathrobes as they wound way through the groves in pursuit. After the druids had set fire to their wooden flats at the shoreline, they had abandoned all charms and incantations.

The fires had really been the coup de gras, as before they actually set anything to flame, they were relying on literal smoke and mirrors, which worked well on soldiers dosed with mistletoe wine and beer.

Focusing now on their final act, the druids headed inland. What they weren't aware of is that their own natural defense was working better than anything they had tried thus far. When it came to the path toward the nemeton of Bran the blessed, smelling like a gnarled old tree, had its advantages.

No sooner than a soldier would catch a glimpse of one of the druids just ahead in the mist, a tendril would loop out from the trees and entangle the unfortunate Roman. In a flash, the lively fauna would strip the armor from the poor gentleman and toss it away looking like it had been crushed under hoof and hammer. As the process continued, the way became more frequented with Romans hanging this way and that from the lower branches of the oaks in nothing but their sometimes-soiled undergarments.

"They went that way," pointed one of the stunned men.

The horseman turned his head nearly upside down to look the foot soldier in the eye.

"Who went that way?" he asked.

"Them's whoever's stripped me to me knickers." the soldier said, letting his arm drop.

"Are you hurt?" asked Ector.

"I don't think so. Lucky for me it's hung me by the feet and not my neck."

"Then, for God's sake, come down out of that tree!"

"Yes, Sir. Right away, Sir! Oh, but Sir..."

The captain lifted his brows to the inverted soldier.

"Wouldya mind cuttin' me feet loose. Whomsoever got the drop on us seemed to have lifted me dagger as well."

You heard a sword being drawn from a scabbard. The sound of metal briefly chopping at wood, and then a thwump as the large man struck the soft grass.

The next random underdressed soldier pointed another direction, his upper body only visible from one side of the crook of a mighty beech. The dampened white of his undershirt flaunted a large red heart that read, *I Love My Mommy*. "I'm certain they were off in that direction, Captain."

"Imbeciles," said Sir Ector, before heeling his horse the way the finger was pointing.

Six more soldiers and six more directions and he felt no, he knew, he was going in circles.

Speaking of circles, the twenty Arch Druids had formed a perfect one around the well of Bran the blessed and were beginning to chant in a way that made the crows nervous.

"I thought the head was buried under the tower of London," said one druid to another while they were joining hands.

"That's a misconception," said he in answer. "What really happened was Bran ordered his head be thrown into the well here, on the Isle of man, so that he returned to the living waters from whence he believed all things sprung."

"Uh Ummm!" Across the circle, a druid wearing white and gold robes cleared his throat and the chanting went silent. The two druids who were conversing followed suit. "We call today on Bran the Blessed. Rise from the waters of Annwyn and give us council!"

The crows began cawing in unison. The trees came alive with black feathers as more birds came to investigate.

"Great voice that calls us in the wind of dawn! Strange voice that calms us in the heat of noon!" cried the druid. "Heard in the sunset, felt in the moonrise, and the stirring of the wakeful night! Speak now in blessing!"

Then all the druids began humming the four sacred utterances. The sound started as a reverberating 'Ah'. It seemed to vibrate inside the circle of druids. Then the sound changed to an 'O' and the birds spread their wings like a hundred idols of some forgotten religion. After thirty seconds all the priests closed their mouths and a heart shaking vibration in the sound of 'Mmm' grabbed hold of the glade. The black birds closed their wings and went silent as the roof over the little ancient well started shedding its shingles among the shaking reverberance.

Just at that moment Ector had been following the sound of cawing birds, as it seemed to be more reliable than any direction he had received from his men. He found himself crawling up a steep incline to peer from some shrubbery down into the glade where the druids were gathered.

Down in the clearing he could see the ancient well losing its shingles amid the strange vibrating tone of the bards. He lay there and watched them a moment, feeling the vibration at the pit of his throat. He experimentally made the same sound and found he felt a strange connection with the party until the sound changed. They had opened their mouths and now made a high pitched 'Eeee' sound that pierced the forest like a clear bell. It sent Ector's ears ringing so he instinctively put his fingers in them to shut it out.

He had squinted his eyes shut and when they opened again, he saw something that made him question everything he knew.

The crows had lit on the top of the well in a huge cluster. Supporting one another so that they made the shape of a giant face. Every druid fell to their knees save the one trimmed in gold who only bowed his head with his arms outstretched above. In the druid's hand was a roll of parchment.

The giant face of birds and their cackling had replaced the piercing chant. Now the black mass settled into a clear semblance and the cawing and cackling quieted to the whisper of feathers rubbing on one another to keep the birds in order. Then the mouth opened, and Ector could see right through the hole.

"Who calls from across the seas of Annwyn and to the isle of the holy head?" said the face, the voice made up of the many different clicks, caws, and cackles of each bird in harmony.

"Great Bran!" said the standing druid, still not yet daring to look upon the face. "It is your loyal followers, the druids of Yns Mon. We come to you in a desperate attempt to understand what is expected of us during this violent season of change."

"Change is what God is," said the face. "Rise brothers of the order and look upon my visage. Remember it well for it will be the last time I grace your race in Rootworld and it will be the last bit of magic that the globe will witness for more than two millennium."

Ector watched as the druids rose and stood in awe of Bran's countenance. But something happened then that made Ector start sweating all over again beneath his armor. The face turned and looked directly at him.

"You," said Bran, and a black bird broke from the image and flew directly over and lit above the bush he was hiding behind. Ector turned away and put his back to the bush, trying to ignore it but the bird above him started squawking. "Roman!" Bran demanded. "Join this delegation, for you too will be charged with a choice this day."

He could hear the druids questioning each other, "Roman? There is a soldier in the glen?"

Ector stood up and revealed himself now taking in the full sight of the magic happening, unable to deny what he was witnessing.

"Yes," said Bran, "approach and join the circle."

Ector pushed through the brambles and walked slowly into the nemeton. Despite his fears, the peaceful old men did not strip him, bind him, and offer him up as sacrifice, which is exactly what the Pope would have them all believe. Instead, they made room for him opposite the golden priest and joined hands with him like brothers.

"Good," said Bran. "Things are as they should be now that we are twenty-one."

The crow which had pestered Ector now flew from its roost and swooped over the outstretched hands of the golden priest, plucking the roll of parchment from his grip and diving down the well beneath the face.

The druids all gasped.

"Hear me well," said the head. "Just as my head was severed for good purpose, the head of the universe is about to suffer the same fate. It is unavoidable for the spiritual realm and the physical realm have much learning to do. Just as we separate the female and males of the order for their education so too must we separate these two halves of the greater whole."

All the men were looking at one another, gauging if their neighbor understood.

"Three of you must volunteer to stay behind with the Roman."

Three hands went up. That of the golden priest, and two others who flanked Ector.

"Good," said the head. "Your job will not be pleasant. You will be stripped of your magic and left with only your greatest gift. Tolerance. The most important value the druid order has imbued your brotherhood with over time immemorial. The rest of you will remain on Rootworld. Teachers who will one day have to introduce the ideas of science and logic to the youths. This too will be no easy task." The head became very still and the crow from the well shot back up from the depths and lit on the stone edge. Under its foot was the parchment, transformed now into a pamphlet of written symbology and words. "Roman," boomed the head. "Your role is pivotal. As an outsider of the order but a witness to our truths, you alone can safely deliver our knowledge to the Cambridge brotherhood of scribes. They will keep it safe until the time comes for its worldwide publication. Come and retrieve the text."

Ector stepped forward and took the compact manuscript then returned to the circumference of the circle with it.

"You four men, bound for the Globe, will be charged with carrying our druidic truths to those of the church who will listen. You must practice patience through generations, as this is no fast process. Intolerance is something that cannot be forced out on the opposite side of the veil. You cannot stop a drowning by throwing on more water. Intolerance can only be weeded out through education. Persevere druids. Start with your new brother."

The face mutated into an abstract shadow and then it lifted higher into the air above the well and reformed.

"And now, for the rite." said Bran. "The most sacred rite of Exile."

All the druids took a step back and gasped.

"It is the only way," said Bran, "to rend the veil asunder. Prepare yourselves."

The druids broke the circle and came to Ector shaking his hand and embracing him. The three druids who volunteered removed their magnificent robes, rolled them up and dropped them in the well. They stood now only in their plain jerkins, long johns, and sandals. Many farewells were passed between them and once everyone was contented, they reformed beneath the face.

The now plain looking man, who once wore gold, looked up at the shifting head of birds and said, "We are ready."

"Remember," said Bran, "tolerance is the secret to success. It is not beliefs that will elevate your soul beyond Abred, but rather your connections to the fellow man."

Then without warning the head expanded and became twice its size and immediately cast the ancient spell of exile.

"ZAMA, ZAMA, ZAMA," the voice boomed, "RACHAMA OZAI!"

It seemed the entire planet shook. The druids and Ector all buckled at the knees and found themselves on the ground unable to stand. The next thing Ector knew, there were only the four of them in the clearing. The rumbling continued and the well crumbled in on itself. Then when everything became calm again and the undecorated druids began taking their feet, Ector thought it was over.

But the crows flew back together and formed the face again above them.

"Remember Roman, companionship is the key to survival, even if your beliefs don't align with one another's." The head went still a moment and the crows that made up its eyes darted to the side and then recentered. "I will leave you now, but I leave you with this. Do you know why I don't find the living world worth it anymore?"

The four men waited patiently for the rhetorical answer.

"Cause I ain't got no body." Then before the head of Bran even gave them time to laugh, the birds flew apart and disappeared into the sky forever.

Moments later, the entire Roman force poured into the clearing, their would-be weapons raised in preparation for attack. Ector looked around with a decidedly clear head and realized that half his troop were in their underwear, most riding broomsticks fitted with pillows to replicate a horse's head. Some carried trash can lids instead of actual shields. Their weapons were wooden utensils, probably taken from the galley they held up in last night.

He started laughing.

"Captain?" asked the nearest ridiculous soldier. "What in Hazeus's name is going on and who are these men?"

"I'm unsure soldier," said Ector, "but these are my comrades, and the Isle of Holyhead has been purged of wickedness."

"But how?" asked the soldier in his skivvies.

"Well," said Ector, "they've disappeared."

Ector put his hand in the air and made a circling motion with his finger and the men all started to fall back toward the shore. This time there were no magic vines attacking. In fact, there was no magic of any sort thereafter. But, on the way back toward the barges that would carry them to Rome, Ector reached into his tunic and pulled out that which Bran had given him. He showed it to his three new comrades.

On the cover was the title, The Book of the Pheryllt.

Chapter Thirty-Two: The End of the MVDs

The mists in the magiscope crowded in around where Morgan lay with Arthur. Arthur was removing the shards of ruby from his tunic, handing them to his sister. "Herne the hunted said someone would like these."

She took the glinting red pieces from his fist as a shadow crossed the sky. The shadow circled around them as the landscape became all the more real. Arthur watched as Morgan threw the shards into the air and Vermatrix caught them on a low pass, then raising her great wings, amidst the orange and blue setting sun, she lit just beside them.

She encircled them with her tail and said, just as she lay her head down between her wings and foot, "That was nice. The bitter taste likes to linger." Then Morgan kissed Arthur as he muttered, "Zama, zama, zama."

Then he shut his eyes and the dragon rested its head into the void of her own elbow, becoming a cocoon around them and for all outward observers, the semblance of a large stone. Then the mists continued to crowd inside the magiscope until the whole thing whirled endlessly with the confounded stuff. The eyes of each of the golden dragon statuettes turned red, indicating that the record was over.

Hazeus put down his Slurpee in disgust. "That's it then?" he said aloud, looking down at the vinyl record spinning with more than an inch of real estate for its needle to cover.

"Well, what happens after that?" he declared aloud.

An oddly familiar young man's voice startled him from behind, "I thought it was pretty good!"

Hazeus turned and saw a young Arthur sitting there tossing a piece of popcorn down his gullet. He couldn't have been any older than when he liberated Excalibur from the stone!

A God Gets his Wings

"What in God's—" Hazeus paused.

Arthur straightened his arm, propping himself up on a palm and uncrossing his legs. "Well, Merddin," said Arthur, giving Hazeus just enough time to consider it, "I could tell you, but that would mean that you would have to believe I own at least half of your knowledge, and I assure you, this would not be the case."

Hazeus sat there for a moment, and then silently said to himself, "What in my name is going on?"

"That's better," said Arthur. "Naturally I am not surprised. You told me this would happen."

Suddenly Hazeus remembered and a bright flash came from the window. Two seconds later a clap of brilliant thunder shook the magiscope in its cradle.

"I do wish you would stop doing that!" cried Arthur, removing his fingers from his ears and picking up the popcorn from the bearskin rug.

"Hey, Zeus!" came his father's voice from the kitchen. He had a skillet in his hand. Probably eggs like usual were in the making. "I wish the weather would make up its bloody mind!" His dad's voice was full of sarcastic accusation.

Hazeus finally took a hint when his shoulders went rigid and sprouted branches like some tree of feathers. He felt suddenly electrified and was unsure if it was a sense of power or more like being strapped into the electric chair. As he had a sudden knowledge of all future forms of execution.

"Ug," complained Zeus. He had always enjoyed the comfort of home. Things had always been so easy. So, innocent. But now it came to this.

"Merddin?" said Arthur.

Zeus did not reply. He'd been suddenly enlightened on this technique by future, or was it past, great people like Steve Jobs and Elon Musk. He waited thirty seconds before he responded. In that time, he was truly hoping that Arthur just might fall asleep or disappear, or something. When he saw that was not going to happen, he said, "Yes, Bear cub?"

At this, Arthur looked more comfortable. "Who is that in the kitchen?"

Zeus looked with reluctance. His father was already making coffee.

Knowing it would sound ridiculous he said it anyway, "That's Dad. I should probably explain who it is I have sleeping over."

"Is this Rootworld, then?" asked Arthur. "Are you going to introduce me to your parents?"

"I can't believe I'm about to ask you this question but, what in the world happened?"

Arthur took no time thinking about it. "Well, Morgan saw something completely different than what we just watched. Lancelot knows what I'm talking about. It was a bit more, eh hum, real."

Zeus shook his head. "Are you still talking about the movie?"

"Oh," said Arthur, "You mean this other thing. I think you just earned your wings."

Zeus thought of the lichgate in the yard and then of all the people beneath the clouds just now learning about the existence of science. All of a sudden gravity seemed a bit more logical than it ever had. "I'm not sure they're ready to meet you yet, Arthur." Then sensing a rebuttal Zeus said, "It's a long way down the mountain from here. Just ask the last friend I sprung on Dad." He looked thoughtful for a moment.

Arthur said, "Lance said to me one time, that If I ever caught a Merlin off guard just to remind him that it will all come back to him eventually."

Zeus considered his new wings and thought he'd always preferred the color of the Merlin's primaries over the goshawk, then he said, "So, what are you saying?"

"That it will all come back to you eventually, I guess."

From among the assimilating knowledge, Hazeus finally picked out the memory of himself telling Arthur that they would meet as brothers if he cast the third spell. "Well, go on, what did Morgan see?" Hazeus finally said.

"She put me in the canoe, dressed in Lugh's sleeve and placed Excalibur on top of my body. The magic on the globe may have been all dried up but there was mist on the lake when she pushed me out onto it. And when the mist swallowed me up, she threw the shards of the ruby up into the air and they became yellow specks of corn which were gobbled up by a peregrine falcon in a daredevil's dive. That bird plucked those bits from the air and cut skyward with a sound like Sadghuru's whistle over the crowd."

Zeus was listening intently and Arthur thought it reminded him of himself, looking up at Merddin during those last moments, begging for straight answers. Inside he shared a silent laugh with himself. This is going to be fun, he thought.

Then he said, "and the mist rose to the sound of the bell at Glastonbury abbey where she would go to give birth to our baby boy. The legend remains on the globe, whether the magic really disappeared, or was it in Morgan all along?"

Zeus's eyes were trying to catch up with his own thoughts on everything when from the kitchen came again, "Hey, Zues!"

A Conversation

Zeus and Father Time were sitting silently at the breakfast table. There was a clink of silverware right before Father time said, "So. What do ya think?"

Zeus was certain he wasn't sure what he was talking about. He stared until his dad dropped both hands back on the tablecloth. A fork in one, a knife in the other. "Really? About Zeus? Ya didn't think I was gonna call ya Hazeus forever, did ya?":

"Oh," said Hazeus, eh er, Zeus. He tried it on again, "Zeus? I guess I like it."

"It happens. When you grow up, sometimes your name drops a syllable. I've been calling you Zeus in private to your mother for years."

Zeus picked up his silverware in the same fashion as his father. He broke the yoke of an egg with his fork and watched it run into the grits. "Uh, Mom still calls you Bobby, I hear."

"Hey," said Father Time. "Because she's your mother. Pretty much everyone at the watering hole calls me Bob."

Mom came into the kitchen and made a beeline to the sink after tussling Zeus's hair. "Like a cork on the ocean. Wouldn't have anything to do with your father's ability to go with the flow."

"Huh?" said Zeus.

His Dad did a little shadow boxing and managed not to put his own eye out with the fork or knife. "I can see things coming, ya know. Master of the bob and weave."

Zeus looked unimpressed.

"Old joke," his dad said afterward and shrugged. Mother Earth seemed to have gotten it because she had been doing a ditty with a dirty fork while he pantomimed a hungry Mike Tyson.

Zeus took the chance while they were both in a good mood. "I had someone stay over last night. He's asking if this is Rootworld."

"Uh huh. Well Son, roots are mighty important. There's nothing like digging your toes into the sand."

His father looked briefly at Mother Earth's Bottom as she was scrubbing out the skillet. She was doing a little swaying to the music coming from the Perplexa device.

"Eh hem. Well, sinking your fingers into something at night beats it," he continued. Not seeming to notice his boy's face change three different shades of hue. "That's fine, Son. We just want to make sure if you decide to gain a conscience, that you do so by growing a good head on your shoulders. You saw with your own eyes how the Globe came up from the great pyramid of Rootworld. Well, there is a reason it's round you know?"

Zeus thought of this.

"Well, maybe you should spend a little more time outdoors. Take a stroll in the woods. I mean, Son, this is…" Suddenly, his father got extremely quiet for a moment and Zeus thought he might be seeing a little grey in the old man's beard. "I mean, this is *our* country up here. You can look at a tree for your own sake and see for yourself that they grow nice and round on top if given the proper room and sunshine."

Mother Earth placed a cup of coffee on the table in front of the old man.

"What I mean to tell ya, Son. And ya didn't hear it from me," then he winked. "Is, if you're going to grow up, make sure when you do, you come out nice and well rounded! What's important, Son, is that you have the ability to tell yourself at the end of the day, good job. Also, you have to be able to tell yourself that you need to tighten things up a bit. Because I'm not gonna be around forever, ya know?"

Zeus didn't want to think about that. Not really. "I think I get it," he said.

"You do?"

"Yeah," said Zeus thinking of stealing his dad's liquor, "that's why you drink scotch."

Father Time scratched his bearded chin, "I don't think you get my meaning, Son."

"No, sure I do," said Zeus. "When you come home from a long day at the office and feel you did a good job, you pour yourself a couple of glasses of scotch as a reward."

"Well, yes," started his father, trying to think of a way to object.

"And if you come home and it's been a terribly unproductive day, you tell yourself to tighten up, and then pour yourself some scotch as to not dwell on the negative."

"Well, the whole point is, not to do things the way I do them, but how I tell you to do them, Son."

"Ah," said Zeus putting a finger in the air. "The second commandment."

"That's right," said Father Time, looking nervously at Mother Earth who was finishing up at the sink. "Do as I say, not as I do."

Mother Earth slopped the warm dishrag onto the center rail of the sink, "And you certainly know the first one?" she asked innocently.

Then both Father Time and Zeus said in unison, "Pa is right as everyone knows, but what Ma says always goes."

"That's right," said Mother Earth.

"One day, Son, there's not going to be anyone around to pat you on the back when you do something good or smack you on the rear when you muck things up. That, you're gonna have to learn to do for yourself."

Mother Earth came to the table, pausing only to kiss each of them on the cheek. She put her own plate of grits and eggs on the table, sat down, and Father Time prepared to say grace, motioning for Zeus to put his silverware down like he had.

"Dear heavenly Sun, hallowed be thy name."

For some strange reason Zeus felt his father might be talking about him instead of that great white hole up there...

"Kingdom come, thy will be done, in the Root as on the Globe. Give us this day our daily bread and..."

Zeus coughed and his dad opened one eye to glare at him.

"Well, what are you waiting on?"

Zeus felt a sharp ache in his shin that started spreading out coldly. So, he thought of bread (this time with plenty of yeast), and there it was.

"Forgive us our trespasses?"

He thought he heard a query in his father's voice for the first time ever during morning prayer. He opened his eyes and took in the view of Mother Earth and Father time holding hands with him around the breakfast table. Their eyes were patiently shut. He smiled.

He supposed they had worked long and hard for the terrible things they were about to do together, so he bowed his head and for once in his heart truly thought to himself, "I forgive you, and may God forgive me for mine."

As he said, "Amen," he realized that he had finished the prayer himself and his parents had followed suit.

A smile passed between husband and wife and the food was served.

As I said before, Even Gods have to eat.

Then, on a little place called Earth, a small God was born.

Epilogue

Mother Earth was doing laundry.

She held up another pair of her husband's underwear to the basement window where the dawn light was coming through.

"My god," she said shaking her head and wading up yet another holy pair and pitching it in the bottomless trash bin. The expired pair of underoo's blipped out of existence when they went over the rim and out of her sight. "He's gotta stop scratching in his sleep," she said.

"Mom?"

She turned and saw Zeus coming down the steps.

"Here," she said. "Who's this?"

"Arthur, Ma'am," said the young man with the beard, oddly peppered with grey. "Big fan."

Zeus stopped on the bottom step and glowered up at him.

"What?" said Arthur blushing. "I'm from Earth! She's the mother!"

"It's okay," said Zeus's mother. "What's up?"

"Well," said Zeus, "we were talking about reincarnation and everything—"

Mother Earth stopped with a t-shirt held up by the sleeves. She seemed to have stopped breathing.

"Oh, no!" said Zeus quickly. "It's not time for that talk yet, Mom. I was just wondering if you'd tell me how you and Dad met."

She breathed a sigh of relief, and then clutched the t-shirt to her chest in joyful reminiscence. It was one that Merle will pick up while touring Las Vegas during his third incarnation. There was a Tesla logo on the front.

"It was at the watering hole," she said, flicking her eyes toward the boys and then gleefully returning to her duty. "He split his trousers." She made a little hiccup noise and covered her mouth pertly.

The boys looked at one another. Then, as if words were things to be coveted above all else, Zeus only let a couple tumble uncertainly from his mouth, "So, you liked Dad because he tore… his… trousers?"

She smiled at him and put another folded shirt on one of the piles. "Of course, not. But that is what got us talking. I am a great seamstress you know?" she said in Arthur's direction.

Zeus nudged him, "Master of the loom and all."

Arthur looked confused.

Zues circled his upturned palms. "Weaves reality?"

Arthur shook his head dumbly.

"Anyway," Mom said.

Zeus rolled his eyes, and both boys turned back to her.

"It was really because of why he was bending down to begin with."

"Wait, he tore his trousers by bending down?"

"Men wore a lot tighter clothes back then!" she said defiantly. "And corduroy is so fragile if you don't know how to stitch it."

Zeus tried not to imagine his father in skintight jeans but failed miserably. What popped in his mind resembled a sack of potatoes mounted on a broom stick.

Mother Earth seeing his crumbled expression said, "We were a lot fitter back then, Son."

Arthur shrugged and Zeus shut his eyes and shook his head at the floor.

"It was quite impressive," she said. Then cleared her throat, "Not your father's pants or underwear." She paused then said, "Briefs by the way. Good old-fashioned whitey tight—"

"Mom!"

"Sorry, but what ever happened to those?" she tapped her chin then resumed folding, "Anyhow, his story was that he was tying his shoes, but I think he was trying to take a sneak peek at me from under his arm. I was sitting on a bar stool at the table behind him and was wearing a miniskirt."

"Oh, my G—" started Zeus regretting he had ever come downstairs to ask.

"Don't judge, Son! I won best legs in the Miss Multiverse pageant of square root seven. But the point is, regardless of whose story is true, what really happened was a bottle of Guiness sailed right through the space that his head had been occupying moments before and struck the bartender square on the chin."

She turned to them and supported herself with her left hand on the dryer, then she clicked her tongue and rolled her eyes. "When he came up from whatever he was doing down there, there was a full-on barroom brawl." She touched her own shoulder with her right hand and said, "And then there was me asking him how on Earth he had done that."

"What did he say?"

"Well, first he said smoothly," then she assumed her best manly timbre, "I've seen it coming a million times," she resumed her normal voice with a bit of irony, "but then he asked, What's an Earth?"

She gave them a moment to process then said, "It was then I knew he was the one. Though I knew he probably had been through all of this a million times before, he still asked me to show him what I had been working on. Well," she corrected herself, "he might have said something more like, let's get out of here, but I knew what he meant."

Zeus seemed satisfied as he was nodding his head. Then Arthur asked, "And what was it you were working on?"

"The Universe silly!" she said, and then seeing that same dumb ignorance he'd shown Arthur she said, "Earth?" Nothing. She made one final effort before writing Arthur off as another one of Zeus's bad influences. "The Globe?"

Arthur's eyes lit up like the bright lights of an El Camino on a deer prone highway. "Ahhh! Now I get it!" he said.

And that's that. Who knows what's going on in Rootworld at the top of Mount Meritites at this very instant. I can only tell you what I remember, and let's just say, it's too much to hold on to all at once. This is what makes being a writer the perfect job for me.

I remember telling Zeus to be well-rounded. And I remember Mother Earth's behind. Boy, do I remember that! I also remember Arthur and Hazeus arguing about whatever happened to the cloak of Paden. A cloak of invisibility is hard to track down once some imbecile leaves it laying around right side out. So that remains a mystery.

What? I can't have been Father Time at one point, too?

Changing places. I am learning that is what existing is all about. Who could ever stand being the omnipotent for more than one season? Maybe when Zeus took the power, I died shortly after and came into my next incarnation? It gets fuzzy right in that area, but his mother and I were into a lot of extracurricular activities. You know, expanding our minds and such.

What? It was her idea, she's the one who brought up the Karma Sutra! Everyone thinks women are the innocent ones.

I'm pretty sure universes are stable as long as there is a Father, a Son, and a Holy Ghost. I know that sounds sexist, but hey, I didn't write the religious texts! At least not as far as I can remember. Take solace in the fact that there's always bound to be a Mott around to keep the boys in check.

Anyhow, my recollections have drawn renewed interest from the old druid but now he says the Oracle tree claims I must build something before I can come back to the mountain. Like always, what it is I have to build has been left in total ambiguity. You know Merddin.

I am sure, however, that this will turn out to be a whole nother story.

THE END

Enjoy freebies and keep up with news by joining our newsletter at

bookflurry.substack.com

COMING SOON

A Novel of Rootworld:
The Doctrines of Yestrasmartis

Way northward on Rootworld, Firewise, in the native tongue, a tree had just finished growing at the center of Ego's estuary. An oghamologist named Yestrasmartis had just placed the final leaf from its virgin budding into his satchel and was ready to deliver it to the Firewise branch of the Rootworld library posthaste.

Earl happened to stop him before he could even get down the slope, much less his report to the mayor, which he was also hoping to avoid.

"So?" said Earl.

It was very unlikely that, 'how was your day', was going to follow a 'so' like that, Yestra thought. If it did, then what would follow, 'how was your day', would be something along the lines of, 'what do you think', or just rather more pointedly, 'what does it say?' Luckily, Yestra had prepared for this.

The long and short of it was that science could no longer be denied. But he wasn't going to spill the beans just yet. He had a daughter to think about. Yestrasmartis had seen it coming from miles away, as he was the lead Decipher on Ogham. He read everything before it was even turned into print. Rumor had it that he could tell from a simple leaf scar what volume any tongue belonged to without even seeing the veins.

Then of course there had been the poems he'd published that everyone seemed to think were prophetic. But the truth was that he wasn't all that smart, and he definitely was no prophet! He owed his ability to the mushrooms. It was they that were doing the reading. Without the mushrooms his mind went all swimmy and he couldn't tell one leaf from another. And those poems, well, those were just how the mushrooms felt parading around inside of his head while enjoying a misty afternoon.

"So, what?" said Yestra, immediately regretting it and cinching his satchel more tightly up under-arm.

Of course, Earl asked, "So, what do you think?" he may even have asked, "So, how was your day?" first, but Yestra heard none of that because he was busy telling himself what he'd do next time he got caught in this situation. It was always hard to hear everyone else's voices when your own was constantly blabbing about at you. Or was it the mushrooms? Sometimes it was hard to tell anymore.

He had found that if he simply let the sentient beings do their thing then all was well. But if he tried directing their efforts then things seemed to come back and bite him when he wasn't looking. It gave him the aching feeling that the fungus might be playing with him, in more ways than one[86].

Right now, he was becoming reasonably certain that there weren't any sentient beings along for the ride. They usually vacated right at the end of a good reading. So, Yestra was clear to do as he pleased, and

---

[86] Could it be? He once thought, that perhaps the smaller the being were, the smarter they were? But, alas, he couldn't tell if that was a thought of his own or that of the mushroom's either.

he definitely wasn't having Earl spread the word about the HAT to anyone this side of the universe.

"Well," he said, "It's all desert! As far out as you can imagine. And then a little further." It wasn't lying if you never even heard a question to begin with, was it? He had this little speech pre-planned.

"What do you mean?" asked Earl now genuinely curious as to what exactly the leaves under Yestra's arm were going to reveal. "Do you mean to say it's telling us that the desert is endless?"

At least that is what Earl would have said, if Yestra had been listening. But as it happened Yestra was raising his internal voice to an octave higher than Earl's as to drown out the question entirely. The end result of this was plausible self-deniability.

"The whole of everything, is shaped like a triangle. Or a pyramid to be exact," Yestra said aloud. He was standing at eye level, though he was considerably shorter than Earl, not to mention everybody else.

Earl considered this development for a moment. "Then why does everyone seem to figure that the shape of it is a wallaby?"

"Well, that's just the shape of the Center sea. Scholars would assume as much that the outside shape would be the same."

"Well, that's what's at the center of the Globe ya know? A pyramid. Can't be a coincidence that the triangle is holding things together over there and nothing holds us together here."

"Uh, Mound Mariatites?"

"Oh, you mean the round tower?"

Yestra affirmed unbelievingly, noticing Earl squint in tandem with each nod of his head. How could someone not know as much?

"But I still don't get why they think the Rootworld land mass is the shape of a kangaroo?"

It was time to plan his escape. "Well, that's what the cartographers came up with."

"But how'd they know?"

"The pioneers," said Yestra, his pupils flitting to and fro. Then after a sizing up the beefy blockade, he said, "Rather the pioneers' bones."

"You mean the skeleton's told em?" Earl asked. Yestra looked like an angel with a halo of light behind him. The angle of the estuary slope up to the tree was such that the great white hole was directly behind him.

"Nah, ya numbskull. The second pioneers who'd came upon the bones of the first pioneers and was smart enough to turn back. Well see, they took the measurements."

"Ah. Now I see." Earl looked enlightened then downtrodden. "Shame that."

"Yeah, shame. I still reckon it's a triangle."

"D'ya get all that from the leaves?" Earl's arms were outspread, making as large an obstacle as possibly for the oghamologist just in case he tried to bolt before giving him any answers.

"Nah," he said, breathing a sigh of relief, "Has to do with the weather. Deserts never get any rain because the clouds don't make it out that far. That means there's no room for them as far as I can figure."

"Yeah?"

"Yeah. Only reason the wind blows, says science, is cuz the heat rises. And science says heat rises cuz the air's gone all cold and frozen up into clouds, then is pushed out and away."

"Yeah." He saw Yestra's eyes dart as if looking for an escape.

"Well, if the clouds are pushing themselves out and away, then the space they have up there must be tapering down like's in a pyramid fashion. Also, could explain why most the water's at the kangaroo deluge in the center."

"You gotta be careful with all that science stuff."

"Ah," said Yestra. He caught that one loud and clear, "I see. You're referring to what the Leyonisians say happened to Arthur."

"I am. Science nearly messed up a good spell there, didn't it?"

He really didn't have time for Dogma. "I'm not certain that was a spell, and you probably shouldn't believe everything you read."

Yestra made his move. First to the left which Earl had suspected. But what he hadn't expected was the blinding light that he was now trying to shield his eyes from with his left hand. Yestra saw the man's pupils constrict and turned to the right, ducking beneath and past Earl's left elbow before he could adjust.

In a flash Earl, was trailing him like a giant after a leprechaun with a purse of gold.

"I only go to mass on Sundays," said Earl close behind.

"If Arthur died to keep all the sin from Rootworld, then why is someone trying to steal from me?" he mumbled under his breath at a steady gait.

"Uh," said Earl, now coming alongside but panting heavily. "I can see you're in a hurry, but could you sign this for my son?"

Yestra kept on moving but looked over suspiciously.

"He's read both of your scrolls," said Earl peevishly.

Yestra stopped and the big oaf kept right on along just as newton's laws of motion said he would. After Earl's feet had finally slowed the mass of his body enough to put it in reverse and return to where Yestra was standing, he handed over the scroll.

Yestra surveyed it. "First edition."

Earl nodded. "He's a fan."

"And you allow him?"

Earl's arms were balled into fists and thumping the sides of his thighs like a magnetic ball pendulum. "He won't go to church," he said, downtrodden.

"I see," said Yestra. Explained the animosity toward science, he thought. Yestra put his satchel down and flipped the clasp spreading the accordion bag open enough to retrieve his quill. He could see Earl's shadow grow as the large man was trying to take a peek. Yestra stood. "Ya know," said he, "you might find that if you show a bit more interest in your son's beliefs, he may show a bit in yours." He thought he may regret saying so but, "Church isn't all terrible, its exclusion is what is terrible."

"And intolerance!" said Earl energetically. "That's what the bishop says that Arthur taught!"

Of that, Yestra was on the verge of being guilty. He waved the parchment and pen around unsurely.

"Oh," said Earl and turned around, squatting so Yestra could reach.

Using the oaf's back, he scribbled his name at the bottom. I could wipe out the ol boy's entire belief system right now by sticking this feather anywhere except in his hat. But then he thought better of it and patted Earl's shoulder who turned and took the parchment with glee. He replaced the quill in his satchel and re-shouldered it. "Now, I really must be going."

"Yestra?" said the man as he began to walk away more naturally this time.

"Yes, Earl?"

"What would you say the forecast is for tomorrow?"

"Slight chance of rain," said Yestra.

"You know what I mean," Earl said.

And he did know exactly what he meant. It was the famous parting words of most people who had a fortuitous run in with the semi-famous Yestrasmartus. "You'll still be around, Dufus." He said, getting an audible sigh of relief. Truth be told, that was just statistics. You always bet on life when in private because even if you're wrong, no one will be the wiser. He was thinking that he really should consider teaching a class at the Academy for the Arts. Prophecy 101, perhaps?

He could see it now. The first years asking if he'd always known he'd end up teaching prophecy. Well, thought Yestra, as he mounted his llama, if that ever comes to pass, I suppose I can honestly say that it was always in the cards.

He waved goodbye and his llama gave a good spit from the side of its mouth before he healed off Earthwise at a canter.

ENJOY THESE OTHER WORKS BY THE AUTHOR:

Chilling tales blend nostalgic Americana backdrops with doses of creepy whimsy à la Ray Bradbury. Wickedly humorous at times, make no mistake – malice lurks behind the smirks. Like classic Twilight Zone, these stories shock more than they soothe.

The Death of Science is a twisted and humorous foray into the vast multi-faceted universe of Rootworld. Like a contemporary Twilight Zone, this satirical science fiction fantasy tale will appeal to fans of both the nostalgic familiar as well as the shockingly bizarre.

Perfect for bedtime reading, this charming children's adventure follows a bugs-eye view of the animal kingdom as a plucky band of fleas and lice seek to establish their own empire. Echoing the whimsical imaginings of Terry Pratchett's The Carpet People, these tiny explorers face giant obstacles with camaraderie and wit. Young readers will delight in accompanying the brave King Fleo and quick-thinking Queen Clouse on a quest filled with thrills as they traverse the wild frontiers of fur and skin. This amusing bedtime tale brings the miniature world of animals and bugs to vivid life.

Children's/ Bedtime/ Adventure/ 40 Minute Read

Doctor Datson is getting older, but that doesn't keep him from still getting into mischief.
When one of his lab experiments re-animates some old fossils, it is up to Truman and

the rest of the gang to track down the dangerous creatures and find out who's responsible.
30 Minute Flash Fiction
Science Fiction/Thriller/Humor

⚜ Jay Horne ⚜

Also by Jay Horne: